Mage Resolution

Books by Virginia G. McMorrow

The Mage Trilogy
Mage Confusion
Mage Resolution

Coming Soon!
The Mage Trilogy
Mage Evolution

The Firewing Trilogy
Firewing's Journey
Firewing's Shadow
Firewing's Hunt

Novel
Upstaged by Betrayal

For more information
visit: www.SpeakingVolumes.us

Mage Resolution

Virginia G. McMorrow

SPEAKING VOLUMES, LLC
NAPLES, FLORIDA
2023

Mage Resolution

Copyright © 2004 by Virginia G. McMorrow

All rights reserved. No part of this book may be reproduced or transmitted in any form or by any means without written permission.

ISBN 978-1-64540-923-6

For Kevin, with much love.

Acknowledgments

Thanks to my agent, Cherry Weiner, for her encouragement and steadfast guidance. And thanks to Erica Mueller and the staff at Speaking Volumes for their expert work in publishing another mage adventure.

Chapter One

"I'd rather tangle with a poisonous seabeast than go to this ridiculous, flamboyant, time-wasting ritual," I grumbled, sounding little better than a whining three-year-old, looking for something expensive to smash against the elegant silk-covered wall. "We should have crept out of Ardenna last night when I wanted to, but no, Anders, you wouldn't listen to me. So it's your fault that I'm stuck here."

"It's not a ritual." Trying his best to placate me, Anders ran his fingers along my shoulder, sending a chill down my spine. Not that I would ever admit it. "There's to be no blood sacrifice unless you insist on one." I smacked his lingering hand away, but he went on, unfazed. "Elena is formally announcing her betrothal, and wants you to meet the future Prince of Tuldamoran since you never manage to be in Ardenna when Erich's around. So don't be unreasonable. Besides," —he snuck a kiss on the back of my neck— "it's the middle of the night, and Elena's guards would look askance if we snuck out like thieves with the queen's treasure."

"There is no queen's treasure. And as for her beloved, what's his name of wherever he's from, I can just as easily meet him without all the fuss and bother." I brushed back a strand of dark curls. "Besides," I added, desperate for any lame excuse, "I have nothing appropriate to wear. And I won't borrow one of Elena's dainty silk gowns that she slithers into," I protested, before the thought even entered his mind. "So I think we should leave. Now."

"Ah, well."

I spun around to face my lover, immediately suspicious. "What?"

"Well, you see . . ." Anders stepped back, seagray eyes full of mischief. "It's like this." Absently running a hand through gray-streaked black hair, he narrowed his eyes, keeping a safe distance between us. "Our, ah, beloved monarch sent you a gift."

Crossing my arms, I narrowed my own blue eyes, inherited from my long-deceased seamage mother, to slits.

"Over there." Anders pointed to the far corner of the lavish chambers.

Royal seahag. I knew she'd find a way to keep me in this crowded, noisy town. "It's not my size. I'm sure of it."

"You haven't even looked."

"I don't need to look." My back to the door, I dared Anders to force me. "I can tell from right here."

"Can I make a royal suggestion that you at least take a peek?" A silky voice with the barest hint of sarcasm and affectionate amusement drifted from behind me, as the door clicked shut, reminiscent of a cell door snapping shut, with me as Elena's hapless prisoner.

"You're playing dirty." I turned to confront the queen. "That's not fair."

"Neither is wanting to sneak off in the middle of the night without warning me. Besides, consider it royal privilege," Elena said dryly, dark blue predatory eyes alert, ready to trip me if I dodged past her post. "Now be respectful for a change, before I report your behavior to Rosanna, and go see what I sent you."

Muttering one imaginative oath after another, and determined to ignore the silent amused exchange between Elena and Anders, I dragged myself over to the corner and unwrapped endless layers of soft paper. Beneath it all, folded with obvious care, was an exquisite white embroidered tunic cut from soft leather, with close-fitting trousers to match. She'd even included extravagant soft white boots. I stopped speechless in mid-curse at the sight of the embroidered symbol on the tunic.

"I think she likes it, Anders. Maybe. I can't really tell."

Trying to find the right words, I turned to find Elena watching with a fair bit of anxiety. "The symbol—"

"Well, lords of the sea, Alex," she said in self-defense, "since your mage talent is so different, so unconventional, compared with other mages." She flushed as Anders cleared his throat. "No offense," she told him, still unaware Anders was far more skilled than a simple mage, "but Alex does have a peculiar ability. And you needed your own symbol." She turned dark eyes back to me, genuinely worried. "At least, I thought so."

I stared at the symbol, tracing the lines of thread with my finger, surprised to find it shaking. "You combined all four symbols, wave, flame, tree, and wind, merging into each other. Clever."

"No one else in Tuldamoran can change all four elements from one to another like you can, Alex. Every other mage is like Anders, who can only control one element, in his case, water, in all its forms," she chattered on to cover her nervousness. "And only Glynnswood mages can change one form to another, but they're limited to two elements."

I wasn't sure whether to be relieved or amused that she didn't mention Sernyn Keltie, the Glynnswood mage who abandoned me at childbirth to Rosanna's care when my mother died.

"Not even the legendary Crownmage could do what you can," Elena added, "were he, or she, to exist."

Anders met my gaze across the spacious chamber as Elena thoughtfully traced a finger along the symbol's pattern, much as I had done. I shook my head. Twice. No one knew Anders was the legendary Crownmage except me.

"Well, anyway, you're my Mage Champion," Elena continued, oblivious to Anders's confusion when I bypassed the opportunity to tell her the truth. "Or you were a year ago. I assume you haven't resigned yet."

"Elena." I tugged at her tunic sleeve. "You've placed the mage symbol beneath the Dunneal crown."

"I know."

"The mage symbol is supporting the crown."

"Yes, I suppose. I didn't precisely think of it that way."

"Anders, can a monarch be such a thick-witted idiot?" When he started to protest, as always taking Elena's side, I inquired of my queen with studied innocence, "Does this mean I'm always at your command? Supporting you whenever you get in the slightest bit of trouble?"

Elena flushed bright crimson. "I didn't mean it that way. I'd never force you to do anything you didn't want to do. I just thought—"

I laughed good-naturedly, enjoying her discomfort. "That's exactly what your devious mind intended, even if you weren't aware of it."

"But—"

"Elena." Anders tossed me a scathing look. "No queen should ever suffer the abuse you get from your Mage Champion, who's also supposed to be one of your closest friends. Her support should never be in question. Go right ahead and exert your authority. Show her who controls Tuldamoran. Teach her a lesson she'll never forget. Go on. She richly deserves it."

"Traitor."

Elena kept solemn dark blue eyes fixed on Anders. "I'd rather not. Despite her immature, willful, difficult, childish, self-centered behavior, Alex does have a conscience. She'll be at my side in a heartbeat if she knows I need her." With a fond smile, a kiss on his cheek, and a crooked grin for me, Elena abandoned us.

"Royal flameblasted manipulative seawitch."

In two long strides, Anders crossed the room to corner me against the wall, leaving not an inch of room to maneuver.

"All right, all right, I'll go to the damn ceremony."

"Of course, you will. That's not what I want to know."

Amused, I stared into cool seagray eyes that held unmistakable curiosity. "You want to know what I can possibly see in an old grizzled mage who's almost twice my age, right?"

He stopped my insults with a deep, teasing kiss. "I know precisely what you see in me. And," he added, pinning me gently against the wall, "I'll even remind you. But first things first."

Halting his words, I touched a finger to his lips. "You want to know why I stopped you from telling Elena your secret."

"Well, yes. We'd agreed to tell her I was Crownmage as a betrothal present. Which is why we came to Ardenna to meet Elena's darling, or at least, why I came." Still puzzled, he kissed the tip of my nose. "I can never tell your reason for anything."

"To answer your rude question, I don't really know."

"Trouble?" His expression turned quickly anxious. "Erich's behaved himself. I know you spoke to Elena after the Mage Challenge once it was clear that he was interested in her affection, but surely she'd know if he didn't love her. Or if he had an inappropriate agenda."

"Would she? Ever since—" I stopped, flustered, remembering Anders didn't know about Jules Barlow, Rosanna's son and Duke of Port Alain, who had desired a relationship with Elena. Nor did he know about Elena's heartbreaking denial. We three had grown up together, friends since childhood, and the regret was an awareness we rarely acknowledged. I shook my head and leaned against the warmth of Ander's chest as he wrapped me in his arms, sensing a conflict I didn't want to discuss. "Ever since the duel," I hedged, hoping Anders wouldn't question my hesitation, "I've wanted to meet our future prince before we tell Elena you're the Crownmage. She's devoted to Erich, and I need to see why."

Brushing aside my tangled curls, Anders nuzzled my neck, tracing the scar that Firemage Charlton Ravess, the mage I'd ultimately defeated and Elena banished, had left as a reminder. "Are you protecting Elena?"

"Me?" I laughed softly, enjoying his caresses. "Never."

* * * *

"Interesting mage symbol."

I snapped my head around and glared, giving Jules Barlow, Duke of Port Alain, a swift discreet kick in the shin. "If you don't behave like a duke—"

Innocent green eyes met mine, as he dodged my boot heel. "I was just admiring Elena's creativity, not to mention the workmanship on that tunic."

Anders tugged sharply at my hand. "If the two of you don't start acting like adults, Lauryn and I will greet Elena and her darling without you." Smiling at Lauryn, the Duchess of Port Alain, who was busy threatening her husband, Anders turned back to me.

"He started it."

"Alex—"

"Mage Champion Alexandra Daine Keltie and Seamage Anders Perrin." Elena's steward announced our entrance, with a ridiculous formal bow in our direction. Lords of the sea, but I despised pomp and circumstance. And Elena knew it, which was why she bribed me to stay in town.

Anders pulled me down the aisle between rows of boring, overdressed retainers and dignitaries, who'd all flocked to Elena's side, hypocritically, a moment after my decisive victory over Firemage

Ravess. "Smile," Anders commanded through clenched teeth. "Look happy to be here."

"I am."

"Liar." He squeezed my fingers in warning as we approached the throne where Elena waited, one black eyebrow subtly raised in tolerant amusement.

"I thought you were confident it wasn't your size."

"It's not. I haven't eaten all day to squeeze into the trousers," I muttered as we knelt with grave respect at the foot of the throne. Glancing to Elena's side, I found her betrothed wearing a cautious, amused look.

"Duke Erich Harwoode of Barrow's Pass." Elena tugged Anders and me to our feet. "Alex is a very old friend."

"And Anders simply an old man," I mumbled, studying Erich from the corner of my eye, all senses alert.

"I'm honored," Erich said with a courteous bow as Elena laughed in appreciation at Anders's expected protest. The duke didn't appear much older than Elena, with blue eyes not so very different from hers either. His face was handsome, topped by blond curls that I remembered from Tucker's Meadow. "And also grateful you saved Elena's throne. I was at the duel, watching in horror. It was an unpleasant experience for you, Mage Keltie, though you were evidently capable of dispensing with the traitor, Firemage Ravess."

Unpleasant? Odd choice of words. "It was necessary." Unpleasant? I laughed to myself, keeping my face clear of bitter emotion, remembering the murderous recklessness my anger unleashed in Tucker's Meadow. It wasn't a memory I was proud of, but one I couldn't easily forget.

Erich's gaze strayed to the embroidered symbol on my white leather tunic. "Elena's fortunate you have such, ah, unique talent."

Staring into those eyes, I realized belatedly I had completely misjudged him. The duke's eyes were nothing like Elena's. His were unreadable, coolly appraising, dangerous, reminding me in that single moment of the glance he'd exchanged with Charlton Ravess before the Mage Challenge started. I'd been uneasy then, and more so now, feeling, with no way to prove it, that he was a deadly risk to my friend and queen.

"Such unique and valuable talent should be carefully protected," he murmured, slipping an arm possessively around Elena's waist.

"Such unique and valuable talent," I repeated in what I hoped was a reasonable tone for Elena's sake, "should carefully protect the queen."

Erich held my gaze thoughtfully before turning to Elena. "You are indeed fortunate to have such a loyal champion."

When Elena sent him a look of such deep unguarded affection, completely unsettling me, I wanted to throttle her until her bones and teeth rattled. Couldn't she feel the danger? What hold did he have over her heart?

"Elena spoke with such high regard for both you and Master Perrin," Erich added smoothly. "I'm delighted to finally meet you both."

"I hope we didn't disappoint you." I clutched Anders's fingers in a suffocating grip.

"Not at all. In fact," —he matched my forced smile— "you exceeded my expectations. I hope I'm not being presumptuous to dare think that at some future time you might extend your protection to Elena's prince."

I'd tangle with a poisonous seabeast before I did any such thing. "No offense intended, my lord duke, but I'm sworn to protect my queen. And Elena is, as I'm sure you already know, quite a handful on her own."

Erich laughed, blue eyes, subtly dangerous, never wavering from mine.

"You're too kind, Alex," Elena said dryly.

"Only speaking the truth, your majesty." With a courteous bow, I dragged Anders from the massive audience hall, not bothering to wait for Jules and Lauryn. I needed to breathe away from the poisonous atmosphere.

* * * *

"Perhaps when you're finished throwing every single item you brought to Ardenna against the wall, you'd like to talk about it?"

Gripping one of Anders's good leather boots, I stopped in mid-toss at the smugness in his voice. I dropped the boot with a loud thud, sighed, and sank next to him on the decadent enormous bed, not a lecherous thought in my head. Before I uttered a word, there was a loud, persistent knock at the chamber door.

Anders gave me a knowing grin, as he went to open the door. "It's the middle of the night, so I presume it's either Elena or Jules." Thoroughly familiar with the unconventional hours the three of us kept when visiting each other, Anders had never once complained. The old beast had instead, in the brief time since he'd tutored me in magic and unexpectedly become my lover, fit comfortably into our circle as though he'd always been there.

"I know it's late," Elena apologized, blue eyes flashing impishly at his expression. "But at least you weren't in bed. I'd never hear the end of it."

Anders bowed with a flourish. "You forget, majesty. I've grown accustomed to late night visits from you and Jules, so I'm very careful of my, ah, timing, when I know you're in the vicinity."

Elena patted his cheek and came in, wandering idly around the room, taking in the scattered clothing I'd tossed against the walls, fallen in various piles. "You have an odd way of packing."

"By throwing things against the wall, Alex believes they'll magically shrink and fit easier into our satchels," Anders said blandly.

"I see." Removing a wrinkled tunic and boot from an armchair, Elena tossed them on the edge of the bed. She sank into the soft pillows of the chair and faced me. "I assumed you'd flee the perilous horrors of Ardenna as soon as you could manage without insulting anyone. I wanted to thank you for staying as long as you did."

"My pleasure."

"Liar." With a bright smile, Elena tossed me a small leather pouch. "This trinket arrived later than planned, for which I'm sorry, but nevertheless—" She hesitated, waving a slender hand at me. "Well, open it."

Curious, I fumbled with the strings and pulled out a copper pendant, the design identical to the mage symbol embroidered on my tunic.

"Even the least powerful mages wear a token of office, Alex. I thought it only fair you had your own." Her voice had turned serious, midnight blue eyes solemn.

As she kept her eyes fixed on me, waiting apprehensively, I smiled genuine thanks and hugged her. "I'll wear it on one condition." She lifted her brow in cautious query. "You'll have to think of a new title for me. Mage Champion sounds a bit too belligerent."

"And you're not?" Her grin was eloquent. "Well, all right. I'll think about it."

"Please do."

"Must it be complimentary?" Elena crossed her legs and added before I could answer, "Speaking of which, Erich was full of compliments for my friends. I'm not sure why, Alex, but he was impressed by you. He kept reminding me how valuable you were as a friend."

As a weapon, perhaps. "It was mutual," I lied, "It's obvious he makes you deliriously happy."

"He does, Alex. I've never quite felt this way before."

Anders sat beside me and wrapped an arm around my shoulder in warning. "We're pleased for you, Elena. You deserve some happiness."

"And speaking of gifts," I took the opportunity to say, "our betrothal gift wasn't quite ready yet either." When she started to protest the need for a gift, I raised a hand. "You'll want ours. Trust me. We just don't want to spoil the surprise, so when it's ready, we'll deliver it in person. Right, Anders?" I elbowed him roughly in his firm stomach.

Wincing, he kissed me on the lips. "If you say so. Just remember, we have six months to make sure it's ready, or it'll be a wedding gift."

When Elena laughed and stood to leave, I called after her, bringing her to a stop, one hand resting on the door. "Just because I despise Ardenna doesn't mean I won't come here if you need me."

"I know that." Blue eyes smiled with affection.

"Or just need to talk."

"I know that, too."

"I'm serious."

She traded an amused glance with Anders. "I know that, too. And so does Erich. Your message was quite clear this evening, Mage Champion."

I flushed with embarrassment for Elena's sake, though didn't regret my message to her lover. "Sorry. I didn't mean to be rude."

Elena laughed merrily at my discomfort. "You weren't rude. You were just protective. You were being my champion."

"No, I wasn't. Well, yes. I'm supposed to be."

Still laughing, Elena pulled the door open. "No, Alex. Not you. It's out of character." Tossing a kiss to Anders, she left.

I muttered a long string of vicious oaths and started tossing things again.

"Well, you did ask for it." Running a hand along my neck, Anders yanked a boot from my hand and pulled me down beside him.

Chapter Two

"Were my grandchildren so horribly behaved in the schoolroom today?"

Three days later, I stopped sorting through a pile of schoolbooks at Rosanna's question and blinked, content to be home in Port Alain. "Of course not. Every one of the little beasts kept me busy with questions about Ardenna and their wise and glorious monarch."

"Ah."

"What are you getting at?" Suspicious, I rested my chin in the palm of my hand.

Jules's mother sat across from me, planted an elbow on the schoolroom table, and rested her own pudgy chin, facing me. I was intimately familiar with that look from the earliest days of my childhood when Rosanna had come to be the only mother I remembered. "Coming back from Ardenna generally puts you in a pleasant mood, because you hate to be there and love being home."

I sniffed with indignation. "Are you implying that I'm not pleasant?"

"Well, yes." Though I started to protest, knowing full well that she was correct, I let her talk. "You've been as cranky as a seahag deprived of its prey. Makes me wonder," Rosanna drawled, never taking her eyes from my face, "what happened in the capital."

I slammed a book on the table. The old duchess didn't blink. "You weren't supposed to notice. However, I'm surprised Anders didn't warn you about my mood." I piled one set of books on the floor near my feet.

"He doesn't tell me everything, even though you don't believe us." When I started to laugh, she tried to look offended. "You're the only one who returned in a foul mood. Though no one else's temperament is, ah, quite as explosive as yours."

"Explosive?"

"Don't talk about unimportant or unrelated matters. Tell me what happened." As I stared at my hands for a long, uneasy time without really seeing them, I had the distant feeling they were getting tangled up. "I won't tell Jules," she said quietly, "if that's why you're hesitating."

"Partially," I admitted, trusting the older woman. "I don't want Jules to tell Elena, even though I know he'd do it with all good intentions. But I'm not sure he's the one to tell anyway, not with how he feels about her." Taking a deep breath, I gave her a quick summary and explained, "I don't have any right to tell her who to marry, but I don't trust him. And I don't know why, other than a possibly coincidental glance that passed between Erich and Ravess at the duel. I was so rattled that morning, worried about defending her throne and her honor, how can I trust anything I saw or heard?"

"Your instinct usually serves you well, Alex, especially when you link it to common sense." A slight lifting of her brows made me extraordinarily wary of her choice of words. Not quite sure if I was being insulted, though odds were that I was, I glared at Rosanna, who only grinned and shook her head. "I raised you from the day you were born. If you want me to list every instance where you made a mistake, I'd be here all day."

"Give me one legitimate example," I challenged, walking wide-eyed into her trap.

She locked her eyes on mine. "Refusing to see or even discuss your father."

Motherless seahag.

I stood and turned my back on her, staring out the schoolroom window overlooking her pampered gardens, seeing nothing but a bright blur of green and a riot of colors.

"You still don't know enough about your mage talent, though you pride yourself on being Elena's Mage Champion. By refusing to see your father—"

"I don't need him."

She sighed behind me. "I'd quite forgotten you don't understand his half of your heritage, even though you selfishly use it."

"Stop it," I whispered, whirling back to face her. "I don't use it selfishly, and you know that. You also know why I refuse to see him."

"No common sense there."

"Damn you, Rosanna!" I tried to keep my voice from shaking, but failed.

"Don't you think he's suffered enough guilt for your mother's death?"

"Go away."

"You need a father."

"I've learned to live without one. I'm not a child. I don't need him."

"Maybe he needs you."

"Maybe he should have thought of that when he abandoned me."

"Ah." Rosanna crossed her arms, and watched me, the sarcasm back, accompanied by a peculiar expression. I turned away again. "I thought you were angry at him for not telling your mother he was a mage so that when she was giving birth to you, she couldn't use her own magic to help herself. After all, she promised him never to use it near him, and didn't understand—"

"Stop it." Heartsick, I rested my head against the window, shutting out her painful words.

"She couldn't have known that his mage talent mixed with hers created a mage child with potential no one had ever seen or envisioned. But now I see you're angry because he left you. It doesn't matter that he wanted to spare you his own guilt. You condemn him for abandoning you like a ragdoll." The wooden chair creaked as she came to stand behind me, twisting me around and wrapping me in her plump arms. "Alex. He made a mistake. Forgive him. He wants nothing from you but what you would give him willingly," she whispered, my pain mirrored in her eyes. "You won't be free of this grief if you don't confront him." Rummaging around in her pocket, she pulled out a lace handkerchief and handed it to me. When I stepped away, putting a fair amount of distance between us, she asked, "What are you going to do about Elena?"

I blinked at her abrupt change of topic, but that was how she wore me down. I shrugged. "Nothing. I have no proof of anything, so there's nothing I can do. Not yet, anyway."

"What does Anders think?"

"Don't you know?" I needled, but she didn't blink. "That I'm being over-imaginative and over-protective, though there may be something there. Maybe." I shrugged again. "If I didn't hate Ardenna so much, I'd stay there for a time just to keep an eye on Erich."

Rosanna scratched her graying head and stared into the air above my head. "What could he gain from this marriage besides the usual lure of power and an exquisite bedmate?"

"That's what bothers me. We don't know enough about him. I don't, anyway."

"Perhaps you should do some research. Alex—" Her voice was gentle as she started toward the door, giving me fair warning. "You know I only pester you for your own good."

"You're only being nice so I don't turn you into a goat."

"You can't do that. Anders told me."

Chapter Three

"Do you think there are any others like me?"

"By the grace of the lords of the sea, Alex, I sincerely hope not!" Anders placed both hands on his chest in mock horror.

"Pretty fast for an old man," I complained as he dodged my fist, putting the armchair in my parlor between us.

"You always underestimate me." When I crossed my arms, waiting for an answer, he released a long-suffering sigh. "You, Mage Champion, are the only one of your kind we know about. Intermarriage between Glynnswood people and outsiders was forbidden after your mother— After you were born," he changed the words to spare me. "Your father," he added, appraising my mood, "was the first to break with tradition when he fell in love with your mother. Most Glynnswood people never sought mates outside their own clans. Your father was also the last to do so, or so we think."

"You never told me that. I always figured they liked to keep to themselves, but I did assume"— I shrugged beneath his patient gaze— "some of them ventured beyond their borders, like Sernyn Keltie."

Sernyn Keltie. Not my father.

"In all your hundred thousand questions I suffered through, you never asked."

"Hmmm." I turned back to the task of sorting through Mother's and Grandmother's notes and arranging them in the small oak chest Rosanna had kept them in, along with Mother's copper seamage pendant. Rosanna had given me half of that pendant, Anders the other. Through some peculiar accident of fate, my magic allowed me to merge the copper halves into one. I never could explain it, since my talent didn't allow me to work magic within one element. I could, however, change copper to water. So my merging of the two halves left me, and everyone else, bewildered.

"What are you doing?"

"I want to keep this chest in a safe place."

"Give it to Rosanna."

"I'd rather it were near the cottage."

"Why?"

Shrugging, I brushed unruly curls from my eyes. "I don't know."

"You won't tell." When I didn't answer or deny it either, he said quietly, "With Jules's expert guidance, Elena handpicked every new mage she appointed to the Crown Council, right after you defeated Charlton Ravess. Erich had nothing to do with that decision."

I stared at him, guilty. "I didn't accuse him."

"You didn't have to. You've been edgy ever since you had that pleasant facetious conversation with him in front of Elena."

I flushed in embarrassment and tried to distract Anders. "Will you help me hide this chest, or must I do it myself?"

He tossed an overstuffed pillow at my head before pulling me to my feet. "It's a good guess you already know where you want it placed."

"I always try to be prepared, as you taught me, master mage."

He ignored my sarcasm and carried the oak chest into the bright afternoon sunlight. Standing aside, he waited as I settled down on an old gnarled tree trunk and stared at the flat, dry dirt beneath the oak tree that commanded the clearing behind the cottage, the tree against which I'd slammed him unexpectedly more than a year ago, scaring me half to death. With confidence, I coaxed the talent awake inside me, felt the cold bite of ice and sharp sting of fire, merging them until the familiar cool warmth spread throughout my body. Concentrating on the dirt, I imagined it as air. Clean, invisible air.

Just so.

"You're too lazy to dig a hole in the ground?"

"Be a good Crownmage and harden the dirt at the bottom of that hole to stone."

"You only keep me here for my talent."

"That's all you have to offer."

Anders called on his own mage talent, which allowed him control of all four elements and the ability to change each element from one form to another, say water to steam.

After he solidified the dirt, I picked up the chest and placed it gently in the depression. "If I change a portion of air to dirt around the chest, could you simultaneously harden it so that it's covered in rock?"

"If you don't make a mistake, sure."

"The only mistake I ever made was to let you stay with me."

Grinning smugly, Anders balanced on steady legs, pushed his tunic sleeves upward toward his elbows, and stretched his arms out toward the oak tree.

"Don't be so flameblasted dramatic." When he nodded his readiness, I felt the cool warmth still awake inside me and clearly saw in my mind what I wanted. A sizable portion of air turned to dirt and hardened, encasing mother's oak chest in solid rock.

Safe from unwanted eyes and ears.

* * * *

"I still think it's an interesting mage symbol."

"You'd think anything Elena did was interesting," I accused Jules good-naturedly the next day, throwing a booted leg over the arm of the guest chair in his book-lined study.

"I'd be more agreeable with you if you'd be more agreeable with me."

"Did you know about this?" I waved the copper pendant on its leather string around my neck in his direction.

He shook his head, ruffling light brown hair in need of a trim. "Of course not."

"Of course not," I muttered, and then tried to act unconcerned. "Elena seems pretty attached to Erich." I watched Jules discreetly through narrow slits, gauging his reaction.

"Attached?" He laughed with honest affection, though his eyes held a trace of regret that was never very far away. "Wherever Erich is, Elena is near. And the opposite is true. They're very much a matched pair."

"Jules."

Something in my voice warned him as he turned away to stare out the window, at the merchant ships and fishing boats crossing the harbor or bobbing gently at anchor. "What do you want me to say, Alex? That Elena never looked at me that way? Well," —he faced me— "she never did. But Lauryn does. I'm not a complete fool. I'd never begrudge Elena her happiness. She deserves it. But you can't expect me not to feel any regret."

"Do you think I don't understand?" I asked, as familiar with their old heartache as I was with my own. "I was concerned about you."

Jules's smile released the tension that hovered between us. "I know. So was Elena. She spoke to me in private before Lauryn and I left Ardenna."

"Then it's all right?"

"Of course, it's all right. Look, Elena didn't even have to give me a second thought, didn't need to worry on my behalf, but she did."

"She's your friend, you stubborn, thick-witted—"

"So are you." Jules flashed a disarming smile. "I find it fascinating how you manage to express your concern so different than Elena does."

"Yes, well. She was raised on diplomacy. I was raised with you." Satisfied that I shut him up, I switched topics. "Does Erich agree with her policies? Or does he have a very different set of priorities?" At Jules's questioning look, I explained, "I'm just curious as to whether there'll be lively debates in the bedroom, that's all."

Jules graced me with a long-suffering look, not catching on that I was acting like, well, the queen's Mage Champion. "He agrees with the important ones. I've heard him commend her handling of the Meravan ambassador in the Mage Challenge affair."

"Then why didn't he raise his voice in support a year ago?" Idly, I swung my legs back and forth. "No one spoke up in her favor. Not one duke besides you. If Erich wanted her to notice him, you'd think he'd have declared his support."

Jules fixed me with a suspicious stare. "What's this all about?"

"I'm curious and apprehensive as to whether he'll support her in the future. That's all." Barely, but it seemed to satisfy Jules for the moment.

"He never contradicts her, at least not in public. I've never heard him mentioned as being controversial or a troublemaker or linked with anyone dangerous."

Wasn't Charlton Ravess, the mage with whom he exchanged that unreadable glance at the duel, considered dangerous? "Well, that's good."

My next words were cut short as a tempest from Shad's Bay whirled into Jules's study in the form of his six-year-old twins. "Alex!"

"Easy." I caught them both in my arms, Carey first as usual. "If you don't learn to walk through open doors, instead of flying through them, you're going to have a flat face like your father," I scolded, fixing them with my stern schoolmistress expression, which was blatantly ineffective.

"You're always so gracious," Jules grumbled. "Now what's chasing you monsters so that you forgot your manners and interrupted our serious discussion?"

"You promised to take us riding," Carey said confidently, inching up to his father's carved chair, the one that replaced the previous chair I'd transformed to water, with Jules in it, to announce my mage powers.

"I did?"

"Yes." A vigorous shake of brown curls.

"Hunter?"

A silent, far more reserved nod.

"That's still no excuse to run in and interrupt your father and Alex like a pair of wild dogs," scolded Brendan from the doorway. Elena's younger brother and heir was squiring at Port Alain. "Now apologize."

Two curly heads mumbled something contrite to Jules.

"And to Alex."

As the boys turned to me and mumbled something else contrite, I ruffled their hair. "I'd be grateful if your father took you riding. I've had enough of his company, anyway."

"I'm sorry." Brendan sighed. "They're getting too fast for me."

"I'm glad you chase after them, not me. Besides," —I smiled, trying a devious tactic— "we were only gossiping about your future brother-in-law." At mention of Erich, Brendan's dark blue eyes, identical to his older sister's, held a fleeting emotion that snagged my attention. "Jules, why don't you take the boys, disappear, and leave us in peace?"

With a long-suffering look, Jules allowed the twins to drag him away. As Brendan turned to leave, freed for the afternoon, I caught the sleeve of his light wool tunic.

"Close the door," I said softly. Intrigued, Brendan shut the heavy carved wooden door and faced me. "You had a peculiar look in your eyes when I mentioned the Duke of Barrow's Pass." When Brendan flushed and looked away, I urged, "Brendan, it's important."

The young man sank into the chair opposite me. "I don't like him, Alex. But I don't know why. And I can't very well tell my sister that, can I? She adores the ground Erich walks on, and he makes her happy." He ran his fingers through midnight black hair, staring at his scuffed boots. "And I don't think he likes me very much either."

"That's precisely the problem I have."

"You?" His handsome face shot up to stare at me in disbelief.

"Anders thinks I'm too imaginative, but from the moment I saw Erich in Ardenna, I felt my skin crawl. No, that's not quite true. I noticed him at Tucker's Meadow the morning of the Mage Challenge, and I mistrusted him then. I thought— Listen, Brendan, it's only a feeling, but I had the impression he supported Charlton Ravess, and I haven't trusted him since."

"I thought I was the only one," Brendan said in open relief. "But I don't know what to do. Erich's returning to Barrow's Pass for a few weeks, and I wanted to send Martin there to sniff round."

At mention of Martin, Brendan's man from the capital, I nodded. "I haven't told Jules how I feel, and I'd rather you didn't for the moment. Martin just might be my answer. Rosanna suggested I do some digging into Erich's affairs, but I can't leave here, not now. Martin won't be missed from your side if you let it be known that his family needs him. Make up some emergency no one can verify." I stood and stretched, muscles stiff from sitting cramped in Jules's armchair. "Rosanna knows about this problem because she knows most everything I fret about. But I'd leave it at that, Brendan. No further than Rosanna and

Anders for now." When he nodded, a small smile tugged at the corners of his mouth, making me wary. "What?"

"Elena told me what you said to Erich about being his Mage Champion. She didn't see it as an insult," he added, at my anxious look, "but I do now." His smile broadened. "I'm glad you told him that."

I placed a hand on his arm. "What I said to Erich doesn't apply to you, Brendan. If you ever need my help, you'd better come find me or I'll hunt you down and dangle you from the highest mast in Port Alain's harbor."

He smiled shyly and hugged me. "Somehow I knew you'd say that."

Couldn't Rosanna see the truth? I didn't need Sernyn Keltie. I had family and friends enough, though I'd refused to see it for so very long. My fault, I admit it. But I still didn't need his guilty apologies.

"Are you all right?" Brendan tugged at my sleeve.

"Yes." I tossed him a sly grin. "Just don't tell your sister what I said. She'll start to worry. I don't want her to think I'm getting too soft."

Chapter Four

"Who sent the letter?" Propped against the huge pillows Rosanna kept on the floor by the fireplace in her sitting room, precisely for me, I waited for her answer, never suspecting it had anything to do with me.

Jules's mother altered her expression to utter blandness as she brushed an invisible speck of dirt from her tunic sleeve, the opened letter lying innocently in her lap.

Instinct screeching, I sat up with a curse. "I don't want to hear what he has to say."

"It's not from him, but about him." When I sat back and looked away, avoiding the accusation in her eyes, she added, "Your father's very ill."

"There are healers in Glynnswood."

"They can't help him."

"And is it his dying wish that I forgive him?" My voice was bitter cold to banish the heartache and grief that had buried itself deep inside for more than a year.

"No." Her tone was bitter cold to match mine, trying to shame me, and, of course, succeeding. "Sernyn didn't ask for you. In fact, no one asked for you, Alex. The letter is informative, not an invitation or request to visit."

Almost tripping in my haste to flee, I stood up, fists clenched tight against my sides. "Yet you expect me to go to Glynnswood."

"Alex," she spoke as she sighed, eyes unreadable. "I'm simply telling you what the letter says. I don't expect you to do anything. In fact, I don't expect you to do anything intelligent or reasonable where your father is concerned."

Stung, I slammed the door behind me.

* * * *

"I don't know why I'm doing this," I mumbled, settling my poor fretful horse by the side of the road where a small clearing allowed some room to maneuver. Anders and I had followed the road north toward Tuckers Meadow, along the Kieren River, for a day at a slow, steady pace. The turn westward to Glynnswood came, unfortunately, before we reached the vineyards of the Marain Valley. Not that we needed to purchase any of their rich wine. Elena, as promised after the Mage Challenge, kept me well-stocked. Anders and I decided to camp for the night before intruding too deeply into the Glynnswood forest, though one step over the border was too deep for me.

"Because it's the right thing to do. And it proves that under all that pitiful excuse for a brain, you do have a conscience." I ignored him, busy rubbing my stiff legs back to normalcy. "Why don't you start a campfire?" Smug amusement tinged his voice as he unsaddled his horse.

"Why don't you?"

"If you recall—" He brushed a gloved hand through gray-streaked black hair. "You're the mage who can change that pile of wood to a respectable campfire. I can only control the fire when it already exists. You forget I'm only a humble—" He dodged the bedroll I threw as I unsaddled my own mount. "Is that part of your fire-making ritual?"

"Listen—" I inched over to where Anders stood clutching my bedroll for meager protection. "I'm only going to say this once. I don't know why I'm here, but I am. I don't want to be here, but I am. So don't make it any more intolerable for me than it already is."

"Or?"

I stared blankly into cool seagray eyes. "Or?"

"I presumed there'd be a threat behind that statement."

"Am I that horrid?" I whispered, blinking back sudden tears.

"Alex." He held me close and stroked my bowed head. "No, of course not. Well, not always," he teased, trying to soften his words. "I'm sorry. I was only trying to make you laugh because I know how difficult it is for you to be here. That's—" His body tensed, from head to toe, arms gripping me tight as they spasmed around me.

"What's wrong?" I stepped back, instinct screaming of danger. "Anders!" I shook him roughly, his face ashen as his body slumped against mine, a bloody arrow in his back.

A bloody Glynnswood arrow.

Betrayed by flameblast Sernyn Keltie. He betrayed me once as an infant, and betrayed me again as a woman. Quelling the rising panic, I reached for the fire and ice to fight back with magic, but scorching pain and an arrow in my own shoulder destroyed my concentration. I pitched forward against Anders, pulling him with me to the hard ground as I fell.

* * * *

A voice murmured in a soothing tone as I tossed from side to side, words more polite and civilized than I was used to hearing in Port Alain. Glynnswood words, Glynnswood accents. I opened my eyes a narrow slit to face my captor.

"Ah. You are awake." A gray-haired woman, eyes like Rosanna when they were gentle and not accusing me of ill-bred behavior, was smoothing back the coarse blanket covering me. "Here. You should eat something to get your strength back." She helped me sit up, mindful of the bandages. "You were fortunate. The wound was not very deep."

I bit back a vicious oath, wincing against the sharp pain in my shoulder, and closed my eyes, catching my breath. "Anders? My companion?" I tensed, waiting for her answer, afraid the news would be bad.

"He is still feverish, but you were both brought to me in time." She gestured to the far corner of the darkened room as I opened my eyes. "He is resting there. Now you must care for yourself. Eat." She picked up a chunk of warm bread, pushing it gently into my hand. "When you feel stronger, we will bring you into the sunlight. You need strength to make the journey home."

I looked at her with open suspicion. "You'll let us leave?"

The healer met my skeptical gaze with confusion. "Why would we keep you here against your will?"

"We're your prisoners."

"Prisoners?" The woman was indignant, yet trying hard to remain civil. "You are not our prisoners but our guests. Free to come and go as you please once you are well. Why would you think we have taken you captive?" Her eyes flashed almost imperceptibly to the darker side of the room. "Ah. The arrows. Our people did not attack you. Your father—" Bright spots colored her cheeks, and she stared down at her hands.

Not my father, not to me. "What about Sernyn Keltie?"

"Sernyn Keltie promises to find and punish whoever ambushed you and Anders Perrin," said a soft voice behind me.

I spun around, flinching in pain from the reckless movement. Sernyn Keltie looked no different from my two brief glimpses of him a year earlier, sadness and old grief ever present in haunted deep brown eyes. "You're not dying."

His eyes widened at the cold, bitter accusation in my voice. "Should I be?"

"The letter said you were dying." I flung the coarse wool blankets away to grab my clothes, folded on the low table beside the bed, but the healer firmly, but gently, held me back. "Let me go! Lies, again. A trick to get me here and—"

"I never sent a letter." Eyes showing clear distress, Sernyn kept his voice even beneath my growing rage.

"Then you asked someone to send word. Lured me here, attacked me, though why that would be necessary, I don't understand."

"Hush." The healer stroked my arms as I started to shiver, the shock and distress doing nothing to help me get well.

But I wanted nothing more from Glynnswood and shook her hands away. "I want—"

"What you want is a clear head to think, something you seldom grace us with, particularly when it comes to your father."

"Traitor," I spat at Anders, as he struggled to sit up. Sernyn bolted across the room to help.

Breathing heavily, sweating still from high fever, Anders had the presence of mind to send me a scathing look. "Think, damn it. Why would your father want you hurt, particularly by one of his own people? Don't be an idiot. Someone who knows he's alive and precisely how you feel about him used Sernyn to hurt you, physically and emotionally."

I met Anders's fevered eyes across the length of the sparsely furnished chamber. Was he right? Had Elena inadvertently told Erich something of my heritage and how I despised Sernyn? There was no other possibility.

"Don't jump to conclusions," Anders scolded, leaning gratefully against the pillows Sernyn propped up behind him.

"Then how did Sernyn's people," I nearly choked on the name beneath his quiet scrutiny, "know where to find us in the forest?"

Before Anders could speak, Sernyn answered my accusation. "The presence of any stranger to these woods is soon noticed among us. We reached you too late. I am sorry for that. We are responsible for your wounds."

"No, you're not." Annoyed, Anders dismissed him and turned back to me. "You owe your father an apology."

"Anders, please." Sernyn placed a hand on his arm, distressed as I slumped down onto the soft mattress and pulled the blankets over my shoulders, turning my back on them all.

Chapter Five

Sernyn kept his distance, and Anders was either too ill or too frustrated to speak to me for most of the next day. "When do you think he'll be able to travel?" I asked the healer in a low voice as she changed the bandage on my sore shoulder.

"Not for some days." Her voice betrayed uneasiness. "Master Perrin lost a great amount of blood, and the fever weakened his resistance."

Lords of the sea, it wasn't her fault. "I haven't thanked you for helping us. And any of the others who brought us here."

She nodded gravely, avoiding my eyes. "I will tell them."

"Were any of them hurt?"

Surprised at my unexpected concern, she looked up. "No. But I will tell them that you send thanks. Now you must eat again." Leaving some warm grain bread and hot tea on the table beside the bed, she left us alone.

"Planning to leave me behind?" Before I could threaten that very thing, Anders spoke, his tone brittle. "I don't think it's wise. The attack was aimed at you, Elena's Mage Champion. I'm only a seamage, remember?"

"I can't stay here." I winced as sharp pain stabbed through my shoulder, radiating down my back, but determined not to let it stop me from escaping this nightmare as soon as possible.

"Indeed, you can't." Anders chuckled to himself. "Why not send word to Jules to have an escort come rescue us?"

"Then word will be out that we were attacked."

"It doesn't matter. Whoever's behind it knows you're not dead. Unless," Anders drawled, covering a smile with one hand, "you'd rather hide here for some months."

"Absolutely not." I shivered, wrapping the coarse blankets closer around my aching shoulder. "When the healer comes back—"

"You need to walk and get your strength back. Go find her. Or," he added, trying unsuccessfully to hide another smile behind the edge of the blanket when I stared at him, "your father."

I stood up with exaggerated caution and held onto the bed frame until the dizzy spell passed. Grabbing my clothes, cleaned and herb-scented, I shrugged into them very gingerly. My boots were impossible. I threw them aside in disgust. Ignoring Anders's feeble attempt to call me back, I went out barefoot to find the healer, stumbling directly into Sernyn's arms as I pitched forward, dizzy again.

He brought me inside and set me gently on the soft bed, tucking the blankets around my bare feet. "You should not be outside alone."

"Afraid I'll escape?" I asked, looking away to brush nonexistent dirt from my tunic sleeve. "Can we send word to Duke Barlow?" My eyes stayed fixed on the invisible dirt. "If he could send an escort to meet us at the inn—" My voice faltered beneath his quiet scrutiny.

"At the edge of Glynnswood? I will send word immediately. By the time they arrive, Anders should be strong enough to travel." Sernyn cleared his throat when it was obvious I had nothing further to say. "Will there be anything else you need?" Impeccably polite, as Rosanna had described him so long ago, his tone was distant, hiding grief and guilt behind a guarded barrier. But for his eyes.

I shook my head like a willful, spoiled child, and then blurted, "Why did you come to Tucker's Meadow?" From the corner of my eye, I caught Anders's surprise. I'd never told him Sernyn had appeared on the fringe of the crowd, watching the Mage Challenge. "To see me fail?"

"To see you defeat Charlton Ravess, as I knew you would." He edged closer to the bed. "I did not know whether my presence would help or hinder you, Alex."

"It helped in a way that would have shamed you, Master Keltie." At the unforgiving bitterness in my voice, Sernyn turned to leave, maybe only then realizing his presence at the duel had fueled my rage and desire to annihilate Elena's enemy, to use my magic in warfare, not peace. Clutching the blankets around my feet, I pulled my knees close to my chest, trying to find the courage to say the one thing I owed him. "I'm sorry about what I said yesterday," I mumbled so low, hoping he didn't hear me, and stole a furtive glance in his direction.

But he stopped, slender frame silhouetted in the doorway, and turned grave eyes to meet mine. "Your words yesterday were the only words you ever said about me that were wrong. Anything else you accuse me of, Alex, is justified."

I swallowed hard and fought back tears. If he was the villain, why was I feeling like a criminal? He didn't even gloat that I'd come to Glynnswood at news of his alleged illness. "I don't need you," I whispered, aware from the corner of my eye that Anders was listening intently. "I never needed you."

"Alex." The weight of twenty-six years of grief and heartache centered in my name. "I do not want you to need me. I want you to forgive me."

"I can't!" Brushing away stubborn tears like a pathetic, unhappy child, I hid my shaking hands beneath the blankets, bowing my head in utter misery.

"I know." He came close to the bed and reached out to stroke the top of my head. Before I could pull away, he turned and walked out.

"Alex."

"Go away."

"I can't go away, and I can't hold you if you're on the other side of the room."

"I don't want you to hold me."

"Yes, you do."

Sea-draggled old mage. I sniffled all the way across the neat, spotless room, and sat scrunched in Anders's arms, weeping, until he rocked me gently to sleep. No different from when I'd first discovered, a year ago, that my father was still alive and had abandoned me, blaming me, or so I thought, for surviving childbirth.

* * * *

Huge brown eyes under a rebellious lock of deep brown hair poked through the half-open doorway. The building held only one bright chamber where they'd kept us fed, clothed, and comfortable. Prisoners, despite the healer's indignant insistence. Startling me, because every single Glynnswood person I encountered was stealthy, I stared at the apprehensive head to see what the rest of the boy looked like, unwilling to be civil just yet.

"Mage Champion?" He edged into the healing chamber, eyes wide, darting a glance at Anders snuggled under covers in the far corner, sound asleep.

Well, it wasn't his fault either. "That's me." I sat up gingerly against the bed's headboard, careful of my shoulder. "Though I'd rather you use my name."

A quick nod. "Mistress Keltie."

Keltie wasn't what I had in mind either. "Alex."

Consternation flashed in his huge brown eyes. The boy couldn't have been more than eleven or twelve seasons. "That is not proper."

"Then don't call me anything!" I snapped, wishing Anders would hurry and heal, and Jules come to rescue us from this hell, though it was only hell to me.

"I have offended you." A quick blink over shamed eyes, he edged closer, dressed like Sernyn in forest-hued tunic and trousers.

Idiotic child. "You haven't offended me. I'm just tired and my shoulder hurts and I want to go home. I'm cranky and rude," I added, as he darted a cautious glance from under exquisite long eyelashes.

"No. You are simply not where you want to be." He managed a shy grin. "But, Alex," he tried out my name, found it inoffensive, judging from the smile that appeared, "it is not such a horrible place to be."

Lords of the sea, if Sernyn flameblasted Keltie had sent this child to charm me, he was succeeding. "Where precisely is this not so horrible place?"

I was rewarded with a broad grin. "Hartswood village at the center of the forest."

"I see. And who are you? My guard?"

"Guard?" The boy flushed with the identical indignation that had so colored the healer's face. "You are not our prisoner. Did they not explain that? I will tell them to apologize."

I kept my face neutral, certain he'd be devastated and insulted if I laughed aloud. "I didn't believe them."

"But it is true. My name is Gwynn. Bretta asked if I would take you outside."

"Bretta?"

A brisk nod. "The healer."

"Ah." I studied Gwynn with open curiosity. "Well, all right. I'm dressed and have nowhere to go. Were you planning to take me far? Perhaps Port Alain?"

Gwynn's smile was disarming. "I wish I could take you home, Alex, but I am not permitted. And you are not strong enough. No." He shook his head. "We are only going outside and maybe through the village a little if you are strong enough. And want to," he added quickly.

"Pity." I sighed, struggling to get up. "We'll have to see how far I can go. But I won't get anywhere without those." I pointed at my boots, polished and gleaming, in better condition than I'd ever seen them.

"Wait." Gwynn pounced on my boots and came toward the bed. When I tensed, waiting for him to shove them on my bare feet, he slanted a reproachful look my way beneath those long eyelashes. "I will not hurt you."

Caught off guard, I stammered something unintelligible that he dismissed, easing the boots onto my feet. "Thanks."

Another disarming grin revealed clean, even white teeth. He held out his arm. "Ready?"

"I suppose." I glanced at my cloak, but he shook his head. So I inched off the bed, grabbing the boy's outstretched arm gratefully until I caught my balance. At the doorway, I stopped, blinking against the brilliant sunlight, enjoying the warmth on my face. Then I caught sight of the villagers, going about their business, and stiffened in alarm and hesitation.

"No one will trouble you." Gwynn's voice was soft beside me. "Elder Keltie has given strict orders." As I scurried outside to avoid discussion of Elder Keltie, Gwynn trailed behind, helping me settle down on the wooden bench alongside the building's wall. "I have offended you again." Head bowed, eyes downcast, Gwynn looked dejected. "I will ask Bretta to send someone else to keep you company."

"You'll do no such thing." I tugged at his coarse woolen sleeve, yanking him down beside me. "Idiot. Sit down. If Sernyn Keltie gave strict orders, and Bretta asked you to stay with me, then both of them must have warned you about me."

"Yes." He studied his feet, swinging lazily back and forth. "But not why."

"Well, hell, I won't tell you that either, but I'd rather you didn't speak of Elder Keltie. What's an elder, anyway?"

Gwynn settled back, leaning against the cool wood of the guesthouse. "An elder guides the people of a village. In Hartswood—" He stopped, flushed brightly, and looked away in confusion.

"I assume Elder Keltie is elder of Hartswood," I said dryly. At his nod, I poked his arm playfully. "Go on."

"It is simple really." Tugging at the unruly lock of thick brown hair that refused to behave, Gwynn shrugged skinny shoulders. "The elder settles disputes, guides the gathering of clan chiefs, makes decisions that affect the village. All such things, Alex."

"How does an elder get to be an elder?"

As a schoolmistress, responsible for teaching the children of Port Alain, I wondered idly if these gaps in my knowledge related to the fact that Sernyn Keltie came from Glynnswood. I'd never taught the children the least bit about this independent region within Elena's kingdom but its name and the fact that it had forests. Evidently, there was much to learn about Glynnswood and its polite people. The village itself was as spotless as the guesthouse, with buildings all low and constructed of wood, surrounded on most sides by the encroaching forest. Everyone I saw milled about with an air of busy good nature. Was I the only one with hostile intent?

Gwynn's voice had an easy, pleasant quality as he rattled on, oblivious to my wandering thoughts. "The villagers choose the man or woman they believe most capable of acting as elder. If the villagers do not believe the elder should remain as elder, they will petition to have the elder step down."

"I see." Surely someone had a grievance against Elder Keltie in all these years. And how long had he been so honored? One year? Two? "How long has Elder Keltie been elder of Hartswood?"

Gwynn shot me a curious glance. "Almost twenty years."

Twenty years? Almost my entire life. I cleared my throat. "Who does the elder go to with problems?" I shut my eyes, content to feel the warmth on my face.

"There is a gathering every summer in Hartswood. All elders come. No one is held higher than any other." I opened my eyes to find Gwynn studying me from the corner of his eye as I yawned politely. "We are taught as children we owe allegiance to the crown in Ardenna, but we do not have one chief elder to represent Glynnswood should the queen demand it. We would have to choose an elder then."

At least they were theoretically loyal to Elena. I twisted to face Gwynn. "You're rather intelligent for a boy. Maybe they'd send you. I'm sure her majesty would enjoy your company."

"I am not a boy! At least," he stammered in embarrassment at the outburst, "not according to Glynnswood traditions."

"Now I have offended you."

"No." He rushed to my rescue. "You do not know our ways. How could you think anything else? But Alex, I am fourteen and do not play with children any longer, and Elder—" He blinked rapidly, fumbling over his words. "And I am a scout for the village and keep watch in the forests and do other things that men do."

An involuntary smile tugged at my mouth. "Is one of your manly tasks to keep a hostile guest content and out of trouble?"

An unreadable expression flashed across his face, and then, "It is an honorable task." A very shy grin transformed his face so that he looked of an age with the twins.

"All right, if you say so. Then let's walk, very slowly, through the village, and tell me what there is to know so that I will stay out of trouble and not offend anyone. I wouldn't have you fail at your honorable task, and I'd rather not be considered by the village to be rude and hostile."

* * * *

"I see you've made a friend." Anders sat up in bed, eyes finally free of the feverish glaze. "There's hope for you yet."

"This is Gwynn, my, ah, guide."

"Indeed." Anders graced the boy with a polite bow from his reclining position, bundled under the coarse sweet-smelling blankets. "I hope you've succeeded in keeping Alex out of trouble."

"She has been safe with me, Mage Perrin."

"Well, yes. I didn't doubt that. But have you been safe with her?"

I tossed a pillow at Anders's head, cursing as pain flared in my shoulder. "I've been a perfect guest. Most of the time, anyway. You'd have been proud of me."

Gwynn listened to our affectionate bickering, brown eyes darting back and forth. "I did not feel threatened at all, Mage Perrin."

"Call me Anders, please. You make me feel old."

"You are."

Bretta came in before Anders could reply to my sarcasm. "The fever is finally gone." She smiled at her patient. "You are much better." Pleased, she turned to me, a hesitant look in her eyes.

"Thanks to your skill."

With a grateful, though pensive nod, she changed the dressing on Anders's wound. "Word has come from Duke Barlow. If you are both well enough to travel,"— she glanced over Anders's shoulder at me— "an escort will bring you to the inn tomorrow where he will be waiting to take you back to Port Alain."

"Are you ready to travel?" With great restraint, I managed to not sound urgent.

"I think so."

As Bretta tucked Anders back under the blankets, I caught Gwynn staring at me in a peculiar way, tugging at his unruly lock of hair. Taking a chance, I asked, "Would Gwynn be allowed to accompany us to the inn? I understand he's a scout, and such tasks might be part of his duty." An unreadable look passed between our hosts. "Forgive me, if it would be a problem—"

"No." Bretta turned curious eyes my way. "No. Not at all. And Gwynn, I think, would be honored."

I chose to interpret the nervous tug on his hair as agreement.

* * * *

"Thank the lords of the sea you're all right."

"I didn't think you cared, Jules."

"I don't. But mother, Lauryn, and the twins do." Green eyes mocked me with old affection as the duke helped me struggle onto a horse, taking great care not to strain my shoulder.

"And Khrista, too," Kerrie, the Barlows' steward who was madly in love with Jules's younger sister, added with a smile as he held my horse steady. "If we didn't come after you ourselves, Khrista threatened to call the wedding off."

"They were worried about me," Anders pronounced as he tried to mount his horse without help. "Not you, Alex. Ah, damn."

I laughed as he slipped and fell forward onto the horse's neck. "Serves you right for being so independent." Settling myself in the saddle, I looked beyond Jules to the small escort he'd brought. Shivering in the cool morning breeze, I turned to Gwynn and the Glynnswoodsmen waiting at the forest's edge. "We're grateful for your help."

The head scout bowed from his half-hidden spot beneath the gnarled oak. "You are Sernyn Keltie's daughter. There is no need to be grateful."

Flameblast Sernyn Keltie. He never even came to say goodbye. I nodded in confusion as the woodsmen started to vanish. All but Gwynn.

"Thanks for keeping me out of trouble."

The boy smiled shyly, glancing at Jules and the Port Alain escort. "Alex? If you ever visit Hartswood again, I would be happy to keep you out of trouble." With a strange expression on his face, he waved and vanished before I could reply.

Maybe it was for the best that Gwynn didn't hear my reply. I didn't plan ever again to set foot in Glynnswood.

Anders edged his horse close to mine. "Are you all right?"

I tugged at the reins of my horse, and turned south. "Let's go home."

* * * *

Impatient and curious, I rapped more than once at the door to Rosanna's study the next afternoon, waiting for the older woman's voice.

"Come in, Alex."

Wretched old witch. How did she know it was me? I opened the heavy oak door to find solemn eyes watching as I settled on the window ledge overlooking her precious gardens. "I've been greeted and hugged and fretted over by everyone, including the squirrels and your ducks . . ." I paused for dramatic effect. "But you."

"You were so busy with the others, I didn't want to intrude."

"Did you have time to see Anders and make sure he was all right?" Guilty, as I knew she would be, the old woman turned away. "Rosanna, I don't hold you responsible for our little misadventure," —I smiled at her averted head and added dryly— "although it did occur to me that you might have engineered the attack to finally be rid of me."

Rosanna's graying head spun around. "You ungrateful, malicious child." When I grinned, her expression softened. "I was frantic with worry for both of you. If anything had happened—" She clenched her fists and settled down in her rocking chair, plumping pillows behind her so I wouldn't see the tears.

"Well, I survived. And here I am, a perfect target once again."

"Do you think it was Erich?"

"It has to be someone who knows Sernyn Keltie's alive and how I feel, or don't feel," I added like a spiteful child, "about the man. And, I suppose, that I'd go to Glynnswood despite those feelings if I knew he was at death's door. Elena knows."

"Elena would never—"

"Of course not. But she's so utterly in love with Duke Harwoode she might tell him anything without thinking there was harm in it. And if he expressed curiosity about her Mage Champion's odd talent . . ." I shrugged, wincing at the sudden pain in my shoulder.

"Oh dear."

"Precisely."

"So you're a threat to him."

"Maybe. But why?" I asked in frustration, tapping a restless finger against the window pane. "Because I support Elena? If he loves her, and, frankly, Rosanna, I don't think he understands the word. Lust, no doubt. But love? Anyway," I continued, thinking out loud, "if he loves her, wouldn't he want to see her protected?" I turned to look out over the lush gardens, which Rosanna never let me near when she was working there, since I didn't know the difference, in her eyes, between a weed and a rose.

"Maybe he doesn't want her protected."

"And maybe Elena's safe only until the wedding. But after that—" I sighed unhappily. "Has Brendan's man returned from Barrow's Pass?"

"Not yet. But speaking of Barrow's Pass, Elena sent my daughter a note. She may not be able to attend Khrista and Kerrie's wedding. It's only a few days away, and Erich" —she bit her lip— "may be delayed in Barrow's Pass."

"I wonder why."

Rosanna sent an anxious look my way. "Please be careful."

"I really didn't think you cared."

"I pretend to care." She waited a beat, and then, "Rather like you pretend not to care in the least about your father."

My leg stopped in mid-swing. "He never came to see us on our way home," I said, suddenly angry. "Why should I care if he doesn't care?"

"From what Anders told me," —Rosanna didn't blink— "if I were your father, I'd keep my distance, too. Sernyn may be many things, but he's not a stupid man."

"I apologized for accusing him of the attack."

"Generous of you, under the circumstances."

I stood away from the window and headed for the door. "Yes, it was."

"You've come back with a number of unhealed wounds."

"And you delight in rubbing salt in them."

The only answer I got was a sigh.

Chapter Six

"The happy couple seemed happy enough," Anders remarked some days later. He threw one arm lightly around my uninjured shoulder as we sauntered back to the cottage in the middle of the night after hours of unaccustomed celebrating.

"They're made for each other." I laughed, snuggling closer under his arm. "Poor Kerrie. I don't think he realizes just how much his new bride resembles Jules."

"He'll know soon enough. Always happens with a brand new unsuspecting husband. Too bad Elena couldn't make it in time. It's always a pleasure—" Anders stumbled over a fallen log, muttering a vile oath I didn't quite catch.

"Pardon?"

"Flameblasted log got in my way."

"Ah."

"Don't be smug, Alex. Listen." He wrapped his arm tighter around me and pulled me close. "Why don't we get married?" When I stopped dead in my tracks in the middle of the narrow road, Anders peered at me, squinting to see my face in the moonlight.

I swallowed uneasily. "I don't want to talk about this now."

"Why not?" He planted a very uncoordinated hand on his hip.

"For one thing, you're drunk."

"Crownmages don't get drunk. I know perfectly well what I'm saying." When I turned and started walking toward the cottage, Anders grabbed my arm and held me back. "Should I take this personally?"

"No. Lords of the sea," I said in frustration, "of course not." I tried without success to pull away from his solid grip.

"Then why won't you even discuss it?"

"Not now. Please."

"Now, Alex."

I closed my eyes to avoid his reaction. "I'm afraid," I whispered.

"Of me?" He dropped his arm in surprise, immediately losing his balance.

"No." I shook my head, steadying him. "Of what you and I could do."

Thoroughly confused, Anders edged his face closer to mine. Threads of gray in his black hair caught the moon's glint. "What more could we do that we haven't already done?"

"You're a Crownmage, Anders." I ignored his lusty grin.

"Yes." He blinked.

"I'm some bastardized version of a mage."

"Indeed." He smiled cautiously, trying hard to follow my point without making a mess of things.

"If we had children—"

Sudden understanding lit his eyes. "Alex. Oh, Alex, it won't happen to you. I won't let it. We won't even have children," he said earnestly, spinning me in a circle. "I won't risk your life in childbirth, not unless we know more about your mage talent and that it's perfectly safe for you to have a child. And only if you want it, too." Anders hugged me to his chest, possibly more to stop himself from falling than from affection. "Foolish idiot. Honestly, Alex. Let's go home. We'll talk about it there."

Relieved, I let him lead me down the path, both of us stumbling and weaving a little. But my relief lasted only a few moments. I stopped walking, alert, instinct screeching, one hand pressed firmly on his arm.

He stopped, edged away from me, searching. "Something's burning." Seagray eyes, swiftly sober, turned back down the path. "The cottage. Hurry."

I passed him, running blind as thick smoke swirled round me, choking me, as I turned the bend. Flames sprang from the windows and darted through the open doorway.

"Alex." Anders was shouting as he caught up to me. "My talent is useless here. I can't put out the flames. Hurry, before it reaches the woods."

I nodded, blinking back tears from the heavy smoke, and the sight of my home, my mother's home, in flames. Furious, I urged the fire and ice awake, merging it to cool warmth without effort, envisioned the flames as soft, gentle rain. Eyes closed, I heard the loud hiss of steam and sank to my knees.

"Water?" Anders came up behind me, coughing raggedly.

"If I turned it to air, most of the cottage would've vanished." I looked in dismay at the charred walls and practically nonexistent roof, knowing the damage was worse inside. My books— "Anders." I turned to him, a sharp word on my tongue, but stopped at the concern in his eyes, and something more, far more dangerous.

"If they wanted you dead, they miscalculated."

"No." I shook my head, pushing strands of hair from my face, leaving streaks of soot on my forehead. "It was a warning. Why else wait until we were on our way back here? Which makes me wonder if the attack in Glynnswood was only a warning, too. Did they fail to murder us because they intended to fail? I can't think." I slumped against his chest, exhausted. "What a mess."

"Let it dry. We'll come back in the morning. At least your mother's notes are safe." Anders gave me an odd look. "Your instinct frightens me sometimes."

My eyes followed his gaze to the large boulder protecting the oak chest. "Me, too. Where should we go?" I said, suddenly lost without the cottage that had been my home and shelter for so long.

"Back to the Hill, of course." He hugged me tight. "The wedding celebration's probably still going on."

* * * *

The celebration was indeed still going on, but much quieter. Khrista and Kerrie had vanished, along with most of the guests, leaving only stragglers behind. Rosanna. Jules. Lauryn. Brendan talking seriously to someone I couldn't see behind Lauryn. Blinking as we entered the bright-lit hall, I blinked again, and saw Elena. And Erich, speaking to Brendan, who gasped in surprise at the sight of us.

Anders gripped my hand in warning. Or perhaps to hold me back from ripping Erich's throat out in front of Elena. Maybe it was coincidence, maybe not. But he wouldn't be foolish enough to set the blaze himself. Confused, I stopped in the entrance to the ballroom.

"Alex! I was just about to steal some wine from Jules and wake you up." Elena waved merrily at the sight of me, her smile transforming into a puzzled frown as though her brain couldn't interpret what her eyes were seeing. "What's all that dirt?" As she came closer, her frown deepened. "What's happened?"

"Ashes," I said quietly, keeping her pristine tunic and trousers at arm's length from the soot I flicked off my once-festive clothes.

Rosanna flew to my side, eying me from head to foot before doing the same to Anders. "Are you all right?"

I met her stare evenly, fighting to hold back tears. "The cottage, all the duke's work, it's all—" My voice faltered briefly as I thought of the old duke and how he'd treated me like a daughter, but I caught it back under control. "It's destroyed." It was more difficult to keep a tight rein on the fire and ice that threatened to explode and consume Erich.

Ignoring the ashes and soot, she hugged me close. "We'll build another."

"Not until I find out who did this." I pushed back from her comforting embrace as Erich's deep voice sounded behind me before Rosanna could answer.

"Elena, this is the second attempt on Alex's life." His earnest voice dripped masterfully with deep concern. Too bad he never learned to mask the coolness in his eyes as they met mine without a trace of challenge and defiance. "It's intolerable. Alex must be protected."

Elena turned to me, oblivious to his lie. "I wanted to talk to you, anyway, after what happened in Glynnswood. I'll have guards posted."

"Absolutely not."

"Why not?"

"Because I don't want it. I don't need it. They don't want me dead, at least not yet." Ignoring my friend's concern, I turned the defiance back to Erich. "All I want is to find the one responsible—"

"Hush." Anders came up behind me and wrapped his arms around my waist, pulling me close. "How about some Marain Valley wine instead?"

Elena met his eyes over my head.

"Don't think you can post guards without my knowledge. I'll send them scurrying back to Ardenna before they've even unpacked their gear."

"I had no such plan," Elena fumbled over her lie. "What I don't understand is why someone is after you." She started to pace, as she always did when distressed, along the length of the ballroom, littered with wedding debris and leftover food and wine.

"Someone finds me a threat," I said quietly, accepting some wine from Jules with thanks. "Me. All I want to do is teach, and some fool considers me a threat." I shrugged, leaning back against Anders. "I won't rest until they're stopped or they manage to stop me. Whoever's behind this little trouble has underestimated me."

Anders kissed the top of my head. "Along with the rest of us, I'm afraid. Lords of the sea know why, Alex, but we're all ready to protect you."

"We are?" Jules said with perfect innocence, green eyes wide, wincing as Lauryn's sharp elbow bit into his side.

"What will you do now?" Erich watched me, ignoring the banter, eyes cool as he flipped a wayward blond strand from his forehead. "You're welcome to stay at Ardenna. I'm sure Elena wouldn't mind, and we could certainly keep a closer eye on you, Alex, to see if anyone is trailing you."

"Thanks, but no." I laughed with feigned warmth, tightening the control over the fire and ice that hungered to devour his heart. "I don't think Elena could tolerate me in such close quarters, particularly since I'd be complaining about Ardenna from the moment I arrived. No, I think I'll stay here, if Lady Barlow doesn't mind."

Considering that the old witch had wanted me to return to the manor from the day I left some years ago, Rosanna kept her expression bland with admirable restraint. "I think I could tolerate your presence for a day or two. Anders, naturally, for a longer period."

"If anyone cares, I mind." Jules kept a safe distance from his wife.

"You may be Duke of Port Alain, but you don't rule here on the Hill. Your ladies do. All of them."

"They do not."

Anders leaned over my shoulder to tug on his silk sleeve. "Trust me, they do."

Laughing at Jules's mournful expression, I caught and held Erich's gaze. A smile graced his lips, icy contempt blazed in his eyes. What had I done to make him my enemy? Destroyed his ally, Firemage Ravess? If that were true, Elena needed to know her lover and future prince was a traitor. "Will you be returning to Ardenna?" If he wanted to keep a close eye on me, the feeling was mutual, and I didn't care that he knew it. In fact, I wanted him to know.

Erich nodded. "For a time. Unless any trouble comes up in Barrow's Pass. I still have responsibilities there," he added, the image of the responsible, respectable duke, entirely distinct from Jules, who, in spite of his flaws, ruled well and fairly. "But please let us know if you change your mind about coming to Ardenna. Elena's Mage Champion needs to be kept safe so she can keep Elena safe. And truly, Alex," — his eyes widened with hypocritical sincerity— "I'd feel better if I could be of help."

"I'm sure you would." And I'd feel safer in the jaws of a ravenous seabeast. "Ah. Well, if I think of any way you might help, I'll send word." I glanced at Elena, who'd finally stopped pacing. "If that's all right with you?"

"Of course. Alex, you don't even need to ask. And if you'd feel safer in Ardenna, then please come. I know you despise being there, but it may be safer."

"Maybe I will. But not now." My smile at Erich promised sweet vengeance. "Not yet. But thanks."

Brendan, who'd been standing behind Erich, watching and listening, caught my eye and winked.

Chapter Seven

"Flameblast whoever did this," I muttered, staring at the pathetic ruins of the cottage. "My favorite boots. All worn and soft just as I like them."

"I'll buy you another pair." Anders flapped a sooty tunic in the breeze to brush clinging ashes from the burned material. He discarded it when he saw it was damaged beyond the possibility of mending.

"They won't be the same." Disheartened, I flung the ruined boots to the pile of hopelessly lost items.

"Always time for something new. Besides, it's a good excuse to spend some of your riches on the local merchants."

"My riches? Old man, I think maybe a piece of rubble hit your head last night. You're imagining things. Riches," I snorted, starting to toss my old cloak to the pile of salvageable possessions, but stopped with my arm outstretched. "Is that why you're still hanging around Port Alain? Biding your time, waiting for me to tell you where I hid my treasure?"

"Sure. The Mage Champion is rumored to be wealthy, so it seemed reasonable to stay nearby in case you talked in your sleep. But all you do is snore."

"Precisely how wealthy?"

"Fabulously."

"You don't think robbery was behind all this?" I waved a hand at the mess we were sorting through, the half-standing walls, charred furniture, the caved-in roof. I shoved aside the grief that threatened to creep back into my heart.

Anders stopped rummaging through the dirt and ashes and gave me a peculiar look. "I was only teasing."

"Yes, I know. But is there really a rumor like that going round?"

His shrug was nonchalant as the cool autumn breeze tossed back his hair. "Remember all those rumors about the Crownmage a year ago, and how all powerful and all—"

"Yes." I dusted my trousers. "And look at you."

He scowled at my smug expression, wounded when I laughed. "Anyway, I don't know of a specific rumor about your wealth, but it wouldn't surprise me if there were rumors flying around for some reason. Especially since you're real, and I'm only a legend."

"I never paid much attention to any of the stories about you, and I certainly don't care about me."

"Maybe you should."

"And let Erich off the seahook so easily? Not a chance in hell." I went back to rummaging, delighted to find a handful of books only half ruined.

"Why don't you ask Jules? He usually has an ear for that sort of talk," Anders suggested, tossing me a boot for inspection.

"Mindless chatter."

"Always with a grain of truth."

"Ah." I sent Anders an innocent look. "Like the rumors of the Crownmage and your, ah, virility?" Too late, I caught his intention from the mischief that flashed in his eyes. One tiny shove and I landed on my backside in a heap of damp ashes. Before he could dodge my grip, I pulled him down beside me, making very sure he had as much dirt and ashes on every inch of his body as I had on mine. Sputtering, Anders grabbed a handful of the wet gritty stuff and dumped it over my head.

"I hope you're searching for my betrothal gift."

We both jumped, startled, and guilty. Elena sat on an uncharred tree stump at the far edge of the clearing, one eyebrow eloquently lifted.

Lords of the sea, what had she heard? "Ah, no." I brushed ashes from my hair. "Actually, your gift is quite safe."

"I see."

"Alex pushed me." Anders cleaned off his tunic and trousers, not paying the slightest bit of attention to me.

"Liar." I caught him off balance, shoved him back into the ashes, and swiftly put distance and the burned remains of an armchair between us.

"What will Elena think?" he scolded, rubbing his face, leaving streaks across the lines of his cheeks and forehead.

"That you're a fool."

Elena crossed her arms, scowling, not at him, but at me. "I'd never think Anders was a fool. Now you, on the other hand—"

"Pity." I plopped down on a fallen log beside her, nonchalant but alert to any clues of what she might have overheard. She'd been sitting far enough away, and we'd wrestled for some moments. So maybe, we were safe. "How is it possible, your Majesty, that you left your beloved alone in bed?"

"He's not in bed." Dark blue eyes flashed with mischief, though her cheeks blazed scarlet. "If he were, I'd still be there."

"Under Rosanna's roof? Shameful."

"She made certain we had the best guest room with the largest bed."

"The old witch never had any morals. Hmmm. I wonder if Anders and I should be insulted. We were guests, too, last night, and our bed wasn't anywhere near as comfortable as yours," I complained, slanting a glance at Anders, whose expression gave nothing away. "In fact, it had quite a few lumps that rubbed against all the wrong spots."

"I'm Queen, remember?" Elena poked my arm. "Though for all the time we spent in that bed, it was nearly wasted. Erich left early this morning to return to Barrow's Pass. A courier arrived soon after you went upstairs last night. He has some matters that need his attention in the next few weeks."

"Doesn't he get weary, scurrying back and forth?"

"Yes, I suppose." Elena shrugged, apparently oblivious to what Anders and I had been discussing. "But it's only until he gives the responsibility to someone else. And that person hasn't been selected yet. Besides, he wasn't planning to return home quite so soon."

I'll bet. "Did he take your troops back with him to add to the tax burden of your poor hardworking subjects?"

Anders queried me with his eyes as he joined us, sitting cross-legged on the pile of salvageable clothes in need of serious washing.

"My troops?" Elena darted a questioning look at Anders. "Since when have you started to complain about paying taxes, Alex? And no, he had his own Barrow's Pass troops. He never travels without them."

"There, you see?" I gave Anders a meaningful glance, wondering which of Erich's guard dogs razed my cottage. "I had every confidence Erich respected the plight of the poor taxpayers and brought his own guards."

"Alex." Elena's bemused expression turned thoughtful.

"Forgive her, Elena." Anders cut in swiftly before she could voice any theory about my comments. "Losing the cottage has rattled her brains. She's worried about taxes because I was teasing her about the hidden riches she's rumored to have. And if you find out they exist, you'll send tax collectors breathing down her neck."

Elena turned inquisitive eyes my way. "Do you?"

"Lords of the sea, not you, too?" I dusted ashes from my tunic in her direction on purpose. "Fools, both of you."

Sweeping the dust away, Elena crossed her legs and rested her chin on one hand, quite the lady, considering the circumstances.

I was immediately suspicious. "What?"

"I wish you'd let me keep a small troop here, or at least have some of the Port Alain guards keep an eye on you, if you're so worried about taxes." An impish grin accompanied that last bit.

"I said 'no' last night. Must I bore you and repeat myself?"

"If it hadn't been for the attack in Glynnswood," she hedged, glancing to Anders for support, "I wouldn't worry. But this attack right after that one–"

"We still don't know for certain that a Glynnswood scout wasn't behind the attack." When Anders' eyes flashed in sudden annoyance, I shook my head. "Just keeping an open mind. They were Glynnswood arrows, Master Perrin. And those skillful, highly acclaimed scouts couldn't find a clue."

"You can't think clearly about Glynnswood, so don't bother to discuss it."

"Alex." Elena placed a hand on my arm as I turned away in annoyance. At her touch, and the intimate tone in her voice, I hardened my heart, knowing she'd try to probe the wound as persistently as Rosanna. "Lords of the sea, take that stony look from your face. I can't talk to you when you look like you're ready to rip my throat out." She knelt in front of me, despite the dirt and dust, forcing me not to look away. "Someone knows how you feel about your father and used it to their advantage. If you suspect there's a connection to Glynnswood, maybe your father should be warned."

"Not by me."

Elena met my cool stare without blinking. "Why not?" I started to move away but she held me firmly in place. "I don't want to interfere."

"Then don't. Listen, Elena," I said hotly, "I know you mean well. But you had a father who loved you and raised you. Everyone makes me the villain. But I'm not the one who ignored him for twenty-five years." Getting to my feet, I broke free of her grasp and walked toward the cottage, poking through the ashes to hide my tears. Kicking aside the remains of the bed's headboard, I shoved my fists under my arms and hugged myself, furious and confused.

"You're not the villain." Elena came up quietly beside me. "But don't you see? For us, the simple answer is for you to confront Sernyn, forgive him, and get on with your life. Easy, I know, for us to say, but truly, we just want to ease your grief."

"Did any of you stop to think that he'd never be concerned about my forgiveness if I hadn't caught him off guard last year?"

"He didn't have to come himself when you arrived, looking for your family," she countered, "but he did."

"His mistake."

With a subtle change in expression, Elena brushed soot from her sleeve. "All right, I won't argue with you. I only wanted to help. That's what friends are supposed to do."

"Well, then. If that's true," —I crossed my arms with a smirk— "make yourself useful and find my riches buried under all these ashes."

* * * *

"Riches?" Jules smiled with delight when I decided to confront him after all. "Of course. The queen's courageous Mage Champion is swimming in riches. After all, you saved the throne, and Elena could do no less than grant you uncounted treasure."

"You're not serious?"

"Indeed, I am. And that's not all."

"Spare me."

"Oh, no. Let's see. Because your powers are so different from every other known mage, it's possible you've been raised by a mountain lion or born under Shad's Bay in a seabeast's cave or flew through the air and—"

"Oh, please," I said in disgust, tracing the covers of the books stacked along the shelves in his study. "I'm sorry I asked."

"Fame has its negative aspect," Jules said wisely, leaning back in a rather precarious position, hands behind his head. I turned to leave when my eyes caught sight of the wooden chair he was lounging so very comfortably in. "Don't you dare." He sat forward so fast he almost toppled over. "I've finally gotten this chair worn and smooth just how I like it. Go play mage and turn someone else's chair into a puddle of water."

"You're so dull." I headed for the door, stopped when he called my name, and turned, gritting my teeth against whatever obnoxious comment he was about to make.

"Just precisely where do you keep your riches?"

I slammed the door with a resounding bang and practically knocked poor Brendan across the length of the corridor. With impeccable tact, he schooled his surprised face to politeness. "Waiting for me?" I appraised him from head to toe like a schoolmistress who discovered one of her charges up to no good.

"Well, yes, as a matter of fact."

"I see." I crossed my arms and studied his dark blue eyes. "How did you know I was in there?"

"Alex, I'm sorry." He lost his composure and flushed bright red, trying hard not to laugh. "But when you and Jules, ah, discuss things with, ah, enthusiasm, you're both a bit loud. Not that loud," he added.

"But loud enough." When the young man nodded with mock gravity, I started to laugh, as did he. "Well, what is it? Have the twin monsters tricked you again?"

His eyes turned serious. "Martin's back."

"Well, let's go find Anders and Rosanna. I wouldn't be surprised to find them plotting together in the old seawitch's tower. We'll try there first."

Brendan smiled as we climbed the stairways to the highest floor. "I'm glad Elena's gone back to Ardenna. I'd feel horrid sneaking behind her back if she were here."

"You'll get used to it. Everyone sneaks around everyone else's back." At Rosanna's door, I knocked loudly. "Take these two, for instance." Brendan laughed aloud as Anders opened the door.

"What are you two plotting?" Anders narrowed his eyes to slits as we walked past him, taking comfortable seats by the blazing fireplace.

"The question should be, what are you and" —I nodded at Rosanna, enthroned in her rocking chair— "the old seawitch plotting?"

"Not a thing," Rosanna's tone was bland.

I turned back to Brendan. "See what I mean?"

"Yes." Dark blue eyes danced in appreciation, and then subtly changed as I nodded for him to explain our visit. "I'm not sure it's much help." Brendan stared at his hands. "Martin's back from Barrow's Pass. All he was able to find out was that Erich had several clandestine meetings late at night with unknown mages. And another one in two weeks."

"Probably the Barrow's Pass Council of Mages," Anders's tone was thoughtful. "Jules meets with the Port Alain Council, doesn't he?"

"In the middle of the night?" Rosanna arched a curious brow in his direction. For once, I was glad her suspicions matched mine.

"Maybe customs are different in Barrow's Pass."

"Why are you so determined to prove Erich innocent?" I demanded, fiddling with my boot rather than stare daggers at Anders.

"I'm not." When I glanced up, cool seagray eyes narrowed in disapproval. "But you're scrambling to put facts together to prove he's guilty. Someone should be objective. And we all know it can't be you."

"He doesn't look at you the way he looks at me," I snapped, remembering the danger in Erich's eyes.

"I should hope not."

"Anders does have a point," Rosanna interceded quietly.

"And," —Anders uncrossed his legs and stretched— "I also have an idea. Since Martin couldn't get closer, but did learn that their next meeting is scheduled in two weeks, which explains why Erich needs to be there, why don't you and I take a journey to Barrow's Pass ourselves?"

"That's a possibility." I turned back to Brendan, thinking. "Did Martin travel through Ardenna?"

"Yes, and then through the section of the Arditch Mountains that runs north of the city to Barrow's Pass."

"It's a good thing it's not winter." I turned to Anders but stopped at the curious look in his eyes. "What?"

"It's too obvious to go that way. Besides, that wasn't my plan." When my suspicion became evident, he composed his expression to unconvincing innocence. "We could bypass Ardenna and confuse any potential pursuers. If we go around the east route, we'll end up in boggy Thornmarsh. So—" He coughed with exquisite delicacy, sending a sidelong glance in Rosanna's direction. "The west route was my, ah, plan. To Glynnswood."

I scrambled to my feet.

"And through Glynnswood."

I scurried to the door, ignoring Brendan's curious stare, and Rosanna's anxious expression.

"To bypass Ardenna and come around Barrow's Pass from the west." Anders caught my tunic as I reached the door.

"No."

"It's the only way."

"I'll go through Ardenna."

"The Mage Champion is immediately recognizable. As I recall, that fact made you uncomfortable on our last visit. And disguise won't work," Anders countered when he recognized the idea leap into my eyes. "If Erich is behind all this, he'll be watching you. With a Glynnswood guide to sneak us through—"

"Absolutely, positively not." I plucked the edge of my tunic from his grip and stormed out. I was never going to Glynnswood again.

Or near it.

Or anywhere in that general direction.

Never.

I'd rather tangle with a ravenous seabeast.

Chapter Eight

"I don't know why I let you talk me into this."

"You know I'm right."

"Hmmm." We'd ridden at an easy pace north along the Kieren River to the crossroads that led west to Glynnswood, but I was weary and not very confident as we stopped for the night. "You're sure Sernyn Keltie's not going to show up?" I asked for the hundredth time. Anders cocked his head to the side and sent me a pained expression. "I want to be sure. I don't trust you any more than I trust Rosanna or Elena. You're all deceitful, manipulative, and interfering. I could go on all day describing your faults." I tossed my bedroll to the ground, raising a cloud of dirt that set Anders coughing.

"Alex, really. Be civilized, will you?" Setting his own bedroll beside mine, he unrolled it with neat, precise movements. "I suggested with great delicacy that Sernyn send another guide. He reassured me he'd never consider putting you in an awkward position. I also mentioned your suspicions regarding the arrows," he added blandly, "without making you sound like an unhinged, narrow-minded idiot."

"I suppose I should be grateful."

"Yes, you should." With a muffled yawn, he crawled into his bedroll. "He said he'd keep watch for signs of suspicious activity."

"Do you believe him?" I knelt on my own bedroll, stretching it out to its full length, one wary eye on Anders.

"Go to sleep." He tucked himself under the covers and turned his back on me.

"Anders—"

"Rosanna was right."

"About what?"

"Everything."

* * * *

A sharp, annoying nudge kept penetrating my grogginess. "Go away. It's too early. I haven't had enough sleep."

"I know," Anders whispered, tickling my ear with his warm breath. "But I think our guide's arrived."

"Lords of the sea, it's too damn early." I rolled over on one side and leaned up on my elbow. And stared, unsure what my reaction should be.

"Your pardon. I did not mean to wake you." Our guide sat on the other side of our nonexistent campfire, legs crossed beneath him, a curious look in very young eyes.

"That's all right." I sat up with unfeigned stiffness, prodding Anders into a sitting position. If I had to be up and about, so did he. "I think."

"I really am a very good guide. When—" Gwynn, because, of course, it was Gwynn who was our guide, flushed scarlet. "When I heard you requested a scout from my people, I asked permission to help you in your journey." His smile was uncertain, his brown eyes wide. "But if you would rather someone else—" He started to scramble to his feet, but a wave of my hand stopped him.

Flameblast Sernyn Keltie. Sending Gwynn was another form of subtle warfare. Somehow, through his letters to Rosanna, he caught her deviousness and knew how to make my life a living hell.

"I don't doubt your abilities, Gwynn, nor would I rather someone else be our guide. You, at least, I know to be honorable."

The young man's expression suggested he wasn't quite sure of my sincerity. "You will not be disappointed." A boyish gleam danced in his eyes for just a brief moment. "Or my father will be angry."

"Just who is your father, anyway? You never introduced us. As a matter of fact," I said, realizing the truth, "you didn't introduce me to anyone. Were you ashamed of me or afraid I would be impolite?"

His cheeks flushed bright scarlet. "I would never think that."

"Alex." Anders scowled, disentangling himself from his bedroll. "You're being rude. Leave the poor boy alone."

"I'm just curious." I watched the boy thoughtfully for a moment, studying his handsome features, wondering why they seemed so familiar, as he tugged at his unruly lock of thick hair. "If his father's so quick to anger—"

The boy flushed deeper, if that were possible, and looked down at his hands. "He is not, truly. It is just that this task is a matter of honor. My father is a clan chief. If I fail you, I disgrace him. And myself," he added quietly.

Curious boy. I watched his face go through a number of battling expressions. "I'm sorry. I'm not quite awake, and I am being rude."

"Yes, you are. And I'm hungry." Anders groaned as he stretched the kinks from his aching back. "First assignment as guide, Gwynn, is to find us a decent breakfast."

* * * *

We learned quickly that Gwynn wasn't lying. He really was an excellent, well-trained scout. The boy found paths through the dense forest every time my untrained eyes swore we were trapped or lost. Two days of quiet, companionable traveling through the hushed woods left Anders and me weary and aching in every joint and muscle, and cranky.

Not Gwynn, who wasn't old enough to feel tired or even know the meaning of the word.

Eyes closed, I sat cross-legged before the mound of dirt and dead leaves thankful we'd finally stopped traveling for the day. The familiar sharp prick of ice and the answering sting of flame easily merged to cool warmth. Forgetting Anders and Gwynn and our journey, I envisioned the campfire we needed, and relaxed as I heard the crackle of burning flame. Satisfied, I opened one eye to find Gwynn shyly watching me. Caught, he looked down and fumbled with some pebbles at his feet. I cocked my head to the side and watched him, waiting. In the last two days, I'd caught him stealing such glances several times.

Gwynn flushed with embarrassment, eyes still averted. "My father told me you saved Queen Elena's crown in the Mage Challenge, and that she granted you the title of Mage Champion."

"That's what she calls me when she wants to annoy me. I think she should change it. It's a bit too aggressive, don't you think?"

At the obvious amusement in my voice, Gwynn looked up. "But you must be aggressive to defend the queen. And Alex, your mage talent is highly respected. It is far beyond what any Glynnswood mage can do."

"I wonder—" I stopped, keeping my thoughts to myself.

"It's an interesting thought." Anders said, catching my unspoken thought as he joined us by the campfire, leaning back against the soft pile of bedrolls.

Resting my chin on my hand, I eyed Anders for a moment. "You don't think it smacks of being an unhinged, narrow-minded idiot?"

Cool seagray eyes twinkled at me, smug for reading my mind. "Not at all."

Gwynn sat there puzzled, eyes darting between us, though he never asked for an explanation. Lords of the sea, I'd never survive going through life so civilized. Growing up with Jules and Khrista and Elena had banished my good manners.

"Did, ah, Elder Keltie mention anything to you about—" I paused, searching for a diplomatic word.

"What Alex is trying to say," Anders picked up where I left off, "is whether Elder Keltie mentioned anything about our suspicions regarding the attack on us in Glynnswood," he finished, preening like a well-fed cat.

Gwynn nodded, brown eyes wide. "He said you thought there was a chance someone in Glynnswood might be involved. Alex—" His expression was earnest as he leaned forward. "If that is true, it would be dishonorable."

"That's one way of looking at it. But I was wondering just how highly respected my magic really is in civilized Glynnswood." At the boy's befuddled look, I explained. "Is it highly respected or highly envied?"

Recognition flashed in his eyes as he yanked at his hair. "Oh."

"It's just a thought."

"She doesn't have many," Anders explained. "So consider it an honor that she has one in front of you." He dodged my fist as Gwynn tried valiantly not to laugh at my expense.

"Are there many mages in Glynnswood?"

"In our village of near one thousand people, there are only forty or fifty mages. It is not very different throughout the forest." He smiled sadly, and shrugged. "My father is a mage, but I have no magic talent."

"I didn't think I had any for a long, long time. But you have your own talent that's just as special." The boy looked genuinely puzzled. "You told us you were a good guide. You are. Your father and Elder Keltie obviously sent a scout who knows what he's doing. For someone who's not quite so old," —I grinned— "you've done much to help us.

Anders and I would never have found the paths that you have." Embarrassed at my open and sincere praise, Gwynn flushed, his expression, to my eyes, horrified when I added, "I'll tell your father myself."

"No." He scrambled to his feet.

Anders arched a brow at me.

"My father said you would not be comfortable with—" Gwynn stammered, tugging at the misbehaving lock of hair that dangled over his forehead, "with the clan chiefs since you are unhappy with Elder Keltie."

How had I earned such an appalling reputation?

I pointed a finger at Anders when he started to speak. "Don't say anything. And get that smug look from those frosty gray eyes. "Well, Gwynn . . ." I turned to the boy, who was still poised to flee. "I'm only uncomfortable with one elder, and you know who that is. Despite Anders's unflattering opinion of me, I'm grateful for your help, and I want your father to know how skilled you are. Hearing it from strangers, particularly the queen's aggressive Mage Champion, should only make him proud of you. Don't you agree?"

Gwynn hadn't moved a muscle.

I was confused. "Sit down. I won't bite. And I won't tell your father if you'd rather I didn't."

Gwynn sat down, the somber look in his eyes giving way to boyish mischief. "You could write him a letter instead."

* * * *

In another three days, we'd skirted the foothills of the Bitteredge Mountains, keeping within the natural protection of the dense woods. East lay Ardenna. Beyond that, a day's journey north, the road snaked up the side of the Arditch Mountains to Barrow's Pass. We'd reached the borders of Glynnswood. Gazing north, I could see the mountains on the horizon.

I turned to Gwynn, who sat on a log, whittling the same small piece of wood he'd been toying with for a few days. "Are you sure you're going to be all right?"

"Am I a good scout?"

"Yes. Of course."

He flashed me a broad disarming smile. "Then I will be all right. I can keep myself busy until you return."

Anders sat beside him, sharing the log. "It may be a week before we return, more or less." When the boy nodded, he said, "If we're not back by the end of ten days, Gwynn, then you need to go home."

"It is my duty to wait for the Mage Champion," he answered with pride, before looking at his feet, embarrassed.

"Gwynn." I crouched before him, forcing the boy to meet my eyes. "If we're not back by then, something's gone wrong. I want your word you'll return home."

"I cannot give it to you. Alex, please. I gave my word to my father that I would bring you back safely."

Anders touched the boy's arm. "If something goes wrong in Barrow's Pass, there's nothing you'll be able to do."

"I will wait until you return."

Stubborn young fool. "If we're not back in ten days' time, go home." I stopped his protest with an outstretched hand. "And see that word reaches Duke Barlow at Port Alain."

Gwynn shut his eyes, thinking. Finally, "All right. And then I will come back with the duke and his troops to look for you."

"Are all Glynnswoodsmen so stubborn?" I asked in frustration.

"That's where you get it," Anders said, dodging my fist. "I always thought it was from your mother."

"Alex. Before you go—" Gwynn stretched out his hand, shyly offering me the wood he'd been whittling.

In silence, I took the piece of wood, turning it over in my hands, stunned to find a perfect replica of the mage pendant dangling from a leather thong at my neck. I gave it to Anders, got quickly to my feet, and walked away, not trusting myself to speak to this very peculiar boy who represented Glynnswood and every bit of heartache that accompanied the name.

"Anders?" Gwynn's voice was soft behind me. "Does she hate it?"

"She loves it." The old beast chuckled. "Trust me. She loves it. When we get back, she'll tell you herself."

Chapter Nine

"There really is something peculiar about that boy." Anders looked thoughtful some hours later when we were taking a short break from our journey.

"There's something peculiar about anyone from that forest."

"That includes you, I presume. I don't understand it," Anders said, enjoying my ill humor, as he settled our packs along the side of the road, "but I think he likes you."

"Gwynn just wants to make sure I don't turn him into a wildhog."

"You can't do that."

"He doesn't know that."

"You must be casting some kind of Mage Champion glamour, even charming that innocent merchant into taking us as far up the mountainside as the outskirts of Barrow's Pass," Anders muttered, half to himself. "Impressive. But I don't understand it. Unless you're getting uncharacteristically soft."

In mere seconds, I thought of a hundred thousand ways for vengeance against the wretch. "Don't forget to tell Rosanna how soft I'm getting." I nudged him in the side, catching him off balance. "It'll be a delight to watch her amazement."

"She won't believe me."

Scanning the crossroads, I followed the tracks of the merchant's wagon wheels as they veered off to the left. The road to Barrow's Pass lay to the right. And I wasn't sure which way we should be going.

"We haven't discussed how we're going to spy on his lordship's affairs." Anders shaded his eyes against the afternoon sun.

"We have two days to come up with a plan."

"So much time?" Anders picked up his worn leather pack and slung it across one shoulder. "Coming?"

We tucked our mage pendants out of sight and made ourselves as unobtrusive as possible, sauntering through the large town as though we'd been there before. But there was no shore. How could these poor people live without the comforting escape to the sea? Then again, maybe that explained Erich's peculiarities. Barrow's Pass was perched on the eastern slope of the smallest peak of the Arditch Mountains, but high enough to make me uneasy. I was grateful there were no bridges to cross. Though the mountains and valley below, bordered by the thick, dense forests of Glynnswood, offered a view to take one's breath away, still, there was no sea. In the distance, Ardenna gleamed with fraudulent promise.

We took a room at a decent inn and discovered that Duke Harwoode arrived home the previous night. In a foul temper, he planned to stay for only one more night. If we'd missed him, I'd have dogged his trail to Ardenna and ambushed the duke just for vengeance.

* * * *

"I'm glad it's not winter." Shivering beneath my heavy cloak, I tried to keep my teeth from rattling as we kept watch in the shadows at the manor gate.

"You said the same thing weeks ago."

"I mean it now even more so. I forgot how chilly it gets at this altitude." I snuggled further into my cloak. "We're too close to the stars."

"It is the middle of the night, and a clear moonlit sky. If you were of a mind, I could be romantic."

"Hush." I put a finger to his lips. "Someone's coming."

We crouched lower in the shadows and waited. A cloaked and hooded figure crept toward the gate, and headed, not for the main entrance, where Erich's guards were posted, but around the back through the manor gardens. Anders grabbed my hand and tugged. I followed as he trailed the hooded figure, stopping so abruptly we collided. With caution, I pushed my head around his body as the duke's midnight visitor knocked twice, waited, and then again three times at a barely visible wooden door. Creaking, the door swung inward. Not a soul was visible inside, only the figure standing outside in the clear moonlit night.

Lords of the sea! I caught my breath as Anders gripped my hand in dire warning. With a swift glance left and right, the man, clearly a man now, threw his dark hood back, white hair catching the moonlight. A vicious scar stood out on his cheek before he crept inside. The blemish placed there by the log beneath his skin that I changed to flame one year ago in Tucker's Meadow.

"We have to follow him." I started to move forward when Anders grabbed my cloak and then my shoulders, dragging me back and holding me tight. "It's Charlton Ravess," I explained, not sure if he had recognized the mage as I tried to break free of his iron grip.

"Hush." Strong arms calmed my shaking body. "I know. But we can't go charging in. Now wait."

Reluctant, I followed his gaze along the manor's wall. On the floor overlooking the gardens, a small light appeared in the window.

"I hate climbing." Anders grumbled an unintelligible oath. "All right. Listen. See that twisted oak that stretches close to the window?" I nodded. "As I climb up—"

"It's in clear moonlit view," I protested.

Anders ran a hand through his hair, biting his lip hard to keep from scolding me. "Just listen, all right? You have to time it carefully. When

I reach the point where I'll be visible, change the air to a wall of fine dirt. Thin, Alex, so that I can eavesdrop, but natural so it blends into the garden."

"Let me climb. I'm lighter."

"There's no time to argue. You can't do both." Before I could protest further, he was gone, hidden in the deep shadows.

When I caught sight of his head at the base of the tree, I called on my mage talent. The sharpness of the fire and ice vanished almost immediately as I blended the two to cool warmth. Taking a deep breath, I envisioned what Anders had described, watching his slow progress. When his head appeared on the point of emerging into clear view, I focused and changed the air to a thin dirt wall. With a brief approving nod, Anders settled himself more comfortably. I focused to keep the fragile wall from crumbling and betraying his presence. Watching his face as he strained to hear, I wavered at the sudden flash of hot anger in his eyes. He shot me an anxious look until I steadied the dirt wall. Long minutes dragged by, draining my strength until I feared I'd lose consciousness. Abruptly, the light was shuttered. Anders crawled down a short length of the tree and stayed well hidden as I transformed the earth wall back to empty air.

I scrambled to hide, exhausted.

* * * *

"I presume the news isn't very good."

Anders remained silent as we made our way back to the inn. Once we were in our room, he started undressing, flinging clothes off item-by-item in angry spurts. Taking a deep breath, he closed his eyes. "I'm sorry, Alex, truly, for doubting you." Clear, cool eyes locked with mine across the length of the lumpy bed.

"I didn't have any proof."

"No. But you have wonderful instinct. I'm sorry."

I sat on the bed and pulled him down beside me. "Tell me."

"It's simple. Charlton Ravess wants revenge against you for humiliating him in Tucker's Meadow. So does Erich." When my eyebrow arched skyward, he said, "You foiled their plan to get Elena off the throne. Now that Ravess has been exiled and no longer controls the Ardenna Crown Council, it's up to Erich to do his dirty work. Safely married to Elena, he'll arrange an unfortunate accident involving Elena, and Brendan, too. By that time, you'll be long gone." Anders paused to take a deep breath. "They're using mercenaries, too."

"If Elena and Brendan are gone, then the crown—" I stopped, puzzled, absently rubbing his back to soothe away the tension.

"The Dunneal crown would be up for grabs by any eligible duke. There are no other blood relations in Elena's family with any legal claim to the throne," he explained. "Whoever's left has either disgraced themselves or managed to die without heirs."

"Wouldn't it make more sense for Erich to wait until Elena has a child? Then he could still rid himself of Elena and Brendan, but control his child."

Anders rubbed his eyes wearily. "They're impatient."

"They're foolish. Ravess plans to withstand another Mage Challenge to defend Erich's right to remain on the throne. After all, I'll be dead, and the Crownmage is only a legend. Little does he know," I murmured.

"One other thing," Anders said an odd expression in his eyes. "When they moved from the window, I heard Edgecliff mentioned, as well as Glynnswood, but nothing more. Their voices were muffled. I'm sorry."

"So maybe there is a third party involved from Glynnswood?"

"Maybe. But maybe they're just making it look like that. Either way, you're not an unhinged, narrow-minded idiot."

"Gee, thanks."

"We have to stop the wedding. I don't want to see Elena heartbroken, but I'd much rather see her alive."

I sat up straight and crossed my legs beneath me. "Then we'll leave as soon as Erich is gone, find Gwynn, tell him we're not returning through Glynnswood, and then" —I smiled in wicked anticipation— "plan a midnight visit to Elena."

"We can't just tell her Erich's a traitor when he'll probably be listening to every word."

I smiled as I started to undress. "Of course not. But at the risk of putting your life in danger, I think it's time we gave Elena her betrothal present."

Eyes sparkling, he helped me tug my tunic over my head. "My life's at risk just by staying with you. I might as well enjoy it." Pulling me down beside him, he kissed my forehead and fell promptly asleep.

I wasted no time doing the same.

Chapter Ten

"You are back early."

Startled by Gwynn's unexpected presence, I edged back, stepping ungracefully on Anders's foot. Ignoring his loud protest, I stared at Gwynn. "One of these days, you'll have to show me how you manage to sneak up on people."

"You're too clumsy." Anders hobbled along, making a big scene about the pain in his foot as he put his worn leather pack on the ground.

"And you're too old. Now go and sit."

Gwynn tried without success to hide his smile as I shoved Anders in the direction of a tree stump. "I could show you on the journey back."

I stole a look at Anders who refused to ease my predicament after I'd stomped on his foot. "Gwynn, about the journey back—"

The boy looked up, brushing the unruly lock of hair from eager eyes. "Shall we leave right away?"

"Anders—"

"He's your distant kin."

At that smug response, I scowled, looked for something to fling at Anders's head, and thought better of it. "We're not going back," I said, regretting my words as disappointment clouded Gwynn's face. "I'm sorry." And I was.

Lords of the sea, he was only a boy and meant nothing to me. Or shouldn't, but there was something in Gwynn that tugged at my heart.

"May I ask why not?" His tone was polite, distant.

I crouched in front of Gwynn and pulled out the wooden mage pendant he'd carved for me, hanging side-by-side with Elena's gift, catching him unawares. Holding it in my hand, I said softly, "Because of who I am. I have to tell the queen what we've discovered."

Shrugging his disappointment aside, he nodded firmly. "It is a matter of honor. I understand."

Surprising myself, I ruffled his disheveled hair and tucked the pendant inside my tunic. "This token brought me luck. Now listen." I rummaged in my pack for paper. "Tell me your father's name. I'll write him a note as I promised."

"He is a clan chief." Gwynn's voice was without expression.

"Yes, I know." Rummaging further, I found pen and ink. "But I can't address it to the clan chief, Gwynn. It would be disrespectful. Now, what's his name?"

Gwynn stood quickly and edged away like a cornered animal. "The letter is not important. I will tell him myself." He stepped back a pace, inching farther away from me, oblivious to Anders who had crept behind him, sensing imminent flight.

I started to laugh as he stepped on Anders's other foot, but Anders had the presence of mind to grab the boy.

"I must go. Please."

Lords of the sea, it was very hard to ignore the loud warning in my head from instinct, which finally slipped the puzzle pieces together. "Gwynn." I held my voice steady. "If you don't tell me your father's name, I'll turn you into a tiny gray fieldmouse."

Gwynn blinked once. "Anders said you cannot do that."

"Traitor." I scowled at Anders. Wedged between Anders and myself, Gwynn was trapped. I locked eyes with the boy. "I ask you to tell me as a matter of my own personal honor."

"Please." Gwynn blinked again, but this time, fighting tears and looking all of six years old. "If I tell you—"

"Will you be in trouble?" When he closed his eyes and nodded, I cursed loud and long, startling both Anders and the boy. "All right, then I'll tell you." When Gwynn's eyes popped open, brown eyes wide with

Mage Resolution

alarm, I turned to Anders, took a deep breath to stop my voice from shaking, and folded my arms across my chest. "I'd like you to meet my brother. Well, half-brother."

Anders' seagray eyes widened.

Gwynn's shoulders sagged. "I have offended you."

"Offended me? Don't be an idiot."

"You are not angry?"

"Not at you. But now I have another grievance against Sernyn Keltie." I cocked my head to the side. "Are there any more of you?"

"Only me." Gwynn's face was so pale, I was afraid he was going to faint. "Alex, he will be furious."

"Then don't tell him." I ignored Anders's mocking smile. "Until you hear from me. He's kept you a secret for an awfully long time."

"Father said you would not want to know that you had a brother." Gwynn's shyness returned. "Is it true? Alex, will I hear from you?"

"Damn that man," I said impatiently, without being unkind. "I probably didn't want to know that I had a brother, not if Sernyn Keltie fathered him. But here you are, and I don't mind in the least knowing you're my brother, only that he lied to me again." I took a deep breath, wondering if Gwynn could make sense of my rambling speech. "As for hearing from me, didn't you promise to teach me your stealthy, deceitful tricks?"

Gwynn nodded with enthusiasm and relief.

"So go home. And tell Elder flameblasted Keltie that you performed with honor. So much so, that I might need your services again." I tugged at the misbehaving lock of hair. "Go." When Gwynn didn't move, I touched his cheek. "It'll be all right, Gwynn. I promise."

With a solemn nod to me, and then Anders, Gwynn walked away, stopped at the edge of the dense forest, and then ran back, gripping me in a fierce hug before vanishing into the woods without a backward glance.

"You handled that in a rather mature fashion."

I faced Anders until we were nose to nose. "Listen, old man. I don't want to hear your snide comments all the way to Ardenna."

"That wasn't snide."

"Oh, no?" I poked his chest with a determined finger. "Gwynn's a child. What did you expect me to do? Hold him responsible for Sernyn Keltie's lies?"

Anders removed my prodding finger from his chest. "Considering your reaction to anything your father does, I don't blame him for keeping Gwynn hidden."

"Hidden? He sent Gwynn to me as a guide."

"An excellent one. You said so yourself."

"Stop being smug."

"Your father underestimated you."

"No, he didn't, Anders. Believe me, he knew precisely what he was doing. Sernyn Keltie knew deep in his heart that I'd instinctively recognize something about Gwynn."

"To make you angry?" Anders arched a cynical brow. "That doesn't make sense."

"To soften me up. He knew I'd grow fond of Gwynn. He used that boy."

Anders stopped my tirade with a lingering kiss. "You're giving your father far too much credit."

"He's devious, Anders. That's why he asked Rosanna to raise me. She's even more devious." I backed away as he tried to put his arms round me.

"Leave the poor woman out of the argument."

I prodded his chest again. "If she knows about Gwynn, Anders, I swear I'll toss her into Shad's Bay and personally find a ravenous seabeast to devour her."

His hand grabbed my needling finger and held it tight. "She told you everything she knows."

"You don't know her like I do. She's always got a secret hidden away."

"So do you."

"Yes, well." I looked past Anders's head to the massive mountains that blocked my view of Ardenna. "Here's another. Did you know there's a back door to Ardenna?"

* * * *

"So this is how you managed to creep in unnoticed all those times last year when you and Elena were at odds."

"Yes." A few days later than we'd planned because of the detour, we arrived at the tunnel's entrance, where I'd shown Anders the secret passage that led to the throne room. I rummaged in my gear for a torch, hoping the tunnel was still passable.

"Elena doesn't mind?"

"Elena doesn't know. And if she did," —I shrugged, not bothered in the least— "I never confessed to some of my trips here last year, so she never had cause to question me." I held the torch away from my body, coaxed fire and ice awake, and effortlessly changed the tips to bright flame.

"Shouldn't you remind her? Alex, what if she needs to flee the city?"

I shoved the torch ahead of me, leading the way, and shouldered my pack. "I've thought of that, but I don't want to remind her in front of Erich."

"Good point."

"I have them now and then. Listen, Elena's pretty sharp. She'll remember if she needs to remember. It's her family secret, after all." With a teasing kiss, I led the way through the crevice in the cold rocks. "Watch out for your bulging stomach, old man."

Anders muttered a curse, and then another. "My stomach isn't the problem. My traveling bag, stuffed full of all those unnecessary items you couldn't fit in your own pack, is the problem." Another curse, a groan, the sound of leather sliding across stone, and a heavy breath. "Next time, I'm going in the front door."

I held the torch closer to see his red-blotched face. "I never have any trouble getting through."

Refusing to respond, Anders waved me away in annoyance. "Lead on." He stayed quiet as we made swift steady progress through the tunnel, climbing slowly upward until we reached the alcove beyond the chamber door. Anders glanced around, intrigued, as I set my pack down on the stone steps, and crept toward the hidden door behind the throne's tapestry. I set a finger to my lips and eased the door open a crack, listening. He crouched beside me, wincing as the crack of a huge oak staff resounded above our heads.

I stifled a betraying laugh at Anders's dazed expression. "We're just in time."

The rustling of Elena's silk robes of state as she sat on the Dunneal throne was followed by the sound of boot heels.

"Erich," I mouthed to Anders, who listened as the royal steward read the first grievance, a minor one brought by a merchant in

Thornmarsh, followed by several others that Elena resolved without controversy.

Until, "Your majesty, my sister's children have been stolen. And there have been others, too."

Elena paused. "Where did this happen?"

"Edgecliff, majesty." Edgecliff, on the western border of Glynnswood. "The duke of Edgecliff sent troops to search for the children, but they've vanished without a trace. I thought that—"

"Surely, this is not a matter for the queen." Erich's deep voice rolled over the poor man's plea. I was surprised Elena allowed him to participate before her wedding. Erich had no legal right to pronounce judgments, not until he was proclaimed Prince of Tuldamoran.

"With all respect, my lord duke." The man paused, silent, until we heard the sound of rustling silk when Elena probably signaled him to proceed. "There have been strange things happening in Edgecliff. People have seen things they didn't understand, though they were too far away to say clearly what they saw. But it was nothing natural," he added, as Erich's boot heels started pacing.

"If you're speaking of magic, didn't you inform the council of mages?" Erich didn't even bother to hide his contempt.

"Erich." Elena's robes rustled softly in warning.

"We did, your Majesty. But they brushed us away when we had no proof. We thought, perhaps, if you could send word to them, they'd help us. Nothing more than that. It's the children that matter, and if there's a chance that something unnatural has taken them—"

Silky smooth, Erich interrupted the man's plea with impeccable politeness. "Before we exert the queen's authority to find possibly nonexistent demons, would you accept a further investigation?"

"Yes, my lord. Of course."

"Then, Elena," —boot heels clicked closer to the throne— "since my duchy is nearer to Edgecliff, let me send a small band with a mage from Barrow's Pass to investigate. Why force an issue when you may not need to?"

Why was Elena letting him interfere?

"And," he added smoothly, "if it is something truly extraordinary, perhaps your Mage Champion can offer some assistance?"

So he'd send me right into an ambush. Anders glanced at me, his expression simple and eloquent.

"If that's satisfactory—"

The petitioner agreed and left, along with Elena and her court.

"What doesn't my lord duke want Elena to know about in Edgecliff?" I whispered to Anders.

"Good question. I think we should warn your father and encourage him to send scouts to poke around the forest."

"You warn him."

With a long-suffering sigh, Anders stretched his muscles. "Yes, Alex. Now what do you propose to do?"

"Get some sleep."

Chapter Eleven

"Her Majesty is sleeping, Mage Champion." Elena's personal guard looked apologetic, as he straightened to attention, and perplexed at our sudden appearance in the castle.

"I'm aware of that. Believe me, I wish I were doing the same. But I have important news that she must hear. Now." Casting a glance first in Anders' direction, I turned back to the hesitant guard. "I'm not leaving until you wake her."

The guard disappeared with open reluctance, muttering something disrespectful under his breath. Anders shook his head in tolerant amusement. Moments later, the guard returned, a sheepish look on his face. Apologizing, he directed us straight to Elena's sitting room, where she was already waiting, and worried.

"Are you all right?"

"Of course." I hid a smile at Elena's obvious state of dishevelment, keeping my expression neutral.

"Damn you, Alex. From your message, I thought you were hurt."

"If I were hurt," I said with exaggerated patience, "I wouldn't be here."

Throwing me a look of utter disgust, she went to Anders and kissed his cheek. "You're always welcome here. Preferably alone."

He flushed bright red. "Surely not in the middle of the night?"

"Any time."

"Should I leave the two of you alone?" I asked dryly.

Elena chuckled, wrapped her silk robe tighter around her slim body, and started to sit, and then stopped with a grin. "I suppose we can't have a midnight chat without a glass or two of Marain wine."

"It wouldn't be civilized." I tossed my cloak over a low chair.

"Well, then, I won't have you spread rumors of my poor hospitality." Elena went to find glasses and returned with an unopened bottle.

"Only three?"

Elena gave me a contented smile. "Erich's sleeping."

"Ah." But I knew better, confident the traitor was listening to every word behind the door. "Tired him out, did you?"

"I always do."

"Good. Keeps them docile."

"So . . ." Elena grinned at Anders' indignant look, and poured wine from the bottle he had dutifully opened. "Why are you here this time?"

"We wanted to give you your long overdue gift."

"Should I wake Erich?"

"No," I said hastily, scrambling to explain at her arched brow. "He's not used to our midnight visits yet. Besides, we thought we'd give it to you in private, and then you can share it with him later. At your discretion," I couldn't resist adding.

Taking a small sip from her glass, Elena brushed strands of black hair from her forehead. "All right, Alex, I confess. I'm intrigued."

"You should be."

"Alex, stop torturing her."

Smug, I settled back comfortably against Anders's knees. "You remember, ah, how you and Jules thought I was the Crownmage?" When Elena nodded, blue eyes narrowed with suspicion. I went on, "I knew I wasn't, though the two of you hounded me without mercy." At Elena's pained expression, recalling the ugly confrontations we'd shared, I paused to choose my words. "What I didn't know until after I defeated Charlton Ravess, however, was that Anders was the Crownmage."

Elena's glass halted in mid-air as her face lost all trace of color. I stretched to take the glass from her hand before she dropped it to the floor, but she pulled her hand back and drained the entire glass. "Lords of the sea."

"Care for another glass?" I held out the bottle.

Elena grabbed the bottle from my hand and poured herself another full glass. "Lords of the sea, Alex."

"You already said that."

"Why didn't you tell me?"

Fair question. "I was in shock myself for a long time."

"What Alex means, Elena, is that she was furious with me for keeping it a secret from her." Anders' smile was apologetic. "I didn't tell her when I arrived in Port Alain, because" —he flushed scarlet again— "well, because I wanted to meet you before committing myself to your cause. But Alex was in the middle of discovering her magic potential by then, as unique as it is. I'm sorry, Elena. I may have made a grave mistake, but Alex was doing so well."

"Remember the theft of my mother's pendant before the Mage Challenge? Guess who robbed it?" I tossed in spitefully to remind him that I still hadn't forgiven him for hiding the pendant to force me to rely on my own self confidence.

Elena looked horrified.

"Well, it worked," Anders defended his actions, which had almost severed our fledgling relationship.

"Yes, but—" Elena sighed and took a long sip of wine. "I'm not sure I can handle these midnight visits anymore." Then she laughed, mischief in her eyes as she grinned at me. "No wonder your cottage went up in flames. You can change one element to another. He can change each element to its different forms. In the night, between the two of you—"

"He's too old."

"You keep changing your mind about that."

"You and Rosanna always take his part."

"Ladies," Anders interrupted. "It's late. Before our queen has an overabundance of wine, I'd like to remind her that my mage talent is at her command. Actually, it always has been from the moment I first met you, Elena."

"Thank you." Suddenly serious, Elena put the wine glass on the low wooden table to her left. "Shall I announce this formally?"

Anders wrapped an arm around me, toying with a lock of my hair. "We thought it might be better if you were to keep it quiet for now. It's always helpful to have a hidden weapon on hand, particularly since someone is out for Alex's blood."

"And Erich?" Elena looked at me.

"Your choice." I shrugged, restraining my immediate reply. "But if you tell him, you'd best tell him to keep it secret."

"Of course. Erich can be trusted, or I wouldn't be marrying him."

* * * *

"Damnation." Jules groaned, green eyes miserable. "I let you out of my sight for a few weeks, Alex, only a few weeks, and look at the news you bring back."

Almost the very moment we arrived back in Port Alain, I gathered the troops together in Rosanna's tower to inform them of Erich's treacherous association with Firemage Ravess. "I'm sorry to ruin your day," I said dryly, "but there's another important matter we need to discuss." As he continued to groan, I made sure I had Rosanna and Brendan's complete attention. "But this point also stays secret. Elena's the only one who knows. Well, Elena, and probably Erich by now, which also means Charlton Ravess knows, too, if Erich tells him."

Rosanna's eyes widened in undisguised curiosity.

"Knows what?" Jules ran a hand through his light brown hair, clearly unhappy, and worried about Elena, this time, for good reason.

"Easy, Jules. This news is good. Anders—" I stopped as I caught sight of his rugged face, scarlet with embarrassment. "It's out of character for you to be humble." When he studiously ignored me, I started to laugh and turned to Jules. "You were right about the Crownmage. He does exist."

Jules's green eyes lit with unexpected delight. "You found him?"

Anders fidgeted with the sleeve of his brown tunic, cleared his throat a few times, fidgeted some more.

"Anders, really. Stop stalling, and spit it out."

"Jules," he said slowly, shooting daggers at me, "though you might find it hard to believe, I am the Crownmage."

Poor bewildered Jules said nothing for a very long time, started to speak, stopped, started again, scratched his head, threw up his hands, and shook his head.

"Jules, it really is good news." When he nodded, a dumbstruck expression plastered on his face, I crossed my arms and stared at his mother. "You look surprised."

"When are you going to believe that Anders doesn't tell me everything?" Rosanna's eyes held challenge, daring me to cross swords with her again. Little did she know that I would, soon enough. "Anyway, it is good news."

"It's wonderful news." Brendan cut in, his young face smiling. "My sister must have been delighted."

"She was," Anders said, adding pointedly, "We told her she had to keep it secret. Not from Erich, of course. She trusts him implicitly."

"Unlikely he'll keep it a secret," Brendan grumbled. "You're right, Alex. By now, Charlton Ravess must know, too. Is that why you told Elena now?"

"Of course. Let them lose a little sleep."

"We have to stop the wedding," Jules said quietly, green eyes searching mine, old grief shadowed by heartache. "We have to tell Elena."

"I don't think that's wise." Rosanna stood to pour cinnamon tea and handed out the cups. "I'm not saying she'll not believe that Alex and Anders are telling the truth, but, well, she's in love for the first time." She avoided her son's eyes with exquisite care. "I'd rather we tell her only as a last resort. We can take comfort in the fact that she's safe until the wedding."

"You'd rather set a trap and let Erich bring about his own downfall?" Anders suggested. When she nodded, he glanced at me. "Then why don't we think about this for awhile and meet again tomorrow? We all have quite enough on our minds."

"That's for certain. I'm really grateful, Alex." Brendan's manner turned shy as he stood to leave. "I've been worried sick about Elena, and now we have proof that she's in danger. At least, we can do something about it. I was beginning to feel helpless."

"Well, we're not helpless or hopeless." I laughed, squeezing his arm. "And Brendan," —I held him back from leaving— "I meant what I said about my mage talent protecting you."

"That includes me," Anders said, coming to stand beside Elena's heir.

"Thanks." Brendan nodded, embarrassed at our words. "I'd better get back to the little monsters. Pardon me, my lord." He grinned at Jules. "But they are."

"I know." He sighed. "Alex spoils them."

"I do not."

"That's what Lauryn said."

"Jules!" His mother slapped him on the shoulder. "Lauryn said no such thing."

Jules shrugged, and escaped with Brendan, leaving us alone with Rosanna, who looked at Anders and then at me, resignation in her eyes.

"There's something else, isn't there?"

"There's always something else," I said quietly. "Your fate depends on your answer, old lady. The wrong one will find you swimming in Shad's Bay with hungry seabeasts."

Though my threat was light-hearted, Rosanna had no trouble reading the serious intent in my eyes. She fidgeted with her teacup, stealing a furtive glance at Anders, looking for a clue. For once, he stayed neutral.

"Did you know about Gwynn?"

The old woman met my gaze without blinking as she admitted, "Your father told me a year ago, when you first met him, that you had a half-brother. Up until that point, I didn't know, Alex. And that's the truth. I swear on my dead husband's grave. Sernyn told me he'd tell you himself when he thought you'd accept it. He hoped" —she held my gaze— "that you would come to accept him and Gwynn in due time."

Unsure what to say, though I'd practiced a head filled with nasty remarks all the way back from Ardenna, I put my teacup down and left the two of them alone, needing to think.

* * * *

Rosanna found me much later in a sheltered corner of her gardens.

"Don't bother apologizing," I said, unable to restrain the bitterness. "You'll only have to do it again the next time I find out some other dirty little secret." Silk rustled softly as she sat beside me on the cool stone bench, keeping her counsel. "I'm so tired of it all." Unable to sit still, I stood and paced, keeping distance between us. "I feel trapped in a web of lies between you and Sernyn Keltie. What more are you keeping from me?" I stopped long enough to catch a glimpse of her somber face. "Gwynn said he's the only sibling I have. Of the three of you, he's probably the only one telling the truth."

Rosanna tucked a strand of graying hair into the knot at the base of her neck. "There was another child, a girl. She didn't survive long." Her voice was pitched low, expressionless. "I don't know very much about your stepm—" she caught back her words, "your father's wife, except that she's from Glynnswood."

"Well, she would have to be, wouldn't she? He couldn't afford to lose another wife in childbirth. Did he marry the woman the moment he buried my mother?" I fought down the turbulent fire and ice building inside me, looking for release.

"Your mother was dead ten years when he remarried." When I brushed my hands across my eyes, angry at my tears and all the lies, she added, "That's all I know, Alex."

"And you expect me to believe that?" When she stayed silent, I left her sitting alone in her gardens. Wandering glumly along the path toward the remains of my destroyed cottage, I headed for the port and the feel of the breeze from Shad's Bay.

I never reached Port Alain.

Where I thought to find ashes, I found instead my cottage, completely restored. Opening the door, with shaking hands, I went inside, sat before the cold fireplace, knees drawn tight against my chest, and wept.

Chapter Twelve

"Alex!"

Carey's shout startled me. Lords of the sea, how long had I been sitting in the dark? With ginger movements, I tried to stretch my cramped legs, numb from huddling against the wall for hours.

"Alex! Where are you?"

Muttering to myself about twins who couldn't leave me to be miserable in peace, I leaned on the wall for support and stood on shaking legs like a newborn pony. "In here." Voice hoarse, I blinked against the light from the lantern Anders held over the twins' heads. As they ran into my arms, I staggered back, grateful for the wall behind me. "I must have fallen asleep," I lied, avoiding Anders's gaze, knowing he saw right through my deception.

"Grandmother said we'd find you here. Do you like it?" Hunter stepped out of my arms, waiting anxiously for my approval.

"Like it?" I ruffled both heads. "I love it. It's just like the old one, only better." Shoving aside my selfish desire to be alone, I let the boys drag me around from room to room, pointing out odds and ends Rosanna had remembered, adding melancholy bitterness to my heartache. Anders trailed behind in respectful silence, holding the lantern.

"Grandmother knew it would make you happy." Hunter stood quietly by Anders's side as we came back to the fireplace, while Carey fidgeted, eager eyes roaming the room.

"I told the boys if we found you here, I'd take them back before it gets too late," Anders said, appraising my mood.

"Walk back with us, Alex," Carey pleaded as though he'd die a painful death if I didn't. "Please. Anders said you would."

Anders shrugged, a wry smile on his face.

"Not tonight." I tugged at a lock of Carey's hair.

"But Alex—" he protested.

"Not tonight," Hunter said with gravity no child should possess, as he nudged his twin. "We'll see Alex tomorrow." Eyes grave, he turned back to me for approval. The child had definitely inherited his mother's sensitivity.

I kissed the top of Hunter's head. "Tomorrow."

* * * *

Jules had suggested we meet in his study after I'd given the children their lessons in the schoolroom. No need to take unfair advantage of Lauryn's good nature, now that I was back. Once I sent my charges on their way home, I went up to the manor house, reaching the study before anyone else arrived. I claimed a seat on Jules's window ledge, overlooking the harbor and the ships bobbing in the bay. Eyes averted, I waited until I heard the others come in, and took a deep breath to steady my nerves.

"I'm grateful for the cottage," I said quietly.

"It was the least we could do." Jules rustled the papers on his desk, moving them to the side. "Mother tried to recreate everything exactly as she remembered it."

"I'll repay you both somehow."

"Don't you even think like that," Jules protested, turning to Rosanna, who'd not said a word. "Mother—"

When she only murmured something to please him, I shoved aside the memory of every small detail she'd remembered to replace, deciding then and there I had no time for confused grief. We had serious business to discuss, but I wasn't up to starting the conversation.

"I have a hazy plan," Anders said, breaking the uneasy silence when he realized I wasn't about to take charge.

"Let's hear it." Jules rocked his chair back from the desk and propped one foot against an open drawer.

"Alex." Anders locked eyes with me, and I felt a knot form in my gut. "Will you listen before ripping out my heart?"

"With that kind of warning, I'm not sure."

Seagray eyes darted to Rosanna, and then back to me. "Suppose we tell Erich that you're being held for ransom by jealous Glynnswood mages who think your impure and unconventional magic should be destroyed. We have the Glynnswood arrows from the first attack, so our ignorant assumption of a possible connection would be credible. And frankly, maybe it's not so ignorant. Something's going on in Edgecliff, bordering right on Glynnswood." Anders paused to stare at his hands. "If we ask Erich for help, behind Elena's back, to, ah, avoid Elena worrying about you, I suspect he'll offer to ransom you himself."

"You don't really expect him to do that?"

"Of course not. He'll let you die and blame it on Glynnswood."

"What about Elena?" I began to find myself intrigued, in spite of my misgivings, at the possibilities.

"She's the tough part." Anders tapped his fingers on the arm of his chair. "Tell her that your father sent word of your kidnapping. It'll have to be after Erich leaves to rescue you." He smiled without humor. "And we'll make sure he leaves Ardenna by telling him we need his help and no one else's. We'll stroke his ego enough to make him go after you himself."

"That shouldn't be hard to do," Brendan muttered, going bright red when we all turned to look at him. "Erich is arrogant enough to believe himself invincible."

"You're right. And if we tell Elena the Glynnswood mages demand her presence, we can get her there, too. Make up some story that they want a sum in gold from her treasury and they'll only accept it from her hands. Knowing your sister, she'd want to go, anyway," Anders continued, grinning at the young man, though his fingers were still tapping an anxious rhythm. "The rest of my plan involves Jules, Brendan, and me. If we take along some of the Port Alain guards, all of us dressed as Glynnswoodsmen, we'll avoid an accidental confrontation between Erich's troops and the real Glynnswoodsmen, who will hopefully help us." Anders stared at me, and then away.

Jules looked puzzled and gave voice to his doubt. "Won't Elena be suspicious when she sees us in disguise?"

"She won't know we're there until it becomes obvious that Erich didn't rescue Alex. Only then will we reveal ourselves. At this point, we need it to be obvious that Erich is holding Alex prisoner. Then we can march in and catch them celebrating your sorry end, Alex." He flashed a charming smile at me.

"I'm touched."

"It gets better." Anders looked pleased, probably because I hadn't yet ripped out his heart. "When Elena confronts Erich, you saunter into camp and expose him. Elena will have enough witnesses to be convinced."

"It's an interesting plan," Rosanna broke her silence from the corner of Jules's study, "if you can fill in the details and get it to work. But I'm afraid Elena will be very hurt when she knows the part you all played, especially since she'll be frantic with worry for Alex."

"There's no way around it," Brendan said. "My sister will know we were lying anyway, once Alex shows up alive."

"I could make it easy for you," I said lightly, "and simply disappear." I turned and caught Rosanna watching me with overwhelming sadness. I blinked and turned away.

"As though we'd miss you." Jules laughed, rocking his chair back and forth. He brought it abruptly to a halt when I eyed the chair with relish. "Don't you dare."

I chuckled, though my humor was forced, and refocused on our problem. "There are too many details that can go wrong," I said in a sobered tone. "Erich may decide not to go. He may be too selfish to risk his own skin. And if he does go, he may not go anywhere near Glynnswood, and there won't be a confrontation. Not to mention, if there's really a connection with Glynnswood, it will only complicate matters. We won't know who to trust." Under Anders's cool scrutiny, I added, "I'm sorry, but too many things can go wrong. I don't like it."

"What choice do we have?"

"Tell Elena the truth. She'll be hurt anyway."

"But which way will be less painful?" Rosanna asked softly, speaking only to me, though Jules and Brendan were oblivious. "That seems to be the crux of the problem. It often is."

"On what basis would you decide?" I challenged, not bothering to hide the chill in my voice, figuring Jules and Brendan wouldn't know what I was getting at. "How do you know how hurt she'll be in either situation?"

Rosanna didn't flinch. "I don't. But I'd follow my instinct and hope she put aside her anger and understood her welfare was my primary concern."

"That's very risky, old lady."

Her eyes widened, alert to the possibility of a peace offering. "But well-intentioned. And I'd take the risk anytime because I cared so much."

"That's an unconvincing argument I've heard before."

"Then you should be used to it by now."

Aware of her relief, I laughed in appreciation and turned to Jules, who watched us with a puzzled look in his light green eyes. "I'm sorry, but I'm not comfortable with the plan. Not yet, anyway."

"We're running out of time," Anders's expression was thoughtful.

"I know. But there's something telling me to wait."

He nodded. "Your instinct has been pretty sensitive lately. Does anyone object to waiting a few days?"

One by one, they all shook their heads.

"Anders," I said, catching his attention when he arched a brow in my direction. "I want to make it perfectly clear, in front of witnesses, that my objection has nothing to do with Sernyn Keltie."

He turned to Rosanna. "Do you believe her?"

"I'm not sure why, Anders, but, yes, this time I do."

Chapter Thirteen

"If any of you rowdy children even think I'd let you track mud and dirt through my new spotless cottage, you're sadly mistaken." Surrounded by my students during a walk that encompassed fresh air and my goal for their next lesson on trading and the local economy, I halted beside the path leading to the cottage door. "We're going to Port Alain to see the new ship that's just arrived from Meravan, remember?"

"Alex, please." Carey tugged at my light woolen cloak. "Everyone wants to see it." He gave me a sidelong glance eerily reminiscent of his bothersome father. "Please."

I graced Carey with my sternest expression, hands on hips, but the child was hopeless. Tapping my boot on the ground, staring at each of them in turn, I released a suffering sigh. "All right."

As they all gave a shout, knowing full well I would surrender, Carey turned down the path, running toward the door.

My cottage door. My new cottage door.

Lords of the sea, what was wrong with it? Instinct screaming in my head, though I hadn't a clue why, I shouted. "Carey! No. Stop!"

The six-year-old hesitated for a second at the threshold, one hand resting on the polished oak door. Breathless, I covered the distance between us faster than I thought possible, belatedly realizing from his wide-eyed expression, that Carey would think I was playing with him. He impishly pushed the door open a little, stunned into silence when I tackled him to the ground, arms and legs flying wildly. Eyes closed, my heart nearly stopped when I heard the thud of a well-timed Glynnswood arrow imbed itself in the thick wood.

* * * *

"I'm not overreacting, Jules. I'm reacting, damn it." Shaking with anger, I refused his attempts to settle me in a chair, though the children were all safe and sound with Khrista and Lauryn. "The longer that Anders and I stay here, the more endangered everyone will be. We'll go first thing in the morning." Pacing feverishly, I threw off his restraining hand.

"You can't just leave." Green eyes defied me as he stepped in my path.

"Yes, we can." I walked around him and started to pace again.

"Anders," Jules pleaded, running a hand through his hair. "Talk some sense into her thick-skulled, stubborn head."

"There's nothing he can say to change my mind." I spun on my heels to face Jules. "Your wife will breathe easier when we're gone. This incident was a little too close to home."

"Lauryn would never—"

"She doesn't have to, Jules," I snapped, wanting nothing more than to end this useless argument. "She's a frantic mother of a frightened little boy who just missed being murdered today because of me."

"Alex." Rosanna reached out to grab my sleeve, trying to get my attention. "Jules is right."

"He's wrong. And I have a plan." Cutting her off, I stopped pacing, shakily brushing a hand through my tangled hair. "Anders's idea made me uneasy. But there's another way, and I think it might work. I'm sending word to—" I tangled my fingers. "To Sernyn Keltie. I want the guide who took Anders and me through Glynnswood to teach me. I need to know how to move as stealthily as he does before we implement the second part of my idea."

Rosanna met my eyes with anxious curiosity as I continued, though she held her tongue since Jules knew nothing of my half-brother.

"Then Anders and I will go tell Elena we know Charlton Ravess is behind the attacks. Without telling her Erich's involved in the treachery, it will put Erich on alert. I'll tell Elena I'm going to Glynnswood alone, leaving Anders to journey back to Port Alain and be available if she needs him."

Anders tugged at my arm. "I won't allow it."

"I don't need your permission," I snapped, irritated at everyone's demands. "Besides," I added with an exhausted smile, softening my tone, "I was hoping you'd agree to follow me at a short distance."

"Ah." Cool seagray eyes appraised me with new interest. "A trap."

"Precisely."

"What if neither Ravess nor Erich show up, but send mercenaries?"

"Then we'll force a confession from the assassin and drag him back to Elena. This trouble can't go on much longer."

"I'll meet up with Anders after you leave Ardenna."

Surprised, I looked up at Brendan's quiet words. I hadn't heard him join us in Jules's study. "Absolutely not."

"Absolutely yes. Listen, Alex." His eyes flashed with a close resemblance to Elena. "I've never used my Dunneal authority with you, but I will if you continue to be so stubborn. With me as witness, Elena will have no excuse to defend Erich when we drag him back to Ardenna to confess. She loves you and trusts you with her life, but I'm her brother and heir. My presence as a witness will quiet any attempt to suggest you were mistaken or deceived."

"He's right." Rosanna's eyes were grim, though her anxiety seemed lessened.

I gave her a knowing look. "Younger brothers are a decided nuisance."

* * * *

"Alex—"

"Lords of the sea!" I spun around, heart in mouth, dropping my bedroll and gear. "For the lords' sake, can't you make noise like a normal person?"

Gwynn's eyes widened with shy humor as he shrugged. "I am here to teach you to be just as quiet."

"You have a definite point. But I should warn you, she's a difficult student. She doesn't catch on so fast." Anders stooped to pick up my bedroll, which had landed at his feet. "I hope you're patient."

"All Glynnswoodsmen are patient." He said it with such gravity I found it difficult to stifle a laugh. "Father was pleased that you sent for me."

"Was he?" I stared at the boy standing innocently in front of me. "Because I asked for you or because I actually wrote to him?"

Gwynn looked sideways at Anders, who kept silent, folded his arms, and met my stare. "Both."

"Anders?"

"Yes, Alex?" The beast managed to convey years of long-suffering patience in those two words, though we'd only been together a little more than a year.

"Oh, hell, never mind."

"Have I offended you?" Gwynn's question was accompanied by eyes round with innocence.

"No." Anders smiled in reassurance, shifting his pack to the ground. "She just needs to get accustomed to you being around. Right?" He prodded my shoulder.

"Go away."

"What have I done now?"

When Anders and Gwynn shared a companionable glance, I poked my own finger in Anders's chest. "Precisely that. You did it again."

"Did what?"

"You managed to take sides with that, that—" I fumbled for words, "ridiculously polite young fool, and now you're both conspiring against me."

"Am I really that horrible?" Gwynn cut in, eyes still wide with innocence. Anders had taught him well in their brief time together.

"You stay out of this discussion. And you" —I turned back to Anders— "do it all the time. With Rosanna, Elena, Jules, Brendan, Khrista, Lauryn, Kerrie. And now this sniveling, stealthy excuse—"

When the two of them exchanged another look and grinned, I stalked away into the woods.

"Do not worry, Anders," Gwynn whispered as I left the campsite. "She is so noisy I will have no trouble tracking her."

* * * *

Painful to admit, but the little beast was good. He showed me time and again how to truly see and hear the life surrounding me. The woods I'd always thought silent were noisy with sound and astonishingly colorful. Hidden paths and trails all became visible. But I still couldn't sneak up on the little pest. He caught me every time, until, that is, we were two days short of our departure for Ardenna.

Gwynn sent me in search of healing herbs and roots, part of my scout training, he'd explained with infinite patience. I found them and crept back without making any noise that wouldn't blend into the forest. Anders and Gwynn were deep in some unintelligible conversation, backs leaning against a fallen tree.

Vengeance is not a worthy cause, especially for a mage, but I never claimed to be perfect. Steadying myself against a tree trunk, I closed my eyes and called the fire and ice, welcoming their sting until they merged into cool warmth. Feeling it spread from head to foot, I sighed with contentment and envisioned just what vengeance demanded.

As the fallen tree changed from wood to ice cold water, I sauntered into camp, humming a nasty tune.

Chapter Fourteen

I wasn't prepared for the serious face that confronted me two days later. So like Sernyn Keltie, and a little like me, now that I knew to look for the resemblance.

"I want to help you trap the assassin."

Over Gwynn's head, I met Anders's eyes. I closed my own and rubbed them wearily with my hands. "I can't let you do that."

"Why not?" Gwynn's face held a wild reckless look that I knew sometimes appeared on my own.

"I can't put you in danger."

"Yes, you can."

"Gwynn—"

"Here, Alex." Eyes carefully guarded, he pulled a wrinkled letter from an inner pocket of his cloak, cleared his throat, and handed it to me. From the flushed skin of his cheeks at my low growl, Gwynn probably figured out that I'd guessed the contents. He flinched when I ripped it open.

Alex-

If you are reading this letter, it is because you will not let Gwynn help you any further. If there is danger, be assured that he can take care of himself. If he could not, then he would not be accepted as a scout.

Forgive me, but I would be more reassured for your safety if he were with you, particularly if there is any truth to your concerns about Glynnswood support for Duke Harwood. And even if Glynnswood proves innocent, I would still wish you to take a skilled woodsman with you. Every little bit of knowledge is useful in your war against evil.

Do not reject his help because of me.
Sernyn Keltie

Sernyn Keltie. How else would he sign it but the way I addressed my own letter to him? I handed the note to Anders in silence. "Does he know that I'm aware of who you are?" I asked my half-brother.

Gwynn shook his head. "You asked me not to tell him." There was a pleading note in his voice, reminding me how young he was.

"If anything happened to you—"

"It will not," Gwynn interjected before I could give voice to my fears. In the short time he'd been in our company, I'd grown very fond of the boy as Sernyn had hoped I would. "Alex, I must come with you."

I crossed my arms. "Why?"

"You are my sister."

Flameblasted pest. I touched his cheek, just starting to grow a light down of hair. "You can come with us on one condition." He held his breath, my fingers still resting on his face. "You can't come to Ardenna." When defiance flashed in his eyes, I explained, "I don't want Erich to know you exist. You and Anders and Brendan will be a pleasant surprise for whoever comes after me." Defiance drained from his eyes as he saw the reasonableness of my words, and I took a deep breath. "I also don't want Erich to know about you because you're my brother, and I don't want you in needless danger because of me. This fight is mine."

"If it is your fight, it is mine, too."

"No, it's not." I ran my finger along his cheek, and then dropped my hand away. "But don't think I don't appreciate what you're saying."

"Alex." He hesitated. "Do you mind very much?" His voice was suddenly shy, awkward, reminding me of Hunter.

"Mind what?"

"Who I am."

"Lords of the sea, Gwynn, no. Hell, no." I ruffled his hair. "But I do mind that you're such a nuisance." Startling both of us, I hugged the boy tight for one brief moment, and then led Anders east to Ardenna.

* * * *

"Lucky the same guard's on duty," Anders whispered in my ear as we waited in Elena's sitting room. "I just wish you'd all visit each other during the day like normal people. But I suppose that's asking too much."

I laughed and leaned back against him, closing my eyes. "It is, but I wish we met during the day, too. I'm tired of all this running around. And if I'm so weary," I teased, "what must your old bones be feeling?"

"Pain and aches, if you must know. Why not wait until morning?" he asked in exasperation, yanking at a lock of my hair.

"Elena would be disappointed."

"I would?" Elena chose that moment to make her entrance, yawning and looking weary but content, in a scarlet silk bedrobe.

And I was bent on destroying that contentment. I wished desperately there was a way she wouldn't be hurt, but I couldn't see any other option. Not unless we somehow made Erich out to be a wronged hero, and I wasn't charitable enough to tolerate that.

"Of course you'd be disappointed if I came during the day. You'd think that I was angry with you. Why else would I be so polite?"

Elena smiled fondly at Anders, tossing midnight black hair over one shoulder. "She's right, you know."

"I've stopped trying to understand the whole lot of you."

Bringing a bottle of Marain Valley wine with her, Elena eyed me as she handed the bottle to Anders. As he popped the cork free and poured us each a glass, she sat opposite me. "Something's wrong. What is it?"

"I know who's trying to murder me."

Her eyes widened as she leaned forward. "Well?"

"Charlton Ravess."

"Alex, I exiled him," she said, bewilderment in her voice. "I made very sure he'd never be allowed to set foot in Tuldamoran again."

"Yes, well, he's found his way back." I took a sip of the cool fruity wine and sighed. "Not your fault. The man's crafty. And that means I'll have to confront him again to get rid of him for all time. He's getting tiresome."

"I'm sorry. I've heard no rumors about him, which is unforgivable. I'll put a troop at your command."

"No."

She paused, glass in mid-air, staring at me, forcing me to explain.

"I have to go alone."

"Absolutely not." Elena set the glass on the ground so hard I expected the crystal to shatter. "I rarely use my authority with you, Alex, but this time you leave me no choice." Unaware she'd mimicked Brendan's earlier statement, Elena stared at me with stubborn defiance in every angle of her slender body. "I forbid it."

"Elena." I sighed with unfeigned fatigue. "I'm tired, and I don't have very much energy to argue."

"Good."

"Flameblast you, listen! Your troops would be useless. I know where Ravess is hiding out, and I'll confront him alone."

"Alone? Really alone? Without Anders?" Elena looked from one to the other of us in disbelief. "Anders?" There was a trace of barely controlled anger and disappointment in her crisp voice as she challenged him.

"It's her battle, and Alex is capable of defeating him again." Anders met her angry glare without flinching. "Besides, someone should remain in Port Alain if you need help. As Crownmage, I'm obligated to take Alex's place until she returns."

"If she returns," Elena said coldly, standing up.

"When I return."

Disturbed, Elena stood by the chamber's huge window, overlooking the darkened city below, and then turned calculating eyes on Anders. "I thought you loved Alex."

I started to laugh before he could answer her accusation. "Nice try. But it won't work, Elena."

"Charlton Ravess almost killed you the last time you fought him."

"He did not." I yawned and leaned back against an embroidered pillow, stretching the kinks from my aching legs. "I had no idea what I was doing then. I do now. I'll be fine."

A look of pure skepticism flashed in her eyes, which should have insulted me, but didn't. "Where are you going?" When I threw Anders a swift glance, Elena cut in before I could answer. "I want the truth."

"I'm heading back toward the Bitteredge Mountains. We think Ravess has been conspiring with some, ah, discontented mages from Glynnswood who don't appreciate my perverse talent." I stifled another yawn. "I need to check that out, too."

"I don't like it."

"Neither do I," I admitted in all honesty. "But it has to end. Carey was almost murdered in my place," I added, telling her what happened, watching her expression soften to anxiety for Lauryn and the boys, and, of course, Jules. She paced again, absently tightening the knot of her silk robe until her slender waist looked in danger of being strangled. "Now be a good queen and don't forbid me."

"I can't believe Anders will let you go alone."

"He's respecting my decision." The gentleness of my words forced Elena to look back at me.

She started to say something but caught back her words. "Damn it. You expect me to do the same, don't you? If you let Charlton Ravess murder you, I'll never forgive you." With a savage glare, Elena left the room and slammed the door behind her.

Chapter Fifteen

Three days later, we were back in the deep, hushed forests of Glynnswood, a place I'd visited all too often in recent weeks. Anders had left me alone in the middle of the night, the seamage token from his wrist now wrapped around mine for luck. I touched it with a gentle caress and fell back into a restless sleep.

Dreams woke me soon after dawn, dreams of Anders, lying still, not breathing, covered in blood; Gwynn, screaming, covered in flames. Pushing the horrors aside, I tried to remember everything Gwynn taught me in our brief time together, expecting any moment my plan would fail. Erich could easily maneuver around Anders and Gwynn and trap me, but would Erich even come? Or Ravess? Perhaps Erich would send Ravess to Port Alain to deal with Anders? Would they know we were bluffing and trap us instead?

What if I were wrong?

But no, Ravess craved vengeance. I did, too, for my sake, and Elena's.

It wasn't until late afternoon the next day that my instinct came alert once again. I stopped walking and held still, listening, newly awakened senses reaching out, interpreting what I was intuitively picking up from my surroundings. All sounds had vanished, replaced with utter, troubling stillness. Something, someone had disturbed the natural noises of the forest. I knew it wasn't Gwynn, or even Anders, who'd benefited from Gwynn's tutoring, as well.

Resuming my walk, I rounded the next curve of the path that meandered along the fringes of Glynnswood and found proof my instinct was spot on. Two crossed logs lay in the center of the beaten path, signaling me of danger. Gwynn excelled at his skill. I'd no hint that the boy skirted past me to place the logs in my path.

It was time enough to end this nightmare.

I chose an easily visible campsite along the side of the forest path and dropped my gear to the ground. Closing my eyes, I felt the sting of fire and ice as I urged the talent free, blending it with practiced ease. A fact that still made me pause in wonder, considering how I'd denied my mage gift most of my life.

Until Anders came and changed everything.

Focusing on the mound of dirt and dead leaves in the center of the clearing, I transformed it to a small campfire. Anders would have scolded me for needless waste of my energy, now that I was in danger, but I needed the security of the cool warmth within me far more.

Lords of the sea, I was frightened. But not just for myself. The dreams kept popping into my thoughts during the day, though I tried hard to banish them or replace the suffering faces with Ravess and Erich. Elena, I pushed out of my mind, too fearful of how this treachery would damage her heart.

I set the bedroll near the fire and swallowed some bread and dried fruit, unaware of their taste, eating only because I knew my body craved fuel. As darkness slowly descended, I shoved extra clothes into the bedroll and arranged it to appear that my defenseless body snuggled within its protection. With enough time to spare, I coaxed the fire and ice to a waiting readiness and drifted into the forest like a native-born Glynnswood scout.

I almost missed the traitor.

There, at the edge of the forest from the direction I had traveled, a dark, shrouded figure stood watching. With an outstretched hand, sheltering a tiny flame, the assassin set fire to the ground at his feet, sending a wall of flame shooting toward the bedroll. His other hand held a knife, the scar on his cheek catching the bright moonlight that filtered through the trees as he crouched in anticipation of my screams.

I looked forward to disappointing him.

Swiftly, the flames became sizzling earth as I released the waiting cool warmth of my talent.

"I didn't think you'd let me catch you so easily, orphan child." The ragged scar reflected the moonlight as Ravess faced me. "In fact, I would've been disappointed if you had."

"I didn't think you'd be so careless." I stepped from the sheltering trees, one eye fixed on the small flame still cradled in the palm of his hand.

The firemage ignored my taunt. "Did your seamage lapdog follow along to protect you?" His eyes bored into mine, and I held my breath, wondering if he truly thought Anders was only a seamage. Had Erich not shared the truth? "Or do you stand alone, now you have proof your father willingly made you an unwanted orphan child? Sernyn Keltie rejected you as a child, and rejects you now, doesn't he? If he truly wanted you, he'd persuade you to forgive him, but no, he made the barest effort to convince you. He keeps an association with you only because you have magic. If you'd believed my words that your father and your queen wanted nothing to do with you except for what your magic could do for them, you wouldn't have placed yourself at risk." His laugh was a dagger in my heart. "They used you then, Mage Champion, and they will use you now."

I didn't trust myself to answer, trying to calm the bloodthirsty urging of the fire and ice to strangle him with my bare hands.

Ravess shifted, removing the hood to reveal thick white hair. "Well, orphan child? Where is your lapdog?"

Good question, soon answered.

"Lapdog?" Anders stepped from the shadows of the huge tree behind Firemage Ravess, a puzzled frown on his face, not acknowledging the heartache I knew he saw etched across my face caused by the mage's hateful words. "I think our friend here has been misled by his trusted ally." The expression in Anders's eyes acknowledged the point that was once again snagging my attention. The firemage had distracted me, but I saw with clarity now, Erich never told Charlton Ravess Anders was the legendary Crownmage.

Ravess stiffened. "I'm more than a match for you, for one old seamage and a girl who knows nothing of her heritage, or how to use it. She refuses to grovel at her father's feet to learn what he might teach, though it can't be very much." He laughed again, making it a trial to restrain the killing force of my magic as he added, "After all, it didn't save the orphan child's unfortunate mother in childbirth."

Anders shot me a hard glance of warning as I tensed, shifting my weight to leap at the firemage and smother the sound of his cruel words.

"I suppose I should be grateful. Mage Keltie's ignorance only makes my task easier." Ravess shook his head in disbelief. "Did you think I didn't expect you, seamage?"

Anders crossed his arms and leaned against an oak tree as though he had not a care in the world. "Seamage?" He laughed, moonlight shining on the flecks of gray in his black hair. "I'm afraid you've been misled. You may be a match for an old seamage and a girl mage," — he smiled with a predatory gleam in his eyes— "but are you a match for the queen's Mage Champion and the Crownmage?"

Ravess's deep brown, seductive eyes narrowed to slits. "The Mage Champion is no threat. I'll prove that quickly enough, now I know what her magic can do. And the Crownmage, as everyone knows, is only a legend."

Anders sighed in exaggerated disgust. "I'm so tired of people believing that." He turned to the mound of dirt covering my bedroll, focused his own talent, and swiftly solidified it to rock. Facing Ravess, he called on the breeze, whipping it into sufficient strength to douse the flame cradled protectively in the firemage's hand, disarming him.

"That can't be." Ravess stared at his empty hand. "It's a lie. There are other mages hidden in the forest."

"Sorry. And by the way, your master, Erich, knew the truth, and kept it from you." Anders edged toward Ravess, whose eyes flashed with sudden anger.

"Don't move," another voice said.

"Ah, perfect. It's about time." I whirled to greet the newcomer in our midst. "I was hoping you'd join us, Erich. You owe Firemage Ravess an explanation and an apology for conveniently forgetting to tell him that Anders Perrin is the Crownmage."

Erich's eyes blazed with open fury as he inched toward me. "I'm sorry we didn't murder you the first time, Mage Champion," he whispered with absolute contempt. "You've caused us nothing but trouble." As Anders moved to protect me, two Barrow's Pass guards stepped out from the cover of the forest, swords pointed at his heart. "Don't try it," Erich snarled as I tried to concentrate and coax the fire and ice to a useful level. "One trick. Just one. He dies." Turning to Ravess, he shrugged with a careless gesture as the firemage started to protest. "You didn't need to know about Crownmage Perrin, and I didn't need to tell you. Not until we disposed of Alex. If I had, you'd have scurried away in fright when I most needed you."

Ravess held himself still, but the scar betrayed him, the scar I gave him quivered with restrained fury.

"Now I have these two under control, I can see that you'll only cause me trouble down the road. In other words," —Erich signaled behind Ravess, who toppled to the ground with a harsh moan, pierced through his heart from a sword through his back— "I no longer need you either."

"Elena will be disappointed in you," I said, determined not to vomit at the cold, unexpected murder, barely controlling the fire and ice, holding it in check until I could use it in safety. "Though I'm not sure what she sees in you, to love you so."

Erich came so close I could feel the angry heat of his breath on my face in the chill night. His sword point tapped my neck, tracing the faint scar Ravess had sketched along my skin a year ago.

"Hurt her in any way," a new voice drifted through the clearing, stopping my heart in dread at the unexpected arrival, "you traitorous bastard, and you'll not live to draw another breath or see another morning." Elena joined the silent gathering, her face chiseled in stone as her own royal troops secured the dense woods surrounding the clearing.

"Elena, love." Erich started to face her but her sword prodded him still, his own sword dangling at his side. "I'm not the enemy, I swear it. There's been a serious mistake, a misunderstanding. Alex—"

"Alex was suspicious of you the first time she saw you at Tucker's Meadow, defending my honor and my throne. I thought it only a clash of personality, but her quiet watch forced me to keep my own counsel. I prayed she was wrong, and that you'd change even if she were right. But then I uncovered clues on my own, though you considered me easy to fool."

"Love—" His voice was silky smooth. "Listen to me."

"To what? Lies? By killing Ravess, you saved me the trouble of executing him for my father's murder, and likely my mother's, as well." Elena's face was stony. "As for your proven part in my father's murder—"

Without warning, Erich shifted, intending to thrust his own sword into her heart. But the duke only stared in perplexed anger at the sliver of flame that suddenly appeared in his hand to replace the sword. With a bitter oath, Erich dropped the flaming brand inches from Elena's breast and watched in betrayed horror as she ran him through without hesitation. Erich fell heavily to the ground next to Ravess's still body.

No one moved. I barely allowed myself to breathe.

Anders met my inquiring eyes, as he assumed I changed the steel to flame, with a question in his own. I squinted in confusion across the clearing for the only possible answer and was greeted by Gwynn's shaky, relieved smile. Brendan stood beside him, oblivious, grieving eyes fixed on his sister, who stood alone in the center of the crowded clearing. Elena knelt to touch Erich's face and closed his traitorous, staring, dark blue eyes. Lords of the sea, she'd known all along he wanted her dead and she still loved him. Rubbing a hand across her tear-streaked face, she stood without looking at anyone else, but me. My heart chilled at the contempt and bitterness in those dark blue eyes before she vanished, in the company of her guard, back into the encroaching forest.

"Elena—"

Brendan caught me back, one hand clamped on my trembling arm.

Desperate, I tried to shake free. "Let me go. Damn it, let me go after her!"

"No, Alex." Young eyes pleaded with me. "Please. Not yet." When I nodded, choking back tears, he went after her alone.

Chapter Sixteen

"Can't we just leave the little wretch here at the edge of Glynnswood? He'll find his own way home. Even if we blindfolded him," I tried to convince Anders, "you know he would. Gwynn could travel through these woods in his sleep."

Anders appraised me as he settled his backside easier in the saddle the next afternoon. "I believe it was your idea to confront Sernyn Keltie."

"Confront, yes," I explained, quieting my horse as it fretted beneath me, grateful he'd refrained from reminding me that Elena continued to refuse to see me. Which, in turn, led to my impulsive urge to escort Gwynn back home, "but I never said I wanted to see him. I could just as easily write him a letter and send it with Gwynn."

"Alex." Gwynn sent me a peculiar look as he tugged at the lock of brown hair that never quite stayed in place. "You are not afraid, are you?"

"Of course not."

Anders coughed with exaggerated delicacy, urging his horse closer to mine. "Then we should go before night falls and we can't see anything past our noses."

"Afraid of the dark?"

"No." Anders blinked, and then grinned. "Just afraid to be in the dark with you. Now can we go on? I'm sure some poor Glynnswood scout hidden in these overgrown woods already knows we're here."

"They wouldn't notice us if you weren't so noisy, trampling through the undergrowth and—"

"Alex—" Calming my horse with gentle words at his unexpected appearance, Sernyn Keltie, dressed in the familiar shades of greens and browns that Gwynn wore, emerged from the woods, uncertain as always with me. And sad. Not my fault, really. He'd brought this heartache on himself.

Without dismounting, I bowed with court formality. Though his people were infallibly polite, I knew he would recognize it as my way of keeping distance between us. "You should know Gwynn has served us with honor." As Sernyn glanced at the boy, I added, almost as a casual afterthought, "In fact, he saved Elena's life."

Sernyn's eyes widened perceptibly as Gwynn fidgeted under his stare. "Then you have done well." He smiled, unable to hide his pride.

"He has done more than well." At the subtle change in my tone, Sernyn turned back to me. I studied his controlled features, the rugged handsome face and brown hair that Gwynn had inherited, along with the gentle, easy manner, and deep brown eyes. I took a deep breath, and then another. "Did you know, Elder Keltie, that both of your children are mages?"

His eyes widened further as he glanced first at Gwynn, and then at me. I caught the realization in his expression as it changed from surprise to pride and, inevitably, to sorrow. "You are angry."

Not a question. And not angry that Gwynn was a mage, but angry he never told me I had a half-brother.

"What do you think?" I clenched my fists against my side to control the involuntary bitter anger. "How else should I feel? You thrust him right under my feet. You knew he'd charm me. You deceived me again."

"I wanted you safe," he explained with haste before I grabbed the reins and took off through the forest, a repeat of our first shocked meeting. "And Gwynn—" Sernyn looked at me without flinching, despite my ill-concealed hostility. "Gwynn wanted to know who you were. I am sorry, Alex. I wish I had told you rather than Gwynn revealing his identity."

"He didn't tell me." That surprised him, which gave me a little jolt of satisfaction. "Did you think I wouldn't see it? Did you think I was stupid?" When his sole reply was a flush of shame, I started to turn my horse back toward the road, but Sernyn grabbed the reins, dropping them swiftly beneath my rage.

"Before you go . . ." His flush deepened. "You must know Lady Barlow sent word should you pass through Glynnswood."

"Should I pass through," I said, openly bitter, instinct screaming of trouble. "Something's wrong. What's happened?"

My father brushed a hand through his full graying hair and nodded. "Her grandchildren have disappeared."

I looked swiftly at Anders. "You don't think they tried to follow us again as they did in Tucker's Meadow?"

"That is not what happened," Sernyn interrupted. "The twins were not alone. The duke's sister and husband were taking the children to Bitterhill, but they never reached the inn there, and never returned to Port Alain." He shrugged in apology. "I am sorry, Alex, but that is all she knows."

"It might have been one of Erich's final orders," Anders suggested, holding his mount steady. "If they were kidnapped, perhaps whoever's responsible doesn't know both Erich and Ravess are dead."

I stared at Anders for a long, tense moment, and then looked away. "If they were kidnapped because of me—"

"You don't know that." When I shook my head, Anders grew impatient. "Damn it, Alex. You don't. There may be any number of explanations. Don't go blaming yourself. It's too soon after Elena's departure and that whole fiasco, and you're not thinking straight."

Mage Resolution

In an unprecedented move, Sernyn put a hand on my arm to get my attention. "Anders is right. You do not know this to be true. You have . . ." He paused, as though considering his words, as well he should. "You have an unfortunate habit of blaming yourself for events over which you have no control."

"Don't touch me."

"Do not blame yourself."

When he dropped his hand, I lashed out again, sick at heart. "Why are you pretending to care? For twenty-five years, you didn't care I blamed myself for my mother's death."

"Alex," Anders's voice held a soft plea. "We're wasting time. We've got to get back to Port Alain."

"Wait, Alex. I want to come." Gwynn tugged at the rebellious lock of brown hair, and I wondered how much the boy knew of the trouble between Sernyn and me. The last thing I wanted was for him to get caught between us.

"Sorry, no. I don't want you near me until, until, young man, you learn how to control that flameblasted talent of yours." I softened the denial with a smile. "I won't risk having you practice magic around me. Ask Anders what damage an untrained mage can do."

"Then I will practice very hard. And Alex—" Gwynn leaned close, his words for my ears only. "What Firemage Ravess said, back in the forest, about father—" The boy was smart and grabbed hold of my reins before I moved away. "Those words were a lie. Father would not take advantage of you for your magic. I do not know all the trouble between you, though I have guessed some of it, and I cannot blame you for what little I do know, but no matter, Alex, I know he would never do what Charlton Ravess implied."

If the boy could defend Sernyn, then I was lost. Without another word for Gwynn, or his father, I freed the reins from my brother's desperate grasp and urged my horse homeward.

Chapter Seventeen

"Thank the lords of the sea, you're back." Rosanna hugged me close before turning to smother Anders. We'd found her pacing in her beloved gardens, worried about her daughter and her son-in-law, and, most of all, her defenseless grandchildren.

"We came as soon as Sernyn gave us your message." When Rosanna released Anders, she stepped back to stare at me. "Tell me about the twins," I demanded, sidestepping a discussion about Sernyn Keltie.

Rosanna's plump face saddened abruptly. "There's nothing more to tell. There's been no word. They've vanished with Khrista and Kerrie. Lauryn's sent Port Alain troops to comb the area between here and Bitterhill. There's been no clue, no sign, nothing, Alex. No ransom note. Lauryn—"

"Has Jules gone with the troops?" I asked, tucking chilled hands beneath my cloak, assuming that's where he'd be, until Rosanna's expression turned wary. "What? Has he gone missing, too?"

Jules's mother plucked at the cuff of her tunic sleeve, avoiding my eyes. "Jules left for Ardenna when Elena sent word of how matters ended, how she killed Erich with her own sword. Lauryn sent word two days later about the children, frantic for Jules to return. There's been no response. We don't think" —she bit her lower lip— "that he knows yet."

"Surely Elena—" I started to protest, but something in her eyes chilled me more effectively than the autumn breeze.

"Elena left Ardenna, with Brendan in charge. Apparently, she left for a few days with a small escort. That escort" —her eyes held mine— "included Jules, and she refused to tell anyone where she was going.

Brendan doesn't even know. I suppose," her voice dwindled to a pained whisper, "she needed time alone to heal."

"Time alone with Jules," I snapped, furious at both of them, and kicked a stone savagely across the garden path.

"And an escort." Rosanna's eyes were troubled.

"That unthinking, idiotic, selfish—" When Anders cleared his throat I spun around to confront him. "What?"

He straightened out his travel-worn tunic, tightening his thin leather belt, giving me time to speak, if I felt the urge. When I simply stared at him, Anders said quietly, "I believe I'm missing a crucial piece of information."

Rosanna looked at me and turned away, preferring to stare down the garden path. Interesting, however, that she didn't forbid me to explain the dilemma.

"Damn it all." I kicked another stone. "Some years ago, Jules had this intriguing idea that he and Elena should become lovers. But he never managed to persuade Elena to take their relationship beyond friendship, so nothing, at least from what I've been told, ever happened between them. Enter Lauryn into Jules's pitiful heart, and Jules fell in love again." I waved my hands in wild frustration, chilled to the bone at what misery this stupid action would unleash. "But Jules never quite stopped loving Elena," I blurted, hoping I was wrong about our assumptions. "And now he's gone to console Elena after she's killed the one man she really did love."

As I hunted for another stone to kick, Anders prompted, "And you believe, what?"

"It doesn't matter what I believe. It matters what Lauryn believes. And judging from Rosanna's expression—" I waved in the direction of Jules's mother, who kept her distance. "Lauryn believes what we do.

And Lauryn needs her husband here far more than Elena needs him, wherever the hell they are."

While I was furious, Anders remained calm, cool seagray eyes thoughtful. "What does Lauryn really think?" he asked Rosanna, ignoring my frown.

Tears glittered in her eyes as she sank onto one of the cold stone benches, as cold as the anger and frustration that chilled my own heart. "Though I can't be certain, I agree with Alex. Lauryn won't talk about Jules. At least not to me." Rosanna turned to me. "She won't leave her chamber, Alex. Will you go to her?"

"Of course." Anders started to follow as I headed up the garden path, but I shook my head. "Why don't you tell the old witch about Sernyn? It'll save you precious time sneaking around behind my back." Once past the garden gate, I flew up the stairs to Jules and Lauryn's apartment, cursing Jules with every step I climbed. "Lauryn." I knocked several times, but there was no immediate response. "Lauryn, it's Alex. Open up, please."

The door slipped open a crack, revealing blue eyes, puffy from weeping and red from lack of sleep. Lauryn flung back the door and fell sobbing into my arms the moment I shut the door. I let her weep, waiting until she pulled back, sniffling.

"I'm sorry."

"I can't believe what you just said," I scolded, shaking her gently. "Lords of the sea, what are you apologizing to me for?"

She graced me with a crooked smile. "I'm sorry for being sorry."

"That's better."

"Be right back." Lauryn disappeared into a side chamber, still sniffling, and returned with a chilled bottle of Marain Valley wine.

"Even better." I uncorked the bottle, and poured us both a glass of the cool, light wine, hoping that it signified Lauryn's agreement to talk about what had happened.

"There's not a sign of them. Why would anyone want to hurt Khrista and Kerrie? Why would anyone want to harm my children? I know they're a nuisance in your schoolroom, Alex," Lauryn made a feeble attempt at humor, "but they're only six-years-old."

Considering my answer, I put my glass on the low wooden table and made myself comfortable on the plush rug in front of the fireplace. "Here's one possible motive to think about." Lauryn watched from her perch on the arm of the low chair opposite me, as I explained my theory. "It may have been related to me in some way. Maybe it has to do with Charlton Ravess," I said with caution, avoiding Erich's name because Erich would inevitably lead to Elena, and Elena would inevitably lead to Jules.

Flameblast them both.

"Maybe the firemage wanted to strike out at me through the boys. I never made a secret of how much I adore them." When Lauryn gave me a scathing look and rolled her eyes, I demanded, "What?"

"I can't believe you're blaming yourself. You'd better stop that right now."

"It's possible."

"Yes," she said evenly, sipping her wine. "Yes, it is. And whoever is responsible for kidnapping them may not know that Charlton Ravess is dead. Or that Erich Harwoode is dead, and his grieving lover needs consoling, since she was the one who executed the traitor with her own bloody sword."

I winced at the open bitterness in her voice. "Ah." I fumbled for something intelligent to say, but came up with nothing.

Lauryn's expression changed. "I know the kidnapping is not Jules's fault, but I can't help blaming him somehow." Her control slipped as tears slid down her cheek, brushed away by an impatient swipe of her hand.

"You don't know—"

She bowed her head, face hidden by long, auburn hair. "No, I don't, do I? But he hasn't made it easy for me to stray from trusting him."

"Elena had a hand in this fiasco."

"Elena just killed her lover, Alex. She's not thinking clearly. If she was thinking with her head and not her heart, Elena wouldn't resent or blame you, now, would she? Jules—" Lauryn struggled for control against rising panic and hurt. "Jules isn't important now. My boys are all that matter. And I want them back."

* * * *

"Where do you think you're going this late in the day?"

"To find Jules." Back in our cottage, I continued packing fresh gear, ignoring Anders's loud, irritated sigh.

"You know where he is?"

"I have a good idea."

Anders stuck his face mere inches from mine. "Does Lauryn know?" When I shook my head, refusing to say more, and instead reached for an extra tunic, he said, "I'm coming with you."

"No." I stopped packing to stare at him. "They may need you here."

"I won't have you traipsing off in the middle of the night."

"I'm the queen's Mage Champion, remember?" I said dryly, tugging a boot over my trouser leg.

"And prone to arrow wounds. You're mortal, remember? If Ravess was behind the kidnapping, his people may still be watching for you. And," he added, when I started to protest, "you're exhausted. When was the last time you slept?" He snatched the other boot from my hand. "When?"

"I'll sleep when I can. Right now, I can't."

"Then tell me where you're going."

I saw my destination in my mind's eye. A bit north of Jendlan Falls to a small, cozy lodge Jules owned quietly. I knew about it. So did Elena. No one else did, which was a good thing, as well as bad. And that was how it was going to stay.

"Don't ask." I grabbed the boot from his hand and stuffed my foot into it, tucking trousers into place. "Anders, please," I argued when I saw he wouldn't leave the issue alone. "Jules should be here. If he's where I think he is, I won't be gone very long." I ran my fingers through his thick hair and kissed him on the lips. "Keep an eye on Lauryn and the old witch. I'd feel better if I knew you were with them."

Anders frowned, and I guessed this episode disturbed his sense of fairness. "This midnight visit might embarrass Jules and anger Elena."

"Just this once, Anders, just this once, I hope there's nothing for him to be embarrassed about," I said earnestly, hugging Anders close, taking comfort from his warmth, "but if there is, the fool won't get an ounce of sympathy from me. And if it angers Elena more than she already is, that doesn't matter either. I've been at odds with both of them in the past, and I'll be at odds with them again in the future. Count on it. But Jules needs to come home."

Borrowing a fresh horse from the Barlow stables, I headed for the road leading northwest to Jendlan Falls. It was late, and I was exhausted, more weary than I'd let on to Anders, but I forced myself to stay alert, calling the fire and ice awake to keep me sharp and ready for danger. On horseback, it was no far distance. Along the road that skirted the falls, I slowed my horse to avoid slipping on the spray-slicked roadway.

Reaching the bridge that crossed the falls, I hesitated, bringing the horse to an abrupt halt. In the bright moonlight, the falls glistened with an eerie beauty, spray catching the light, sparkling briefly like fading stars. But the beauty didn't disguise the fact I needed to cross the bridge.

At night.

Alone.

Flameblast Jules. He'd pay for this grief.

I had a decision to make, either a swift dash across the bridge on horseback or a slow, agonizing crawl on my hands and knees, dragging the horse behind me. With a vicious, crude oath, I guided the horse toward the middle of the narrow road and prodded him to a mad desperate gallop.

Eyes closed tight, I shivered as icy spray hit my face, prayed fervently to the lords of the sea when the horse slipped on wet stones, and cried in relief when we reached the opposite end and I was back on solid ground. If Firemage Ravess could have witnessed the queen's Mage Champion in fear for her life on a bridge, wouldn't that have made him laugh?

Wiping tears from my wet cheeks, I guided the horse north to the hunting lodge nestled in the woods. Tying the reins to the post outside the lodge, I barged past the guard who tried to prevent me from entering the building, my expression forcing him to step aside, no questions asked.

Elena, at least, had the decency to feel awkward, if not embarrassed, although she tried to hide that reaction behind an icy welcome. "No wine, Alex? That's rude. I thought all midnight visits demanded a certain amount of civility, though your actions—"

"Where is he?"

Elena narrowed her eyes. "What business is it of yours? Or have you come to tell me that Jules is a traitor, too?"

Maybe Lauryn was right. Maybe I couldn't expect Elena to think clearly. But I wasn't as forgiving as Lauryn. I pushed past Elena in the direction of the chamber she'd come from, all rumpled and disheveled from sleep.

"He's not in there." Elena's soft voice rattled my determination. "He wanted to be, but I wouldn't let him. Deep inside, I must have suspected you'd play the good schoolmistress and make sure we all behaved like perfect little children."

At her sharp, hurtful words, I turned with infinite slowness to face Elena and swallowed uneasily at the unrelieved grief and near-hatred in her dark blue eyes. Grief for her dead lover, and hatred for me. I hardened my heart and gathered my courage. "I don't give a damn whose bed the two of you fall into. That's not why I'm here."

"Then why are you here?" Jules appeared at the door to another chamber, just as rumpled, not bothering to hide his irritation, which only filled me with resentment.

"I'm here because you're needed at home. The twins and your sister and Kerrie are missing."

"What are you muttering about, Alex?" Jules shoved a hand through disheveled hair, his expression disdainful. "Of course they are. They were journeying to Bitterhill when I left for Ardenna."

"They never arrived in Bitterhill," I snapped, my voice seething with rage, thinking of Lauryn and the boys and the flameblasted bridge I had to cross again on my way home. "And they never returned."

When all color drained from his face, I couldn't even find the energy to be glad I'd so disarmed Jules.

"I'll send troops immediately." Elena edged toward him, after an anxious glance at his ashen face.

"Don't bother," I said. "Lauryn's sent Port Alain troops to scour the area."

Jules met my gaze without flinching. "Where does Lauryn think I am?"

"She doesn't know I came here. Your secret's safe." I turned away in disgust and pulled the door open, letting a chill wind flutter through. "As to what your wife thinks about why you're missing, ask her yourself."

Chapter Eighteen

"Alex! You are back."

A hand tugged at my shoulder with relentless persistence, tempting me to coax my magic awake and turn the pesky intruder into a sniveling little mouse. And then I remembered, with deep regret, that I couldn't do that.

"Go away." I pulled the woolen blankets back over my head, satisfied Gwynn couldn't possibly find me now. Gwynn? I tossed the blankets from my head and sat up quickly. Too quickly, losing my balance and falling over the side of the bed onto the cold, hard floor. "Flameblast you, Gwynn. What are you doing here?" I slapped his hand away and fumbled back into the inviting warmth of the bed.

"Anders sent me to see if you had returned." My brother looked sheepish as he tugged at the brown hair hanging in his eyes. Though he looked sheepish, I knew better. He'd been dallying with Anders far too much in recent weeks.

I propped myself up with overstuffed pillows, sat back, and crossed my arms, but not before squinting out the window. I couldn't have had more than a few hours sleep since tumbling into bed in the middle of the night. "I thought you weren't allowed out of Glynnswood until you were trained to control your magic."

Gwynn leaned back against the window ledge, blocking the bright sunlight. "You are right."

"If I'm right, why are you here?"

"Are you unhappy to see me?"

"Maybe."

Gwynn sidestepped that comment, having learned from the first moment we met I didn't always say what I meant. "Duke Barlow has returned home." When I nodded without further comment, he added, "So is Master Kerrie."

"Kerrie?" That woke me up. "Is he all right?"

Gwynn looked disturbed. "I do not know, Alex. He is— I do not know. They will not tell me anything."

What had happened? "All right, nuisance. Get out of here so I can get dressed." Gwynn left my bedchamber without a word. Pulling a tunic halfway over my head, I shouted at the door. "You still haven't told me, you pest, why you're here."

"Father wanted me to keep him company."

I snapped the tunic down so fast I nearly strangled myself, scrambled into trousers, and stormed into the sitting room, fumbling to stuff my feet into boots. "Why," I demanded, "is Sernyn Keltie here?"

Gwynn tugged at his hair again and shrugged. "He would not tell me that either," the boy apologized, though I sensed more of a pout than an apology in his tone.

"Does anybody tell you anything?" When Gwynn shook his head, the pout more pronounced, I grabbed my cloak and flew through the door. "Let's go find out."

I jumped behind Gwynn as he mounted the horse waiting outside and held on tight as we galloped up the hill. Uneasy and anxious, I shoved my fears aside and ran into the manor's main hall the moment my brother brought the horse to a standstill. With Gwynn dogging my heels, I stood at the door to the manor's smaller audience chamber, catching the motley group very off guard.

Lauryn, standing coolly at Jules's side, back stiff with tension, in earnest talk with Anders. Rosanna, in an intense conversation with Sernyn in the corner near the blazing fire. Dangerous couple there.

"Will someone please have the decency to tell me what's going on?"

They all turned to stare at me.

"Did you get enough sleep?" Anders shuffled toward me, with a glance over my shoulder at the nuisance.

"Did I get enough sleep?"

"I need you alert," Anders cut in smoothly, taking my hand and pulling me along into the huge chamber. "Though I know you can't guarantee that." When I didn't answer, his eyes grew serious. "Kerrie wandered back home. Wandered, Alex. Port Alain guards found him walking along the road dazed, feverish, clothes worn and filthy. The port healer's with him."

I refused to look at Lauryn. Cowardly, yes, but I couldn't. "No sign of Khrista or the boys?"

"No." Anders shook his head. "All we can get out of Kerrie are incoherent ravings about a crazed woman in horrible pain. None of it makes a damn bit of sense. Or it didn't," —he paused, holding my gaze, warning of danger to come— "until Sernyn showed up."

Here in Port Alain.

With a shy glance at Rosanna, Sernyn Keltie nodded at me. "I would not have imposed on Lady Barlow—" Catching the involuntary gleam in my eye, warning of unkind thoughts, he chose to ignore it. "A scout arrived in our village soon after you left the forest with rumors of a woman casting peculiar spells north of Bitterhill, near the foothills of the Bitteredge Mountains." He shrugged in apology. "It seemed important that I bring this box." He held out a small oak chest, a tiny version of the one that held my mother's notes, the one I'd hidden away before the cottage burned down.

I didn't move.

"Emila was fascinated by mage talent. She began to study Glynnswood mages when she and I first married, because our talent is so different from mages in the rest of Tuldamoran." His voice faltered at my cool expression, but I couldn't take pity. It was his lack of confidence in his own magic that contributed to my mother's death. "I thought, maybe, Alex, there was some clue in her notes that might prove helpful in discovering what is happening."

Without a word, I took the small chest from his hand, the carving as elegant as the one I had. Avoiding Rosanna's perceptive eyes, I stroked the wood with a tender caress, wondering what more my mother knew.

"Perhaps the woman is a renegade mage. Perhaps she is a Glynnswood mage. You do not know very much about our brand of magic."

"Perhaps some cool Marain wine and a loaf of brushed oats with honey would make your reading easier." Rosanna's bland suggestion acknowledged my urge to bite off Sernyn's head if he made any further insinuation about my refusal to learn about the gift I inherited from his part of the family.

My tone formal, I headed for the door. "I'll be in the schoolroom, Lady Barlow, if anyone needs me."

"It's good to have you back, Alex." Rosanna lifted one brow crookedly as I met her bland gaze.

"I'll just bet it is." I started for the door again and caught sight of Gwynn ready to follow me. "You stay here. And stay out of trouble." Yawning, I strode toward the schoolroom, still half asleep. Opening the door and a window for fresh air to keep me awake, I tossed my wool cloak over a chair and settled down. I found a place for the oak chest in the middle of my cluttered table, as a knock sounded at the open door. I called out a greeting, not bothering to look up. "Thanks," I muttered, taking the offered tray with the bottle and glass, along with the loaf of brushed oats, and set it down, shoving aside a pile of well-read books.

"Alex."

I looked up in surprise at Jules's voice, not expecting him. "Go away."

"Please listen."

"You're wasting my time." I stretched for one of mother's notebooks, crammed full with her neat handwriting, but his hand closed over mine before I reached the book. "Make it fast, Jules." I shrugged off his hand.

"I told Lauryn the truth. About—" He flushed and turned away. "I told her it was me, not Elena. And that nothing happened, but that—" His face burned with shame as his voice dropped to a whisper. "That I wanted something to happen with Elena, but more important, that it was a mistake."

"You don't deserve Lauryn. After everything she's done for you, and still, you treat her like dirt." I clenched my fists in frustration. "It's as though, I don't know—" I slammed my fist on the table. "As though everything's all right until Elena shows a weakness or there's the slightest chance she might accept you, and you pounce on Elena, and Lauryn means nothing." I turned my back on Jules in disgust. "Even Elena deserves better than you."

"Elena's not thinking clearly now. Listen, Alex, I know you think she blames you for Erich's betrayal—"

"Go away, Jules." After a moment, I heard his sigh of resignation as he shuffled from the schoolroom, closing the door behind him. I couldn't pity him, not then, maybe not ever. Shoving aside thoughts of Jules and Elena, and Lauryn in their combined misery, I opened the notebook and started to read.

* * * *

"Imagine Elder Keltie insinuating that I don't know anything at all about my Glynnswood heritage."

Anders studied me with tolerant amusement. "Frankly, Alex, I was shocked at his audacity. I couldn't believe his nerve."

"Bastard."

"That's no way to talk about your father."

"I was talking about you. But the term definitely applies to him, too."

"Oh." Trying without success to stifle a chuckle, Anders uncovered a basket of warm apple cinnamon bread, sweet pears, and another bottle of Marain Valley wine. "Did you find out anything useful?"

"Did you? How's Kerrie?"

Anders peered over the bottle he was uncorking. "Still feverish. I'm worried about him, to be honest."

"If he's in such a state," I said, as reality intruded, "how safe are the children?"

Sighing, Anders poured me a glass of cool wine. "I didn't want to talk about Kerrie because I knew you'd start thinking about Khrista and the boys. Not that you haven't been," he added, not sure of my mood.

"I've been concentrating on my mother's notes so I wouldn't think about the twins. I know that trick, too." I smiled without humor, resting my chin in the palm of my hand.

"So what have you found?"

"Did you know that Glynnswood folk weren't originally from Glynnswood?"

Anders raised black brows in open curiosity. "No. Your mother never told me that. For that matter, neither did your father. Where'd they come from?"

"Spreebridge. Some obscure land north of Ardsbrook that no one ever talks about and probably never heard about. No wonder my brother's so peculiar."

"Only your brother?"

"Did my mother ever tell you her theory about Crownmages?" I asked, knowing how close they'd been when my mother was alive, treating Anders like a younger sibling in need of a watchful eye.

Anders eyed me in wary speculation. "Is this a serious question or am I walking straight into a trap?" He tossed me a pear.

I caught it neatly. "Serious."

He shook his head, thinking. "She had a lot of ideas about the Crownmage, but never focused on one."

"Yes, she did."

"Well, I never saw those notes," he said crossly, polishing a pear on the sleeve of his rumpled tunic. "And who knows where else her notes will turn up. I had no idea your father had any hidden in his pocket. All you Kelties and your secrets." When I shot him a nasty look at that last comment, and then proceeded to sit up straight and shuffle the papers until my desk was neater, he grew impatient. "Don't play schoolmistress. Just tell me her theory."

"All right, hush. She thought Crownmages might be so rare, showing up every few centuries or so, because they required a rare blend of all four mage bloodlines. Seamage, firemage, windmage, and earthmage. And," I drawled, "since mages are notoriously narrow-minded—"

Anders didn't blink as he finished the thought. "They keep to themselves, so that seamages produce seamages, firemages produce firemages, and on and on. Am I right, schoolmistress?"

"You get a gold star. Let's take it another step, shall we? If that's true," —I bit into the crisp pear, catching the sweet juice dribbling down my chin with a cloth— "then your family was rather, ah, social."

"You mean promiscuous."

"Whatever."

"And look what they produced."

"I'm trying to forget."

"Liar." When I continued to bite into the pear, unperturbed, he added, "So where did you come from?"

"Good question. Mother apparently thought nothing odd about marrying Sernyn. She was a seamage, her mother was a seamage, and he, that lying bastard—" Anders crossed his arms and sent me a scathing look. "Don't be annoying, smug, or officious." I took a cool sip of wine to wash down a bit of pear that threatened to choke me. "She didn't know about his magic. Worse, she didn't even know Glynnswood had mages until after they were married. That's why— Damn it."

I set the glass on the table and turned away to stare out the window. Anders waited with kind patience until I could speak again, pretending not to notice my wet cheeks. Finally, I cleared my throat and faced him again.

"You know that Sernyn didn't tell her about himself, about his own repressed magic, but made her promise not to use her own magic when he was around. So my mother didn't tell him a lot of things. She kept a very explicit journal of what she feared, Anders. And one of those fears was that she would make him unhappy, that he'd be upset because of her mage talent." I took a deep breath. "When she was pregnant with me and not feeling well, she started to worry, thinking her magic was causing the trouble—"

Anders reached over to stroke my cheek. "He's suffered again and again and yet again if he's read these notes. Let it go, Alex."

"I want to, but it's so hard," I whispered, swiping away the unwelcome tears sliding down my face.

His fingers traced my cheek, and then my lips. "I know. But you have to try harder. You owe it to your mother."

I kissed his fingers. "That's not fair."

"But it's true."

"Obnoxious fool."

He sat back and grabbed the wine bottle, beaming at me. "That's much better. Now, go on."

I bit his finger before he pulled away and held out my glass for a refill. "From what mother could piece together from Sernyn and Glynnswood legend, a Crownmage, eons ago, brought the Spreebridge people to the Glynnswood forest as an experiment. An experiment, can you believe it?" I fumed, trying to recall my mother's words. "The Crownmage knew these people had some sort of different mage talent, like Gwynn, who can change only one element to another within limits, as he changed Erich's sword into flame. That Crownmage convinced a group of his countrymen to move to Glynnswood, offering them only the lords of the sea know what, and proceeded to, well, experiment, I suppose."

Anders bit his lower lip. "How?"

"He was a bit promiscuous."

"I see."

"Yes, well, nothing ever came of his attempts to merge bloodlines. All his women miscarried, except for one." I took a long, soothing sip of Marain wine. Anders didn't bite, but waited with apparent patience, though I knew he wanted to strangle me, until I reached for a chunk of cooling apple cinnamon bread.

He snatched it from my hand. "Tell me."

"She died in childbirth, and the child went mad. No one could control the child, who used her talent wildly, hurting people until they drove her away. Conceivably, she may have survived in the wild forest and started her own bloodline. Perhaps," I said, in all seriousness, "there's a mad renegade descendant of that pathetic child running loose north of Bitterhill."

"Perhaps." Anders studied me for a long intense moment. "Alex, you're not telling me everything."

"I was hoping you wouldn't notice."

"You make it so easy."

"The child's talent was precisely like mine."

He watched me, considering. "So, there's probably Crownmage blood in your family somewhere. And maybe an insane version of you loose in the woods. But that's not what's bothering you, is it?"

"No." I stared out the window again. "It frightens me to think what kind of mage child you and I could produce."

Anders knelt at my side, but I looked away. He tugged at a strand of curls. "I told you I'd never let you risk yourself."

"I know."

"Alex—" He placed a finger under my chin and forced me to meet his calm seagray eyes. "I meant it." When I began to sniffle, he smiled. "If you start crying again, I'll tell Rosanna how soft you're getting."

"Bastard."

"Thank the lords of the sea." He grinned in relief, giving me a hearty kiss. "I was afraid you didn't love me anymore."

"Did you think I loved you at all?" I shoved him away and stood, biting back a groan at the ache in my back. "Let's go tell the others." I led him back to the parlor in the main house, where a small group of conspirators huddled together as though for comfort.

"Come in, Alex. We were just discussing you." Rosanna smiled, ignoring my pointed glare.

When I stopped in the doorway, Anders bumped into me from behind, shoving me forward. "Did he really stay here all this time?" I stared in disbelief at Gwynn, stretched out in front of the fireplace, overstuffed pillows cradling his head.

"You terrified the poor child," Rosanna scolded, pushing her chair back from the small wooden table.

"Poor child? You travel with him and see how much compassion you feel for the little wretch." Sending her another glare, I caught Sernyn's eye and dangled the small oak chest in front of him. "Did you read these notes?"

"Alex." Anders, still behind me, placed his hands on my shoulders and drummed his fingers in a rapid rhythm. "Don't do this."

I shrugged his hands away. "Did you?"

Sernyn looked past me and exchanged an unreadable look with Anders. "Yes. Several times."

"Recently?"

Anders's hands found their way back to my shoulders and pressed down hard.

"Yes." Sernyn answered my questions with impressive serenity, his eyes telling me without a doubt that he understood my point.

Anders shoved me across the floor and forced me into an armchair.

"How's Kerrie?" I asked, finally managing to chase the beast away before sinking back against the huge well-worn pillows, more fatigued than I thought.

Rosanna's expression sobered. "There's been no change. Jules sent other troops in the direction of the Bitteredge Mountains in case the rumors Sernyn heard were true. Alex, I'm so worried about them," she admitted, letting down her guard.

"Me, too. I think it's possible we have a renegade mage on our hands. Maybe. I don't know." I caught back a yawn. "I wish Kerrie were coherent. I hate feeling helpless."

"I have sent scouts to investigate the rumors." My father gave me a peculiar intense look. "If it is a renegade mage with your unconventional talent, then she would be Glynnswood's responsibility."

"You know we'll have to go after her." Anders tugged at my sleeve from his perch on the chair beside me.

I nodded, rubbing my eyes again. "All I want is an uninterrupted night's sleep. But yes, you're right. We have to go after her, but not with troops." I wasn't fast enough to catch another yawn. "I know Jules will argue, but they'll only slow us down."

"I will not."

Slowly, I lowered my hands from my eyes and peered over my knuckles at Gwynn, leaning up on one elbow. "You will not what?"

"Slow you down." He tugged at the unruly lock of hair, slanting a guarded look at Anders, before turning those huge brown eyes in my direction.

"Don't you even think about it. Your father won't allow it."

"Yes, he will," Sernyn confirmed my worst fears. When I stared at him in disbelief, Sernyn returned my glare without blinking. "Gwynn has proven capable of taking care of himself. Besides, Alex, he is a mage. In fact, you told me so yourself."

Cheeky. I stood abruptly, clutching the oak chest to my body. "If anything happens to him—"

"It will not be your fault." Sernyn's expression held immense caution, though his words were courageous.

"Don't you ever know when to stop?" I snarled.

"I will not stop until you see the truth of my words."

No one dared to breathe, waiting for my rage to explode. With control that made me nearly breathless, I spun on my heels and left the chamber.

Chapter Nineteen

It was clear from the ferocity of Rosanna's digging and tugging at unwanted weeds in the cool autumn morning she was frantic with worry.

"Want some help?" I took a seat on one of her strategically placed rocks.

"Stay away from my flowers," she snapped, brandishing her spade like a knife, and meaning every bit of the threat.

"Anders taught me the difference between a weed and a fern."

"He tried to teach you. I tried to teach you. Your mind goes blank when it comes to plants and trees and flowers. Stay away." She waved the spade again before turning back to the stubborn weeds.

I squinted against the bright morning sunlight. "I'll bring them all home."

Rosanna's frantic digging stopped as she sat back on her heels and sighed. "I keep thinking of how frightened they must be."

"Not Carey."

She laughed in appreciation. "You're right. Not Carey. He's probably planned a thousand ways to escape." Rosanna turned away.

"They'll be all right." She started attacking the ground again. "Rosanna—"

"What's happened to all of us?" She stopped moving. "Jules—"

"Jules made a mistake. If he's lucky, Elena will forgive him for trying to force something that was never there, and still be his friend. And Lauryn will forgive him for being a fool and still be his wife. If he's lucky." I frowned, running my hands through tangled curls. "However, I wouldn't blame either Lauryn or Elena for not forgiving him."

"He told me you found him." Quiet, watchful eyes studied me.

"I'm surprised he admitted anything."

"He also told me about Elena and her trouble with you." Rosanna sighed, looking beyond me. "She'll get over it. Be patient. As for Jules—"

Sidestepping her remark about Elena, as I'd sidestepped my friend's hostility in my own heart, I said, "I found Jules for Lauryn's sake, though maybe she'd rather I hadn't. Maybe I should have left Jules hiding in the woods." I toyed with a weed Rosanna had tossed aside.

"Ah, yes. The woods." Rosanna's eyes flared with purpose. "Your father—"

I shot upright, brushing dirt from my trousers. "I didn't come here to discuss that liar." When Rosanna acknowledged defeat with a loud, resigned sigh, I made my way back up the path to the upper floors of the manor, poking my head around the huge wooden door to Kerrie and Khrista's bedchamber, where Lauryn was tending her brother-in-law. "How is he?"

Lauryn waved me inside with a tired smile, shadows ringing her blue eyes. "He's calmer. I think the fever's finally breaking."

On tiptoe, I edged in and made myself comfortable on the window ledge by her side. Kerrie looked haggard, hair still damp from the fever, as he lay bundled under woolen blankets. "Has he said anything that's made sense?"

"Not yet."

"Are you all right?"

Lauryn stared at my leg as it swung slowly back and forth, and shrugged. When I touched her arm, she shook her head as though to clear her thoughts, and spoke about something unexpected. "Gwynn's as bad as the twins."

"As misbehaved and troublesome? I could've told you that."

"No. That's not what I meant. The boy adores you."

"Not for long if I don't keep him away from Anders."

"He adores you just as much."

I laughed and prodded a teasing finger at her slender arm. "It's not quite so obvious to me."

"Stop that." Lauryn turned away. "He doesn't love anyone else but you." While I struggled for something comforting to say, Lauryn kept her face averted and busied herself smoothing the blankets over Kerrie, tucking him in needlessly. "Kerrie?" Her hands stopped moving, clutching the blanket.

I stretched over to see what had caught her attention and found a pair of bright eyes watching me from under a pile of wool. The brightness of those clear eyes vanished as Kerrie shut his eyes tight.

"Khrista." He started to push back the blankets. "Khrista!"

"Oh no." I lurched to his side the same time Lauryn did, struggling to hold him back down.

"The boys. Let me go." Kerrie clenched his fists in frustration, finding strength to fight us. "I have to go—"

"Stop it." Lauryn's soft voice had an edge that halted Kerrie's frantic movements for a moment. "You'll not help any of them if you go running off naked and weak into the woods. Do you hear me?"

"Lauryn, please." Kerrie shakily grabbed his sister-in-law's hand, and then turned to me when he recognized her stubbornness.

"You can help them best by telling me what you remember."

"I have to go after them." Kerrie struggled, but long days of illness and exposure had taken their toll. "Don't you see?"

"Yes," I agreed, keeping my tone reasonable, "but no one can go after them until you tell us what you remember. If you don't tell us anything, you won't go anywhere. I can promise you that."

Never angry with either of us, Kerrie's face burned with fury, but not foolishness. He sank back, exhausted, against the overstuffed pillows, resigned for the moment to captivity. Lauryn stood waiting at the foot of the bed.

"Lauryn?" I grabbed her sleeve. "Why don't you get Kerrie something to eat?"

Every inch of her slender body screamed defiance. "I have a right to know what Kerrie knows." Crossing her arms, she gave me a cool sidelong glance and turned back to her brother-in-law. "Tell me."

Kerrie closed his eyes. "Outside of Bitterhill, we came upon a narrow stream. Alex," —he gave me a peculiar look— "it was so bizarre. I didn't think anyone else could do what you could do."

I took a deep breath. Maybe my mother's notes were right. I nodded for him to go on without denying or confirming anything.

"While we were waiting to cross, the stream became a wall of flame, frightening the horses. Hunter and Khrista were thrown when the horses bucked, but not hurt. I remember holding on to Carey, trying to control my own mount." Kerrie paused for a breath and accepted some water. Stifling a cough, he fell back against the pillows. "I almost had my horse under control when the flames became a wall of stone. And then flames again. That was the last I saw before I heard a raspy voice behind me. Then something heavy cracked against the back of my head."

The apology in his eyes said it all. Weary, he shut his eyes tight again.

Lauryn hadn't moved from her position, fingers gripping the bedpost so tight her knuckles were white. "Go on." She did, after all, have a right to hear it and know the truth.

So did I. Especially if we were dealing with a mad renegade mage.

Pale with illness and despair, Kerrie glanced at me. "That's all I remember."

"Where were you taken?" Lauryn's knuckles were stretched taut on the bedpost, her voice clipped.

Didn't she understand? Or didn't she want to?

"I wasn't." His voice was flat as his eyes stayed locked on mine. "Where did they find me?"

"Wandering along the Bitterhill road. Feverish and incoherent." I squeezed his hand as tears slid down his cheeks.

"I don't know where they are," he whispered miserably, "but I have to find them."

"Anders and I will find them."

"It was my fault."

"Hush. You sound like me," I scolded, recalling my father's criticism with bitterness. "Anders and I will go. There's a renegade mage loose near the Bitteredge Mountains, and you can't do a thing to stop her. However," —my grin was fierce— "we can, and we will."

"But Alex, please." When I shook my head, he turned to Lauryn, and stretched out his other hand. "I'm so sorry."

"Damn it, Kerrie," Lauryn scolded, blinking back her own tears. "You do sound like Alex. And listening to her is quite enough to drive anyone mad."

* * * *

"Lauryn doesn't want me here."

"And I don't want you with me," I snapped, losing the control I struggled to maintain from the moment Jules appeared in the manor's main hallway. When he announced his intention, I wanted to strangle his skinny neck.

Anders came behind me and held me close. "His children and his sister are in danger. He has a right to come with us."

I stared at Jules's haggard face, green eyes defeated, and refused to banish the chill from my voice. "Then let him take his troops and go alone. I won't travel with him. He may have a right to go, but I have a right to refuse his company."

Miserable, Jules glanced at Anders before facing me again. "Brendan arrived last night from Ardenna."

"With a private note from Elena? How touching."

Anders's fingers gripped my shoulders as Jules's face burned with shame. "Stop it. That particular thorn isn't your concern."

"You're right." I shrugged off his restraining hands and spun around to face him. "My concern is to track down the renegade and get Khrista and the boys back in one piece. Are you coming with me?"

Cool seagray eyes appraised me. "Of course."

"Without Jules."

His gaze darkened. "No, Alex."

I turned my back on him, betrayed. "Then I'll go alone."

Jules reached out a hand to touch me, embarrassed as I stepped away in disgust. "Go on, then, Alex. I won't have you go without Anders. I'll stay behind in Port Alain."

I didn't bother to answer or look back at Anders as I headed outside for the cottage path, nearly tripping as I stumbled into Gwynn and Sernyn Keltie, who caught me with gentle hands as he studied my face. "You are troubled." When I shrugged free of his grip, he said, "Anders told me you were leaving at first light."

I nodded, taking careful note of Gwynn trying hard not to be noticed.

"Please allow Gwynn to go with you."

"Why not just send him after me without permission? It wouldn't be the first time you did what you wanted despite what I might have wanted."

Gwynn's eyes went wide, appalled, and not yet comfortable with my erratic hostility toward his father. "Alex."

Sernyn silenced the boy with an upraised hand. "You have enough to concern yourself with without unwanted companions." Smoothing back a loose strand of graying hair, he regarded me, and shrugged in apology. "Lady Barlow told me there was a problem." He slanted a glance at Gwynn, who looked confused. The boy didn't need to know anyone's dirty little secrets.

I sighed and turned away, eyes unfocused on the gardens, blooming with autumn colors. No one spoke for a long moment. When I faced Sernyn again, I was surprised at the intent expression in his eyes. "I don't want Gwynn in danger."

"And I would feel better if he were with you." Gentle insistence, but not gentle enough.

"I can take care of myself," I said irritably, and started to walk away. "I did it for twenty-five years."

Sernyn snatched my tunic sleeve and held me back. I raised a brow, looked pointedly at his hand on my sleeve, and then at him.

"Getting brave."

"When your safety is an issue, yes."

"And wasn't it all those years?" Fresh pain and old grief appeared in his eyes as I taunted him again, confusing me with conflicting emotions. "Why did you come the day I showed up in Glynnswood that first time?"

At my abrupt question, he shrugged in bewilderment. "I wanted to see you. I wanted to see how you'd grown." When I started to utter something nasty, he raised a hand to stop me. "I did not hesitate, Alex. When the scout reported you were searching for your kin, I immediately put down the leather strap I was repairing and left the house to saddle my horse. Alex, understand," he whispered, "if you were safe and distant in Port Alain, I could almost pretend I had no guilt to bear. But when you arrived upon my doorstep, I could no longer avoid you."

"Avoid?" I spat out the word, satisfied at his flush of embarrassment. "And are you sorry you didn't lie and send word I had no more kin in Glynnswood?"

"How can you ask me that?" As I started to respond, he placed his hands on my shoulders and held me still. "Forgive me. You have every right to ask, but I have never regretted coming to you. My only regret was that I reopened a painful wound and caused you intolerable grief." He gently squeezed my shoulders. "The question is better asked of you. Are you sorry that I came to see you?"

I broke free of his grasp and walked away, turning my back on him, aware of Gwynn's silent worry. Lords of the sea, I wanted to strangle Sernyn Keltie. I shook my head, pausing a few steps away. "I don't know." At that honest admission, I hugged myself hard, trying to ignore his disappointment. "Regardless of how I feel, I still don't want Gwynn in danger."

"Then I will simply send him after you in the dark."

* * * *

"Lords of the sea! You're not coming, too?"

Rosanna stood in the doorway of the cottage, framed by the late afternoon sun, struggling to keep her expression bland. "Don't you think I can be of help?"

"You'd be as much help to me on this journey as I'd be in your gardens."

"Nothing like an insult to welcome a person." She came into my sitting room and draped her cloak over one of the armchairs. "Shall I make some tea?"

I put my hands on my hips and stared at her. "What do you think?"

"I see." Her eyes darted round the room until she found what she was searching for. "Perhaps some of this might lighten your mood?"

"Perhaps." I gratefully accepted a glass of Marain wine from her outstretched hand. "You asked yesterday what was happening to us." I twirled the glass in my hands. "Good question. I wish I knew the answer."

Rosanna fluffed up some pillows, tossed them onto the armchair opposite me, and made herself comfortable. "What's troubling you?"

I searched for sarcasm in her eyes, and came up empty. "A lot of everything, I guess." I paused for another sip, savoring the fruity taste. "I'm worried about Khrista and the boys. I'm afraid of what we'll find. I'm afraid—" I stopped and looked away.

"For one moment, forget I'm Khrista's mother and the boys' grandmother," she said softly. "Tell me the truth. I have a right to know."

I laughed with bitterness at her choice of words. But she was just as right as Lauryn, even Jules. "Kerrie couldn't tell us much. I'm afraid they're hurt or worse. Rosanna . . ." I forced myself to face her without flinching. "I'm terrified that they're dead. If the renegade mage is uncontrolled or mad, I don't know what we'll find. Or even if we'll find them." I drained my glass and slammed it on the table. "I'm sorry. I shouldn't have said all that and—"

"What? Echoed my own fears?"

"What if I can't help them?" I wrapped my fingers around the glass again.

Rosanna appraised me for a long tense moment. "Will you try?"

I blinked in confusion. "Of course."

"Then that's all we can expect of you, Alex. You don't have to go, but you will."

"Of course, I have to go."

She held up a pudgy hand. "No, you don't. But you will. And we're all grateful. Don't you think we'd rather you didn't? Beyond worry for my daughter and the twins, we're worried for you and Anders. And so"—she gave me an impish smile—"is your father."

"Oh, him." I waved the glass in annoyance and reached for the bottle.

"Yes, him."

"Well, that's another thing."

"Why am I not surprised?" When I didn't go on, she said, "The mere fact you're talking to him is miraculous."

"Talking?"

"I was being diplomatic."

"Don't bother. And don't pursue it. I don't want to discuss Sernyn Keltie." Grumpy, I sipped the wine without really tasting it and sank into the chair opposite her.

"What else do you want to discuss?"

"Jules." When she nodded for me to explain, I said, "He has a right to come with us, but I'm still so furious with him." I huddled in the chair, cold despite the blazing fire.

"Would it help to know Lauryn would prefer Jules be anywhere but here?"

"I don't blame her. Anders lectured me that it's not my concern, and it isn't, but that doesn't mean I have to take Jules with me."

"No, and you don't have to, but I'd feel better if you had more protection."

"I can take Port Alain troops."

"Alex." Something in her voice caught my attention. "Jules needs to get his wits together, and he can't do it here."

"You want me to coddle him?"

"I want you to smack some sense into the fool's head."

My turn to restrain amusement. "All right." I slouched in the chair and crossed my legs, dangling one foot loosely over my knee.

"What else?"

"Elena."

"That will take a little time."

"What if she never forgives me?"

"She will. She's grieving right now, but she's not a fool. After all, you didn't make Erich a traitor. He did that all by himself." Rosanna scrutinized my still unhappy expression. "There's something else."

"You're annoyingly perceptive."

"I try to be."

I slouched even further. "This renegade—" Rosanna was watching me like a hawk, seeing right through my careless manner. "She, at least we think she's a she, may very well have my talent."

"Sernyn told me that."

"She has probably had it, or used it," I amended, after catching the brief glint of an unspoken remark in the old lady's eye, "longer than I have. And don't say I could have had it longer either." Her expression turned bland, as I added, "Even though you'd be right."

"I wasn't thinking any such thoughts."

"Liar." I glanced down at my fingers, surprised to find them tangled.

"What are you afraid of?"

"If she's truly mad or stronger or—"

"You won't be alone. There's Anders and Gwynn."

"The boy hasn't a clue what to do with his talent."

"He did manage to save Elena's life."

"It was an accident," I grumbled, unable to coax my hands free of each other.

"You can teach him on the way." She paused, watching me try to untangle my hands. "What are you really afraid of?"

"Failing. Having Anders or Gwynn or even your foolish son get hurt, or worse." I forced my hands apart and clenched them into fists.

"The renegade mage, she's the part of my talent that frightens me. Not controlling it, abusing it, enjoying the power."

"You've managed to remain a civilized subject of Tuldamoran so far," Rosanna said dryly, though her eyes were somber.

"You don't understand. You can't know what it's like. Fighting Charlton Ravess in the mage duel was one thing, until my anger nearly overwhelmed me. I'm sure you heard in sordid detail what I did to him, how I used my magic to maim the firemage and nearly kill him. That incident revealed a part of me that shames me. And don't forget," I added before she could voice a protest, "how I used my magic to get back at Anders for spite when he kept pushing me to go faster and further. That was unforgivable. Anders was my friend." My hands clenched together again, the knuckles bone white. "Don't you see? I enjoyed the power, Rosanna. I used it to hurt Anders and nearly obliterated Charlton Ravess. I've never admitted that out loud."

"Alex." Her tone was chiding. "You used it to defeat a traitor and save a crown. As for Anders, you used it to prove something and to spite him. I don't believe, despite your own self-doubt, that you'd have pushed matters so far with Anders if you knew he'd be hurt."

"You don't know that for certain."

"Be reasonable."

I shook my head. "I like to think I wouldn't have."

"Then maybe it'll do you some good to see this renegade mage abuse her talent." Rosanna's tone had subtly changed to affectionate mockery. She drained her wine glass and grabbed her cloak, flinging it around her shoulders. "Think of it as looking in a mirror. That should keep you honest." Instead of replying, I bowed my head, studying my hands, skin stretched taut over my knuckles. Rosanna stopped by my chair, her fingers gently stroking my hair as she often did when I was a child. "There's stubbornness, pride, spite, and anger in you, Alex, but not a shred of malice. Emila and Sernyn, yes, Sernyn, too, could never have created a monster, and I would never tolerate one." She tugged at a strand of hair. "And you could never become one, even though there are times we all swear you breathe fire and smoke." She kissed the top of my head. "I still want my schoolmistress back in one piece. Not to mention Master Perrin, my gardener. So you be careful."

* * * *

I woke in the middle of the night, cold sweat clammy on my body, a scream echoing in the stillness. Anders held me close, stroking my head, until I stopped shaking.

"Your fingers are getting tangled in my hair."

"Sorry. Just trying to help." He freed his fingers from one intricate knot and sat up, leaning against the headboard. "Want to talk about it?"

I squeezed my eyes shut as he fumbled for a lamp, and struggled to sit up, facing him. "I can't remember, but it was horrid."

"You're worried about what we're facing."

"I'm not worried. I'm terrified. There's a profound difference."

Anders kept his gaze calm as ever, a trait I could never imitate. "You won't be alone. And," he added smugly, "I'm a Crownmage. That should count for something."

"You're Lady Barlow's assistant gardener."

"And your lover. Which reminds me—" He arched his eyebrows in an open leer. "We should take advantage of your brother not watching."

I leaned across the bed to kiss him. "I told you we shouldn't let that nuisance come with us. Not that we'll be alone anyway, with Jules and his guards. Flameblast it, Anders." I snuggled closer to feel warm and safe. "I left Glynnswood to come home, where I can be safe. I want my dull, unexciting life back. I want to yell at the little monsters in class and snarl at Rosanna and throw sarcasm at Jules."

"I know."

His serious tone caught me off guard, when I'd been expecting a light-hearted reply. And so I didn't tease him when his fingers played with my neck, nor fight him when they caressed my shoulders with tenderness. I needed Anders. I needed his comforting reminder of who I was and how he felt about me. Grateful, I gave as much as I took. And even managed to fall deep asleep afterward.

Chapter Twenty

We'd taken the coast road toward Bitterhill, huddling beneath wool cloaks against the sharp wind that blew with seasonal fury, tugging us closer to the seawall. After a long, tiring ride, we set up camp, with Jules's small band of troops keeping watch during the night. To pass the time, Anders took on another hopeless apprentice mage.

"You're not concentrating, lad." Anders scowled at me when I laughed. "What are you grinning about, Mage Champion?"

Enjoying the entertainment, I leaned back against a convenient log, my feet to the campfire. "It's gratifying to hear you scold someone else for a change."

"I'm not scolding Gwynn. Not really," he added when my brother flushed scarlet. "But he evidently shares some of your stubborn tendency to do the opposite of what I tell him."

"But Anders," Gwynn protested, recalling my own words a year ago, "I am trying to do what you tell me. It simply will not work."

"Your sister said the same thing."

"It's all right, Gwynn." I leaned over to pat his head as though he were an overgrown puppy. "Anders hasn't a trace of patience when he's playing supreme master Crownmage and training a brand new apprentice. He's so old he's forgotten how it is to fumble through unfamiliar talent."

Anders scowled again. "Why don't you teach him?"

"I will. After all, I'm a schoolmistress."

"Among other unflattering things, best not said in a young man's presence," Anders muttered, as he stood to stretch the kinks from his back.

"Did you hear those bones creak?" I whispered to my brother. "Or was that an earthquake?" Gwynn's brown eyes were wide, darting back and forth between us, uncertain whose side to take. I took pity. "Go away." I waved Anders in the opposite direction. "Go bother Jules. Make sure he's not getting into any trouble." Anders shot me a nasty look, but left us alone. "Ignore him," I reassured Gwynn, stifling a yawn. "He was a cranky old beast when he was teaching me to handle my magic."

"Anders told me what happened." Gwynn met my gaze without flinching, though I could tell he was uncertain of my reaction, "You know, Alex, when the wind flung him against the tree."

"You mean when I caused the wind to fling him against the tree." My mood turned somber at that troubling memory, so recently discussed with Rosanna. "I could have done him serious harm. It's a good lesson to remember, especially for me. And I'm sure it's an incident Anders will never forget, either."

"You were afraid of your talent."

"Because I didn't understand it, yes, I was terrified, but more important, because I almost hurt Jules when I was a child, and then Anders when I was grown. I had no one to train me, Gwynn," I said, "though it was no one's fault." I didn't need to say that, could have blamed Sernyn Keltie for abandoning me, but couldn't, not in all fairness, not now.

Gwynn lowered his head, scraping some dried mud from his boots. "Father told me how frightened he was, too, Alex, of his own talent." When I didn't answer, the boy looked up shyly. "I am sorry. I have offended you. I did not mean to pry."

When I grinned, I shook my head at his obvious relief. "Yes, you did mean to pry, you little nuisance." I pulled at the rebellious lock of his brown hair. "Did he tell you why I'm so angry with him?"

"Yes, though I had guessed some of the story." Open affection and loyalty flared in his eyes. "I would have been angry, too, Alex. I told him so. I wish I had known about you when I was little. It is not fair."

"What?" Odd how an admission like that still unnerved me. "That you couldn't pester me and drive me mad all those years?"

"That, too." He grinned, the smile transforming to a young man's awkwardness. "I did not know what I was missing until I met you, Alex. I always thought I was alone, but now I have a sister. I told father that, and told him, too, I wish he had not abandoned you to Lady Barlow when you were so small," Gwynn blurted in embarrassment, turning bright crimson.

"Made him feel more guilty, did you?" I shoved him playfully.

"Yes."

"Good. He deserves every bit of it. But, here's something I don't think I ever admitted to you, little man. I'm angry, too, that he kept you away from me." His pleased expression warmed my heart, though what I said was true. Rosanna and the old duke raised me as one of their own children from infancy, and I'd never lacked for love or affection. But I had always, in my heart, felt I didn't quite belong, that I had no family of my own. And now I had Gwynn. "Back to your lesson. Don't think you can distract me. Close your eyes and concentrate." When I felt sure that he was trying, I closed my own eyes. "Feel the heat of the flame and the sharp cold of the ice," I said, keeping my voice soft. "Painful at first, always. Separate them in your mind, make them distinct as two coils of rope, then blend them together, weaving them until you feel a cool warmth, a comfortable cool warmth throughout every inch of your body." I opened my eyes to watch his face. "Can you feel it?"

He nodded, eyes shut tight.

"Open your eyes slowly, still feeling the comfortable cool warmth." As he did, I pointed to the pile of dirt between us. "See this dirt in your mind as a small flame. See it in your mind first. See precisely what you want to create. And then see it in front of you."

He was concentrating so hard I was afraid he'd faint. A small flame perched on the mound of dirt between us.

"Flameblast you, Gwynn. You did it!"

With a proud grin, the poor boy did faint.

* * * *

"Thank the lords of the sea," I muttered the next day, wrapping my cloak tight as protection against the cold air blowing in from the Skandar Sea. "Another mile and a comfortable, warm bed."

"Getting soft?" Anders didn't hide his amusement. "I always forget how Rosanna coddled you."

"I'm only thinking of your old bones." I stopped to stare beyond the Port Alain guards riding ahead of us, a knot forming in the pit of my stomach.

"Trouble?" Anders peered intently as Jules rode his mount forward to confer with his guards.

"Queen's troops." Although I managed to keep my tone flat, Anders shot me a warning glance. Aware of Gwynn at my side, I bit back a cruel comment. As we neared the Ardenna troops, I saw there were not as many as I feared, nor was Elena in their midst.

Their captain approached me as we came to a stop. "Mage Champion?" He cleared his throat, face flushed, looking very young and nervous, and started again. "The queen has sent a message for you."

"Go on."

"She's found evidence in Edgecliff, from a captured mercenary that the late Duke of Barrow's Pass and Charlton Ravess were conspiring with mercenaries to make it seem that folk from Glynnswood were behind the trouble in the forest and the attacks on you. She's sent word along to your father to warn him." When I stayed silent, unwilling to comment, he added with open disgust, "The mage sightings in Edgecliff, though none of the duke's doing, were ignored by him when he'd promised to handle the matter. It was another way for him to harm the queen, by letting it appear she was unable, or unwilling, to protect her people."

"I remember when he offered to investigate the matter," I said, recalling the day Anders and I eavesdropped on that particular audience. "So he's guilty of letting wild magic go on undetected and uncontrolled."

"Yes, an act for which the queen, wrongly, Mage Champion," he said with earnest loyalty, "holds herself responsible. In any event, she sent us" —the captain indicated his small band of crown troops with a wave of his hand— "to offer you assistance."

I started to refuse her help, but Anders caught my pigheaded expression and intervened. "Thank you, Captain. We'll need all the help we can get."

* * * *

I snuggled deep within the heavy blankets, enjoying the decadent feel of the soft bed as I stretched my legs in bliss. Finally in Bitterhill, we'd taken several rooms at the inn along the northern fringe of town. Eyes closed, as my legs wandered onto the far side of the mattress, I absently wondered into what hole Anders had disappeared. On the point of sleeping, I was jolted awake by a brisk repeated knock on the door. "Lords of the sea." I moaned in despair. "Who is it?"

"Jules."

Jules. I pulled the covers over my head, reluctantly remembering Rosanna's request to knock some sense into her son's foolish head. "It's late."

"I know. I'm sorry."

He didn't tease about a midnight visit. Hell. I shrugged into my wrinkled tunic and trousers, fumbling for a lamp. Disheveled, I yanked open the door.

"May I come in?" Jules looked so forlorn that I almost pitied him. Almost. Not quite. "Please, Alex."

"I'd rather you didn't, but I've been accused of being uncivilized once already today." I edged back from the door and sat on the bed, legs crossed beneath me, trying very hard to be patient.

Jules ran a hand through tousled brown hair as he sat on the edge of the chair by the shuttered window, ready to bolt. "I spoke to Elena before she returned to Ardenna the night you came after me in the hunting lodge."

Across the bridge. Twice.

"Jules, I'm tired. What do you want?"

Miserable green eyes met my own. "I wish you didn't hate me."

Stifling a sigh, I admitted, "I don't hate you. I'm disappointed in you. I'm angry, no, I'm furious, with you. I want to rip out your heart and feed it to the seahawks. But I don't hate you, Jules."

"Well, that's a relief." A trace of amusement flickered in his green eyes.

"All I keep thinking about is Lauryn. You don't deserve her." I clenched my fingers into a fist and banged it against the bed. "But it's your problem. Face the truth. Elena doesn't want you as a lover," I said with intentional cruelty, steeling myself against his anguish. "Only as a friend. Be thankful she doesn't hate you, particularly since you tried to step in so soon after Erich was dead at her hand. I can't imagine what you were thinking."

"I wasn't thinking." He bowed his head in shame. When he spoke, I strained to hear him. "I told her that, admitted the truth. Alex, it's not that I don't love my wife." Green eyes bright with tears stared at me. "I do. Honest. I just don't know what was in my head, except that Elena was free."

"Besides the fact that you weren't free, Elena doesn't want you the way you want her," I said quietly. "Let her go, Jules."

"I will. I can. I have no choice." He nodded in mute agreement. "But how do I stop Lauryn from despising me?"

Odd that I felt compelled to comfort him. "The first thing you have to do is bring the boys home."

"And then?" A flicker of hope shone in his eyes.

I reached out to touch his cheek with a gentle caress, disturbed, more than I cared to admit, by his surprise. "And then we'll see. Let's get past that step first. It may be the hardest."

Chapter Twenty-One

Now that we were inland, Gwynn was more subdued. I thought I'd lose my mind, or he'd lose his tongue, from spending too much time with Anders. Back in his home element, the boy took the lead with confidence from the Port Alain and Ardenna guard, guiding us toward Edgecliff, north of Bitterhill. That was where most of the sightings had been witnessed and Elena had found evidence of conspiracy or, at the very least, negligence.

"You'd better know where you're going," I threatened my brother, brushing a willful strand of hair from my eyes as I resettled my backside in the saddle.

"You have admitted I am an excellent guide."

"Good. Not excellent." I eyed Jules, who brought his mount closer. "Have we far to go?"

"No, my lord." Gwynn turned to Jules and answered with quiet courtesy. "We should arrive at Edgecliff by nightfall."

"And then?" Jules wrapped the reins around his hand to keep his horse abreast of Gwynn's.

"If you're asking how we find the mage, I have to confess, I've no idea," I answered, glancing around at the troops surrounding us. Anders gave me an odd look as Jules and I spoke in a civil manner. I hadn't told him of our midnight conversation.

"Alex." Gwynn looked back over his shoulder. "I have an idea."

"I can't wait to hear it."

He grinned as I pushed my horse forward to match his pace. "Edgecliff is on the borders of Glynnswood. The town itself is not very large, nor friendly to strangers," he explained, "especially uniformed strangers."

"And you're not a stranger?" Anders prompted behind us.

"No. They would talk more readily to me."

The late afternoon sun caught the gray streaks in Anders's black hair. "He's right, you know."

"Just this once," I muttered. "Don't encourage him."

"I don't have to. He's got the same blood in his veins that you do. Only his disposition is more pleasant."

"Are you implying that my mother was unpleasant?" I pulled my horse almost to a standstill, daring Anders to make a snide comment.

Anders laughed and tugged at my reins. "Of course not. Emila was sometimes stubborn, often willful, but never unpleasant." He narrowed his eyes. "Maybe you're some kind of changeling."

"You'll regret your words, old man."

"Anders," Gwynn interrupted; a neutral look in his eyes as he avoided mine. "Father told me once that from what Lady Barlow told him, Alex was nothing like her mother."

"That's it." I slapped Anders's hand from my reins. As he yelped, I urged my horse to the side, away from them all, still protected by the flanking guards, who looked uneasy at the disturbance I created. "I've heard enough."

"He didn't say you were unpleasant," Anders argued reasonably as I ignored him. "Only that you're different."

I shook a fist at Gwynn. "You'll regret your words, too."

"Don't threaten the boy," Anders scolded.

"It's bad enough you threaten the rest of us," Jules said dryly, daring to enter the conversation.

"Feeling better, Duke Barlow?" I snapped, honestly glad to see color in his cheeks and a little backbone in his spine, even though it was at my expense.

"Yes." He met my gaze, echoing my thought. "As long as it's at your expense."

"You'll—"

"Regret my words, too." Jules laughed softly, finishing my threat.

"Alex, don't you find it odd that you have a distinct habit of threatening all the men in your life?" Anders arched a brow, but kept a safe distance between our horses.

"Don't you find it odd that they all come back for more?"

"Maybe we men should reconsider."

"I should be so lucky."

"You'd miss me."

I rolled my eyes skyward. "Don't flatter yourself."

"You would," Gwynn said with such conviction that I laughed aloud. "You would miss all of us."

"You, little brother, I'd miss least of all."

* * * *

"I would."

Anders's sleepy voice was muffled against my hair. "You would what?"

"Miss you."

"Ah," he murmured, half asleep, tugging at a strand of tousled curls. "I did hope you would."

Caught in a peculiar bittersweet mood, I turned to face him and leaned up on an elbow. Moonlight caught the flash of silver in his disheveled hair. "You've made an amazing difference in my life."

Andres blinked in surprise. "No. You've made an amazing difference in your own life." He yawned and nuzzled my neck. "When you decided to open your mind and heart, Alex, I was just lucky to be there."

"Anders." I bowed my head, leaning it against his warm shoulders. "This isn't easy for me."

"Keeping me awake when it's hard enough to sleep on a frosty ground?" He tugged at the strand again, wrapping it around a finger.

"No." I laughed and shook my head. "I've never really told you how much I love you." There. Not as hard as I feared. Not when his eyes warmed with open, steadfast affection.

"And I've never really told you how much I love you either," he admitted with ease, "maybe because I've been afraid to scare you away. Nevertheless, we've managed to get the message across in a hundred thousand ways." Anders smiled, tracing the lines of my cheek, and just as suddenly, his eyes went abruptly grim. "What is it? What's wrong? You're trembling like a newborn colt."

"I'm frightened," I whispered, trying hard to banish the terrifying images that kept appearing in my imagination. "I don't know what we'll find in Edgecliff and how we'll deal with it."

"We'll do what we've done these last months." His even, white teeth shone bright against the shadows of his face as he grinned. "We'll create a marvelous plan and discard it as soon as things start happening. And then we'll muddle through and do precisely what we have to do precisely when we have to do it." He kissed the tip of my nose with a dramatic flourish. "It always works."

"The renegade mage is like me."

"We don't know for certain." He waved at the sleeping bodies surrounding us. "You're not alone. And even if you were, you're so angry at the twins being kidnapped, you'd manage to handle her all by yourself." He kissed my lips and then my neck. "Now, since I'm completely awake—"

"Completely?"

"Yes."

"Every bit of you?"

"Every bit that counts."

"Then we should take advantage, I think." I wrapped my arms around his neck, enjoying the touch of his fingers on my back.

* * * *

Edgecliff was just what its name implied. A dirty, barren town perched at the edge of a cliff, a very small cliff facing across the Jendlan River, the fringe of the Glynnswood forest and the Bitteredge Mountains beyond. The town was so unattractive that we skirted around it and camped beyond its borders.

"You didn't tell me about the bridge," I complained to Gwynn, trying to keep my tone light and nonchalant, "if it even deserves to be called a bridge." I'd never admitted to Anders about my midnight dash to the hunting lodge, nor did I intend to mention it now. I wondered, though, whether Jules had considered what I'd done that night to find him.

Solemn eyes met mine. "You did not ask me."

With a melodramatic sigh, I slumped against the damp log at my back. "I liked you better when you respected me."

A horrified expression came into my brother's eyes. I looked around, thinking my father had somehow appeared. "I have always respected you."

"Wretched liar. I also liked you better when you were afraid of me."

An eerie Anders-like neutrality settled in the boy's eyes. "I was never afraid of you. I just did not want to trouble you."

"I never liked you."

Neutrality vanished, replaced by an open grin. "Lady Barlow said I could always tell when you like someone because you give them a difficult time." Pride and smugness overcame his usual common sense and training, as Gwynn forgot to dodge my fist as I shoved him backward.

"How dare she?" Another playful shove and Gwynn fell back on his heels. "That old witch lied about everything."

"She did not lie when she said you were a good person, Alex."

I snapped my head around at the utter sincerity in his voice. "You're serious."

"Yes. Of course."

"May the lords of the sea protect me from adoring little brothers."

Gwynn reached out a hand to touch my arm. "You are a good person, Alex. You did not have to like me, or accept me so easily. But you did."

"I couldn't help myself. Even though you're a pest, you were completely irresistible." I stretched to ruffle his hair and tugged at the rebellious lock of hair. "Now, tell me about that tiny, narrow make-believe bridge."

"It is narrow."

"Do we have to cross it?" I glanced over Gwynn's shoulder to see the bridge, but darkness had fallen. "Is there no other way around it?"

Gwynn shook his head. "It is the only way. And it is only on the other side that recent mage sightings have occurred."

"Just my luck. You're sure?" When Gwynn nodded, I turned to Anders, who had just joined us. "Remind me to complain to Elena about this travesty. I'm sure she collects enough taxes to have her bridge repaired. If I'm her Mage Champion, how can I protect her if I've broken my neck or worse on a collapsing bridge?"

"It's not that bad," he said, tossing some twigs my way. "You'll see."

I didn't broach the subject of the bridge until Anders and I snuggled close in our bedrolls. Actually, Anders mentioned it, and I defended my honor.

"Jules suggested that you, ah, might have a slight problem with the bridge." Anders tugged a strand of hair when I didn't immediately respond. "I know you're awake because you're not snoring."

I turned to face him, and hid my face in his chest. "He's being kind, for once, if he described it only as a slight problem. Anders, I'd really rather not go across."

"We have to, if we're to get to the other side."

"I can't. You don't understand." I'd already started having nightmares.

"No. I suppose, I don't. Would it help if you were blindfolded?"

I punched his chest lightly. "It's not a joke, Anders. I'm terrified of bridges. Don't you remember how Elena told you she and Jules used to hide across the bridge by Jendlan Falls when we were children, knowing I'd never have the courage to follow them." Not until I had no choice but to find Jules and drag him home to his wife.

There was a long pause, and then, "All right. But wait until the morning," he tried to appease me. "You'll see, Alex. It won't be that bad."

It was worse.

The cliff wasn't that high, so the span wasn't that high. And the river wasn't that wide, so the span wasn't that long. But it was weather-beaten wood, with holes where the wood had rotted clear through. Nightmare enough when I trembled at the sight of a solid, well-maintained bridge, but this disaster brought involuntary tears to my eyes and stole the breath from my lungs.

"What are you looking for?" Anders asked as I peered up and downstream, trying to shield my reaction.

"A boat." I crossed my arms. "I'm not crossing that."

"A boat won't help in the turbulent water. We'll tie a rope around each other's waist and—"

"All right. Go ahead." I waved him away. "Let me know what happens. I'll be waiting right here."

Anders gave me a very peculiar look, though he didn't comment on the now-obvious terror in my eyes. "So," he drawled, "are you going to act like a coward in front of your little brother?"

"Coward?" I blurted, before hastily regaining control. "Not me. I'm just showing common sense."

"Gwynn will be disappointed in you."

"He'll get over it. I won't. I'll be dead. That thing," I pointed at the bridge, ashamed at the way my hand was shaking, "is suicidal."

"The twins will be disappointed when they know you didn't have the courage to save them." He turned his back on me and walked away.

And I was seething with anger and sheer terror.

"Alex." Jules came to tug at my cloak. "You don't have to do this. We'll manage without you."

I shook his hand from my cloak, unable to hide my trembling. "I've come this far. I have no choice."

"Yes, you do."

"I crossed the bridge to find you at the hunting lodge because of the children," I admitted, "and I'll cross this flameblasted bridge, too, because of them."

"I know you did, Alex, but—"

"But Anders is evil, and to spite him, I'll do it. And he knows it. I'll do it," I repeated, storming toward the bridge, adding over my shoulder, "without killing myself just so I can rip out his heart when I get to the other side."

Anders kept his distance as I let the Ardenna captain secure a rope around my waist, and then test it, his determined expression indicating clearly he'd get me across to safety no matter what happened. Gwynn was in front of me, nimble as a monkey, Jules behind to steady me. Odd that Jules's presence comforted me, despite the tricks he and Elena played on me eons ago. But he knew I wasn't joking, he'd been an eyewitness to my fear as a child.

My heart pounding so loud I feared Rosanna would hear it in Port Alain, I wiped my sweating hands on the sleeve of my woolen tunic and prayed fiercely to the lords of the sea. We inched across, shifting our weight with extreme caution. Perspiration drenched my tunic despite the morning chill, and I couldn't stop shivering.

The holes were gaping, the rushing river surged below, and the bridge supports were nearly nonexistent. Every step felt as though it were my last. By the time I reached the other side of the river, my shaking feet safe on firm ground, I realized something I hadn't considered in my panic. A truth that enraged me until I feared my mage power would escape unwittingly and harm my so-called lover.

"You could've used your mage talent to harden the wood to stone," I accused Anders, pointing a finger his way the very minute I could speak with any semblance of calm. "It would have helped. Why didn't you?" I snarled, reaching for his throat, forgetting I was roped to Gwynn and Jules until my body jerked backward.

Anders edged away, hands upraised, as Jules reached out to stop me from stumbling on my backside.

"Why didn't you?"

Anders shrugged. "To prove a point."

"To prove a point? I could've been killed." I fumbled for the knots around my waist, slapping Gwynn's hands away as he tried to help me untangle myself.

"No, you wouldn't," Anders said, his eyes unreadable. "Gwynn and Jules wouldn't let that happen. You dishonor their ability."

"You dishonor our relationship." Finally free of the restraining rope, I strode across the ground between us, and slapped Anders hard, the sound echoing in the heavy stillness.

The blandness in his eyes turned swiftly to surprise, and just as swiftly to hurt. He caught my hand as I raised it again. "That's enough."

"Not for me." I blinked back tears. "You proved a point with my mother's pendant, and I never forgave you for that." Recalling his deception days before the duel to save Elena's throne, in which Anders hid my mother's mage pendant that I used for confidence and luck, I pulled my hand free. "I'll not have you do this to me again. Not ever." I turned away from the sorrow in his eyes and went to find my gear, shoving Jules's anxious hands aside.

As I reached my traveling pack, gathered into a pile with all the others, a man-height wall of flame surrounded the pile, and abruptly sputtered into a trickle of running water, and then back to flame. Then nothing, but a low echoing noise that might have been laughter.

Gwynn darted to my side. "Alex!"

"Hush!" I snapped, straining to hear, not daring to breathe. Nothing, not a sound. "She's gone." I hoped so, because I didn't think I had the strength or even the wits to fight a crazed mage. Not after the trauma of crossing that bridge and venting my rage on Anders, who kept his distance when Jules rushed to my side.

"Are you all right?" Jules put a hand on my shoulders and peered into my eyes, studying every inch of me.

"I haven't been ensorcelled, if that's what you're afraid of."

"I was afraid you'd been burned," he said, with a gentle shake of reproach. "When that wall of flame shot up, you were so close."

"I was burned, but not from the mage."

"We'd better move from here," Gwynn suggested, an unfamiliar troubled expression in his young face at my bitter words.

I didn't answer, but reached for my gear and slung it over my shoulder. With the horses left behind on the other side of the river, I'd packed only as much as I could carry and followed Gwynn into the dense forest, all senses alert and my heart aching.

* * * *

"What's the matter with you?" I nudged Gwynn's dirt-stained boot with my foot, after we'd stopped a quarter mile within the woods and settled down for the night, startling him from his reverie. "Your mind is on the far side of Tuldamoran, daydreaming."

The boy shrugged and hugged his knees to his chest.

Concerned, I knelt beside him on the soft undergrowth. "What is it?" I brushed the rebellious lock of hair from his eyes.

"You and—" He lowered his head, flushing to the roots of his thick hair, and took a deep breath. "And Anders."

Ah. "Anders toyed with me when he shouldn't have. I wasn't being funny, Gwynn. I was truly frightened on the bridge, terrified."

"I know. But—"

I arched a brow in query. "But?"

"You were so mad, Alex," he blurted in a whisper.

"I still am." I sat back on my heels, studying Gwynn's handsome face. "Listen to me. Anders was wrong to play with me like that. And," I admitted, "I was probably wrong to slap him."

"But he loves you."

My arms folded against my chest, I stared at him. "That doesn't give him the right to do what he did. So—"

Gwynn's face wrinkled in distress as he met my cool, calm gaze and hugged his knees tighter. "I do not like it when you fight with him."

"I don't particularly like it either. But I'm not ready to forget about it just yet." I put a hand on his head and leaned on it as I struggled to my feet. "Nuisance. Go to sleep. It's late."

"Alex?"

"Hmm?"

"Where will you sleep?" Gwynn flushed a deep, betraying shade of scarlet, caught between reacting like a boy and a young man, knowing too much more than was good for him and too little to appreciate what he didn't yet know. His eyes were so full of dismay I wasn't sure how to answer.

"Don't worry about me. Go to sleep."

I found my bedroll, stretched out and ready, gear stacked to the side. Anders's doing, I assumed. Well, his courtesy wasn't going to help him. Pushing all thoughts of my lover aside, I fell asleep, only to wake screaming at the top of my lungs in the middle of the night, waking the entire camp. Port Alain and Ardenna troops scattered, searching for something to explain my bloodcurdling shriek. Gwynn and Jules leaped to my side, Anders right behind.

"Sorry," I mumbled in a shaky voice, embarrassed at being the center of unwanted attention. "I'm all right. Just a dream."

Jules exchanged a studied look with Gwynn, and the two of them disappeared to reassure the guards that I hadn't been attacked by a renegade mage. Anders crouched on the far edge of my bedroll, watching me.

I turned my head away. "I don't want to talk about it." I tried to yank the bedroll free of his body, found it impossible, but kept a death grip on the coarse material nevertheless.

"You mean you don't want to talk to me about it."

"Whatever." I nearly fell over as the bedroll jerked free.

"It's not very good for morale when two of the primary parties are not being civilized with each other," he scolded, running a hand through sleep-rumpled black hair as though he wasn't sure what else to do with me.

"There's not a shred of civility in what I'd like to do to you right now," I said, ice in my tone, meaning every word. The nightmare echoed in my head with memories of the bridge, and I wasn't quite ready to forgive Anders. "Go away."

"So you'll stay angry?" He held out an outstretched hand, an offer of apology and peace, but I turned my back on him.

"My choice."

Chapter Twenty-Two

"She must know we're here." Jules propped a dusty booted leg on the fallen log I was resting against the next day. Green eyes, dull with fatigue and worry, were unsure of my unstable mood. Well, so was I, with good reason. "I keep feeling eyes on my back. It's eerie. Bad enough she's a renegade mage, Alex, but the fact that she's mad—" He shivered and pulled his heavy cloak tighter around his broad shoulders.

"We have to lure her out of hiding."

"Is that wise?"

I shrugged, my thoughts in turmoil. "If she keeps on vanishing, as she did with Kerrie weeks ago and then with us yesterday, it means she's tracking us. If we knew where Khrista and the boys were stashed away, if she has them, we could lead her or trap her there, or come up with some kind of plan. But we don't know if they're with her."

Or alive anywhere in Tuldamoran.

"I don't like it." Anders spoke quietly from across the clearing, holding my gaze. "We have no control over her."

"We do if she falls into our trap."

"Still," he hedged, brushing a twig from his cloak, "it's dangerous."

"Then think of a better idea! Every moment we waste sitting here places Khrista and the twins in more danger." I bit back more angry words when I caught the troubled frown Gwynn tried to hide from me.

"We should be prepared to track the mage the moment she appears and vanishes." Jules ignored the open hostility, finger-combing his bedraggled hair. "Alex is right about Khrista and the boys. But how do we lure a mad mage?"

"With mad tricks." I kicked some pebbles away from my feet, throwing out the only plan that made any sense or had the most chance of succeeding. "If I show her what I can do, perhaps she'll be intrigued and come closer."

"What about Anders and me?" Gwynn interrupted with a fair amount of hesitation, eyes shadowed from lack of sleep.

"You're the surprise." My voice held bitterness, though none of it directed at my innocent brother. "We'll see if Anders can manipulate a renegade mage with as little effort as he manipulates me." I stood up, hardened my heart against the regret on Anders's face, and went to find the Ardenna captain. "Tricks and deceit," I muttered under my breath. "We're very good at that."

* * * *

And we were. Not very long after I'd spoken to the captain and explained my plan, I planted my backside on a rotted tree stump in the middle of our campsite. I coaxed the sting of ice and fire awake, gently merging them to the familiar cool warmth. As it spread through my body, I stilled my thoughts, pushing aside anger, worry, and fear. I thought only of mage talent and deception, ignoring the tension of the guards nearby, Jules to one side, Gwynn to my other, Anders at my back, waiting; his own Crownmage talent ready. With tremendous difficulty, I squashed the urge to release the fire and ice in a numbing, earth-shattering vengeance. Rosanna would've been proud, but I was shamed by the overwhelming hunger for release.

Instead, I put on a small demonstration of power, setting the pile of dirt and dry undergrowth a little distance in front of me to blazing flames. I let the flames crackle, slowly changing them to water as the hiss of steam filled the eerie silence. Back once more to dirt, and then to flame.

And waited, though not for long.

I felt the brush of potent raw talent on the fringes of the dense forest beyond Gwynn as an uncomfortable tugging at my own talent. Turning my head with measured slowness to avoid any sign of threat, I saw the renegade mage, much younger than I'd imagined. Pretty perhaps, but rough living and harsh conditions had weathered her appearance. Her eyes, bright blue, were mad, and, more than mad, greedy.

The renegade raised her arms in a slow movement that chilled my spine, and I braced for the release of raw and potent power. The flames on the ground before me turned to mud, and then flames, and then empty air. Not what she planned, apparently, if the frustration in her mad eyes gave any sign by which to judge. And over and above the frustration was pain. She shouted in a rough voice, clutching her body as though it were ravaged from within.

And it was. As was my mother's body when giving birth to me.

"Fire!" She screamed, angry and anguished at once, tears of agony falling down ragged, scarred cheeks, adding words in a language I couldn't understand. "Burning." She sank to the ground in pain. "Ice. No more. Fire. Ice." Panting, trying to control her mage talent, she screamed the words over and over, and over yet again.

I started to shake and whimper like a bruised child. "No. Please, no," I whispered, falling forward on my knees, hugging myself hard, looking for shelter from her savage magic and the pain she was suffering.

"Help me," she pleaded, untamed talent ravaging her body, ravaging the camp as flames, debris, and chaos ran rampant. Noise, unbearable noise, drowned all else but her anguished pleas for help.

I was suffocating, shouted something incoherent over the rushing noise of the whirlwind she'd created, and locked my hands over my ears to drown out her cries.

Fire and ice.

Fire and bloody ice that had killed my mother.

Jules ran to my side, crouched beside me, as Anders and Gwynn together tried to restrain her madness, but the poor woman had vanished as suddenly as she'd appeared. Deathly silence fell over the camp, the only sound my uncontrolled, heartbroken weeping. My arms wrapped around Jules's legs for support as he stroked my hair with surprising gentleness, whispering over and over that I was safe.

Anders knelt at my side. At the familiar touch of his hands, I released my grip on Jules and sank into Anders's arms. He rocked me with gentleness as he had that night so long ago when I first met my father, grief-stricken then, as now. After what seemed like endless hours, my breath grew less ragged, and I pushed myself upright. Anders didn't stop me, waited to see what I needed, unconditional love and affection shining clear in his eyes. Humbled, I whispered quiet thanks as he touched my face with a tentative caress, searching for what was in my heart, as he knelt still at my side.

Gwynn hovered nearby, flask in hand.

"Water?"

"Alex." He threw me a wary grin. "I know better."

"Good boy." Grateful, I took a long sip of the cool Marain wine and sat back on my heels, staring at Gwynn, compelled to explain. "The renegade was so very much like my mother. The fire and ice she screamed about in childbirth, Gwynn, was me. It was my raw magic lashing out at her, and she couldn't do anything to stop me." His deep brown eyes widened in sympathetic understanding right before he threw his slender arms around me in a fierce hug. I started to cry again, but this time it was Gwynn who rocked me until I quieted. "Lords of the sea," I complained, finally pushing him away. "If word of these ridiculous tears gets out, Rosanna will think I'm human."

"Not to worry." Jules nudged my knee. "She knows better."

* * * *

"They were able to track her." Jules sat opposite me after dismissing the Port Alain scout some hours later. "There's a cave not too far from where the foothills of the Bitteredge Mountains start to rise. It's an odd cave, inaccessible except by a rope ladder she guards with care."

I pushed aside my hopes, afraid of disappointment. "We'd better take a look. There may be some clue to lead us to the boys and Khrista."

"I will go now." Gwynn sat up quickly, leaving my side for the first time since my tearful outburst.

I placed a heavy hand on his head to keep him seated beside me. "You're not going anywhere."

"But Alex, I am the smallest and stealthiest. You always tell me so. I will climb up the ladder before she knows I have been there," he pleaded, tugging at his hair. "You know I am right."

"Listen to me."

"But Alex—"

"Flameblasted nuisance." I grabbed hold of his forest-hued cloak and dragged his handsome face close to mine, shaking him hard enough to rattle his teeth. "You listen to me, Master Keltie." Eyes wide, he nodded, slanting a sidelong glance at Anders. "You can go and spy to your heart's content tomorrow when she's gone from the cave. Chances are she'll probably be back here, watching us again, waiting to see if I'll do any more mage tricks for her. Besides—" I sliced into the protest ready to leap out of his mouth, "if you go now, and the renegade grows suspicious, she may harm Khrista and the boys."

"Oh."

"Oh." Heaving a melodramatic sigh, I rolled my eyes skyward. "You can't possibly be my brother. You don't think." Releasing his cloak, I shoved him away.

Gwynn smiled in open relief at my sarcasm. "At first light, I will go."

"All right. Yes. Fine. Just so we understand each other. Now go to bed." I struggled to my feet, shocked at the fatigue in my body as I stretched and yawned. "You, too," I said quietly to Anders.

Cool seagray eyes questioned me. In answer, I stretched out a hand. Anders grabbed hold as I pulled him to his feet. As we settled our bedrolls down side by side and slid beneath the welcoming covers, Gwynn watched from the far side of the camp, a satisfied smile on his young face before he turned away.

"Anders?"

"Hmm?"

I ran my hands under his wool tunic along his back. "Gwynn seems to think we need privacy."

Moonlight shone on gray-streaked hair. "Do we?"

"I think so."

* * * *

"Alex! Anders! Duke Barlow!" Gwynn flew into camp, sliding to a halt beside my bedroll, scattering dry dirt and pebbles in my face. "I found them!"

I woke, sputtering and brushing dirt from my cheeks, as Anders sat up beside me. "In the cave?"

"Yes." The boy's smile was huge when Jules struggled out of his own bedroll and fumbled his way to our side, brown hair tousled from sleep.

"Are they all right?" Jules grabbed my brother's shoulders and squeezed tight. "Are they all there?"

Gwynn's head bobbed up and down in excitement, looking no older than Carey or Hunter. "They were sleeping. Lady Khrista—" Gwynn hesitated and looked at me for guidance. When I nodded, he took a deep breath and faced Jules. "I think she is ill, my lord. Her hair was damp as though she were sweating. And she was lying down, her face flushed. She may have a fever. I am sorry. I could not tell for certain."

Jules still gripped my brother's arms. "The boys? Gwynn, what about my children?"

"One was sleeping. The other—" Gwynn beamed from ear to ear. "He was surprised when I poked my head over the ledge, but I waved him to silence, and he nodded."

"Hunter?" I asked Jules.

"Probably. Carey would've been shrieking."

"He was very serious, my lord," Gwynn added, hoping that detail would help. "I wish I could have stayed to reassure him, but I had to leave. From the spot where I watched, hanging by the ledge, I saw the renegade coming back. So I left. I am sorry. It was hard to leave them behind."

"At least you saw them. They're alive, and they know help is near. That was most certainly Hunter, if he was serious." Jules's green eyes showed the first spark of life in days. "If you'd been caught helping them escape," he reassured my brother, "you would've been defenseless against her. We'll take care of the rest. You've done quite enough."

"We need a diversion." I stifled a yawn, punching Gwynn in the shoulder to let him know I was proud of him. "I'll take Gwynn and half the guards back toward the river bank." Another yawn escaped. "Pardon me. Anders, you go with Jules and the rest of the troops to free Khrista and the twins."

Anders wrapped his arms around my shivering shoulders as we sat entangled on the bedrolls. "You go with Jules. I'll go with Gwynn."

I craned my neck around. "Why?"

"Because we can't risk you—" His words faded at my arched eyebrow.

"Behaving like a fool, and falling to pieces?" I pushed him away with feigned confidence. "I'll be all right. It was just unexpected."

"Are you certain?"

"Yes. Absolutely."

"And I must be with Alex because it is partly Glynnswood's responsibility that the renegade is mad." Gwynn's brown eyes were solemn, so like Sernyn Keltie, that I couldn't resist toppling him over on his side.

"You must be with me because I want you where I can see you." With renewed energy, I worked myself free of the tangled bedrolls and helped Anders pack our gear. Within moments, the camp was ready to move. I led Gwynn and our half of the troops toward the Jendlan River. We didn't have long to wait.

Instinctively, knowing she was near, I gestured for silence. Port Alain and Ardenna guards obeyed without question as I strained to hear, catching the sound of low, eerie laughter that sent involuntary shivers running down the length of my spine. Laughter, and something more. Shutting out the sounds of the river flowing past, I felt raw energy edge nearer. And keening, a wild cry of mourning.

I caught the captain's eye and signaled him. In silence, he fanned his troops around to outflank the renegade's position. Cool warmth ran through me as I held my talent in check, not daring to provoke the mage until Jules and Anders had time enough to make their rescue. With caution, the renegade appeared at the forest edge, framed against the close-knit pines, facing the river.

And facing me.

Reaching out with both hands, she shut her eyes tight against the brilliant sunlight streaming through the branches overhead and groaned. "Fire burns," she muttered. "Ice cuts. Help me." Flames singed the ground at my feet as she switched to an unintelligible language once again.

I didn't move, though I wanted nothing more than to flee. "Quiet your mind," I urged. "The pain will stop."

"No." She moaned, clutching her sides.

Flames caught the rotten log near Gwynn's boot. Without effort or thought, I changed the flames to a pool of water. "Quiet your mind." My voice droned on in soothing tones. "Don't use your mage talent. Don't—"

One arm, dressed in rags, draped over a low hanging branch as she leaned back against the trunk for support.

"Rest."

A high-pitched keening destroyed the stillness of the forest, soon followed by a shout of joy. "Alex!" Carey, safe at last, bolted unexpectedly from Jules's arms and crashed through the undergrowth, heading straight for me, too near the pain-maddened renegade mage.

Too late.

Eyes wide in fury and betrayal, the mage stretched both arms in my direction. "No! Mine." Turning around to find more betrayal, Khrista and Hunter free, she muttered, fire erupting in all directions, raw talent reckless and wild.

Anders, running behind Jules, shoved Khrista into the arms of a Port Alain guard and worked his way toward the renegade, keeping out of her sight.

Watching his every move with my peripheral vision, while keeping my eyes locked on the mage, I shoved Carey to safety behind my back into Gwynn's waiting arms. "Get him away," I hissed. "Now."

Mage Resolution

Gwynn moved to get Carey out of sight.

The renegade screamed defiance and darted after my brother as I sent a wall of flame to bar her passage. Enraged, she turned her fury on me. "Mine!" Turning the dry log at my feet to blazing flame, the mad woman laughed as fire caught the hem of my wool cloak.

Without thinking, I changed the flames to water and scrambled after the renegade as she flew toward the bridge.

The flameblasted bridge.

"Anders!" Running as fast as I dared, I shouted in panic and terror as I approached the bridge. Lords of the sea, I'd no choice but to cross.

"It's all right," Anders called out. "It's all right, Alex. It's safe. I promise."

And it was. I looked out over the span in relief to see that he had changed the rickety wooden supports and span to firm stone, though my fear still nearly paralyzed me. The mage screamed again in rage and pain as she leapt at the Port Alain guard who scurried across the bridge with Hunter clutched in his arms. Flames engulfed the poor guard, who fainted from the intense pain as I changed the flames to water. As the wounded guard fell, Hunter tumbled within reach of the deranged renegade, who snatched the boy from the ground. I shot behind her position when Hunter's soft cry of fright distracted her attention.

"Anders!" I watched in horror as the renegade lunged toward the edge of the bridge, Hunter in her arms, Anders moving in her direction, inch by inch.

"No closer," the mage warned, clutching her side again as fire and ice ripped uncontrolled through her body.

I crept closer to her, holding my breath and shoving aside the paralyzing terror of the bridge beneath my shaking feet.

"I need them," she whispered, making no sense to me.

Anders was closer, seagray eyes fixed on Hunter, who watched with implicit trust as the mad renegade carried him closer to the edge, the rushing waters loud below. I held my breath as she grunted, swinging Hunter until he was positioned precariously on the narrow ledge, just out of my reach. Gwynn moved onto the bridge from the further bank, Carey clutched in his arms. Anders stared calmly at my brother for a brief second, some message passing between them. Without warning, Gwynn set Carey down and flew to the renegade's side as Anders leaped forward to snatch Hunter from her grip. In moments, Gwynn shoved the mage toward the ledge where she tried to maintain her balance, hands gripping Gwynn's cloak with desperation. In anger and disgust, my brother cursed and shoved the mage backward and over the edge.

Losing the battle for balance, the mage pulled Gwynn over the edge with her, clinging to his cloak with a death grip. Jules crossed the short distance to them moments before me. He caught Gwynn's vanishing cloak as the mage's weight bore him down. The heavy material started to rip and escape through Jules's straining hands. I reached his side and tugged on Gwynn's cloak, stretching to reach his skinny leg, painfully aware of the deep waters below and the ease with which I could be carried over the edge with him.

In the eerie silence, Jules's heavy breathing was deafening as he pried the renegade's hands from my brother. Her screams were full of bitter curses as she fell into the depths of the rushing Jendlan River below. As we yanked Gwynn to safety on the bridge, the twins lunged into my arms, sobbing. Forcing myself to stay calm, I tucked the boys against my chest and walked slowly, infinitely slowly, off the bridge, step by frightening step, until we were safe on solid ground. As Jules snatched both boys from my aching arms, Anders swept me up in a fierce hug, dragging Gwynn into our embrace.

Exhausted, I signaled the captain, who came to my side. "We need a healer for the duke's sister. Send word ahead to Glynnswood, please," I said, trying to think through the maze of my jumbled thoughts. "And send word, as well, to Port Alain. Tell the duke's mother and his wife that Lady Khrista and the twins are safe." As the captain hastened to obey, my brother joined us, looking no worse for his misadventure. "Are you all right?"

"Fine, Alex, though hanging upside down from a bridge was not something I would wish to do again, even if you and the duke were holding on tight." His cocky grin made me feel old, but I was glad, terribly glad, that Gwynn was safe.

"Next time, I might decide to drop you on your head. Listen, I have a favor to ask." Eying Anders, who hadn't moved far from my side, I explained, "Can you lead them back to your village? I've sent word ahead to notify a healer you'd be coming, and then—"

"You are not coming to Hartswood?" Dark brown eyes stared at me, sorrow and disappointment crystal clear when I shook my head. "Because of father?"

"I don't know. Maybe." I ruffled the boy's hair. "It doesn't matter. What I do know is that I'm weary and drained and need to go home to Port Alain."

Gwynn started to argue, exchanged a glance with Anders, and subsided. He stood straight and tall, cheeks flushing bright. "I will miss you, Alex."

I grabbed the boy by the shoulders and hugged him close. "I'll miss you, too, though you're a beastly nuisance. Take care of yourself. Next time I see you," —I released my brother, eying him from head to toe— "I expect you to show me some magic. Understand?"

"Perfectly." With a grin, and a quick hug for Anders, Gwynn led the duke's party back toward his people.

Chapter Twenty-Three

"You're looking content," I said to Khrista, some months later, when we'd all banished the horror of the kidnapping from our minds. Or so we thought and told each other.

"Content? Be honest. I'm looking fat." Khrista laughed, one hand resting protectively on her swollen belly as she settled down on a low armchair near the parlor window to enjoy the sun's soothing warmth.

"You're looking content," I repeated, not wanting to be accused of suggesting my friend was as round as a barrel of ale. "As does Kerrie, though ever since he's married you, the poor man's been a bit dazed and bewildered."

"Ah, well." Khrista turned her head away, one long brown braid swinging down her back. Her movement wasn't fast enough to hide the peculiar expression that flashed in her eyes, making me wonder, not for the first time, if she was still troubled by her capture. She spoke little about what happened, though Lauryn and I urged her many times after Rosanna had given up. "Poor Kerrie didn't know any better."

"We all warned him about making a terrible mistake, you being Jules's sister and all."

"I'm sure you did." Her laughter at my good-natured teasing was forced, and stopped the moment she clutched her abdomen. "It's certainly a boy, Alex. Kicking up a storm the likes of the tempest that hit us when we were out on the bay almost two years ago." Her face, no longer calm, paled with strain.

"That's not ordinary kicking."

"I'm fine, Alex." Guessing my intent, she held up a shaking hand to hold me back. "It's nothing. I swear it."

"It doesn't look like nothing from where I'm sitting. I'd feel better sending for the Port Alain healer." I stood to leave but didn't get far. Khrista's hand grabbed the sleeve of my tunic with a strength that surprised me, nearly toppling me over. "Khrista—"

"I'd like some water." Clear defiant eyes held mine.

"Not until you tell me why you stopped me from calling the healer."

"Yes, well." She waved a hand in dismissal, which did nothing at all to ease my concern. "Please get me some water."

Unhappy at the manipulation, I kept Khrista in sight as I poured cold water from the ceramic pitcher. "Here. Though I don't see how it will help you."

She laughed as I shoved the glass into her outstretched hand. "I'm all right."

"It's happened before, hasn't it?"

Khrista flushed and looked away, setting the glass down on the carved wooden table alongside her armchair. "Yes."

"How often?"

"Only a few times." Her skin burned hotter.

"Liar." I watched Khrista intently, some instinct warning me, though the message was garbled. "Why wouldn't you let me call the healer?"

"Because she already knows about my baby's active kicking." When I crossed my arms, trying to make sense of this fact, Khrista picked up the glass and twirled it between her hands. "She doesn't know why it happens."

"I can't believe an expectant woman has never been troubled by these kinds of symptoms before," I said in exasperation, not ever having had my own child. "See another healer then. Go to Ardenna. I'm sure Elena will send you to the best healer in the kingdom."

Not that Elena would send *me* to the best healer. I hadn't seen my friend in all these months, and couldn't find the nerve to ask her forgiveness, though it was nothing I caused. Her distance was emotional, and I'd decided to let her find her way back when she was ready.

Khrista stopped twirling the glass and shook her head. "It's not necessary. The kicking and all the sensations that accompany the kicks don't last long. It's always the same. Burning first, then ice cold. And then it's gone as though it never happened. It's—" She squinted at my sudden involuntary move. "What?"

Lords of the sea, no, please. Fire and ice clutched at my own insides in recognition of her horrible words. My own mother's dying words.

Feigning a yawn, I shook my head. "Sorry. Restless night. Anders's snoring was unusually loud." I crossed my arms and glared at my friend. "But getting back to you and my future student, promise me that if the feelings get any worse, you'll go to Ardenna."

"I'll promise if you stop pestering me. Now go and bother Anders."

I left Khrista alone, haunted by her choice of words. Shoving my concerns aside for the moment, refusing to think about the implications of those words, I wandered down the stairs to the main hall, not sure where I was headed. And then, guided by some bizarre instinct, thought better of my indecision and returned to confront Jules's sister. I settled myself on the window seat, overlooking Rosanna's beloved garden, and traced a design on the frosted glass, a design that echoed the mage pendant I wore around my neck.

"Khrista—"

"I'm all right, Alex."

"Yes, I know."

"But?" Her beautiful face looked drawn and fatigued, though she smiled, trying very hard to convince me.

"But I have to ask you something." Lords of the sea, give me strength and courage to say the right words. "You've known me all my life, so you know," —I paused, took a deep breath to still the shaking— "well, you know I'm not asking this particular question because I'm curious. It's important."

Her face averted, Khrista managed a casual tone. "Then ask."

"Are you certain Kerrie is the father of this child?"

Utter silence. When I'd expected anger or tears, Khrista instead wrapped her heart in cold silence, shutting me out as though she'd slammed an oak door in my face.

"It's important," I repeated. "I swear to you, Khrista, please, believe me, I'm not prying to be nosy. It's important."

"To whom?" She came alive with an abruptness that caught me off guard, eyes flashing in warning. "Your sense of honor and decency?"

I struggled to keep my voice even. "That's unfair and untrue." When she turned away again, hugging herself tight, her swollen abdomen strained against her gown, and I knew, from her lack of response, that she was carrying a mage child. "Your life and the life of your child depend on your answer."

"What's it to you, then?" she spat at me, tears forming in her green eyes that so rarely gazed on me with anger. "What's it to you, Alex, now that you force your way in here with no regard for my honor or feelings or—"

Lords of the sea, I didn't have a choice. "My mother died in childbirth from the sensations you've described."

That ugly sentence stopped her cold, as I'd meant it to. "I thought they never knew what happened," she said, voice tightly controlled, though her knuckles were white as she clutched the arms of the chair.

"Your mother never told you the whole sordid story?" I kept my own voice steady as Khrista shook her head in denial. Why was I not surprised that Rosanna protected my privacy, knowing I still blamed myself for a death I'd innocently caused? "My mother was a seamage, and my father a Glynnswood mage."

"I knew that."

"Well, my mother didn't. Sernyn Keltie was afraid of his talent, terrified by it, and so he never admitted the truth to my mother. Not knowing this, knowing only that he had little tolerance for magic of any sort, my mother promised not to use her own gift when he was nearby. And so" —I took a deep, calming breath— "all through her pregnancy and childbirth, the baby, me, Khrista, tiny unborn me, lashed out with raw talent. My father didn't understand what was happening until it was too late, and my mother never used her magic to save herself. She didn't understand either." I met Khrista's bright eyes with tears in my own and turned back to the window, seeing nothing beyond the tracing of my finger on the windowpane. "If she had, she might still be alive."

"I'm so sorry you had to repeat that."

I shrugged, retracing the design, not trusting myself to answer.

"I'm not a mage, Alex. I've never had any tuggings of magic. Not at any time, as a child or now."

"Maybe you never recognized it, but there must be something there," I insisted, needing to resolve this puzzle before it was too late. "Even so, if Kerrie isn't a mage either—" Khrista's sudden movement caught my eye. "Tell me."

"No." She blinked back hot tears. "I thought it was a dream, a bad dream. Oh Alex, I was ill, fevered, delirious. Oh no, Alex, no, please, no." Khrista started to tremble, all color draining from her face. "There was a man in my dream. He had a tiny scar on the left side of his chin. I remember that clearly because his face was close, so close. But it can't be." She hugged herself hard and started to cry. "Maybe it wasn't a dream. Maybe—"

Understanding what she was trying to deny, I flew from my seat on the window ledge and took Khrista in my arms, stroking her silky hair. "Hush."

"Alex." She sobbed. "Kerrie will never forgive me."

"It wasn't your fault."

"If it's not his child—"

"Hush. It wasn't your fault. The only important thing right now is to make sure that you and the baby are all right. We'll deal with Kerrie later." I rocked her, stroking her back until she calmed. "It'll be all right. I promise." Though how I could make such a promise I refused to think and left Khrista stunned with worry while I went in search of the baby's grandmother, numb with misery and foreboding.

I watched Rosanna from my spot on the edge of a stone bench along the garden path, a very chill stone bench, whose iciness penetrated my trousers. "Why are you digging in the gardens in the frost?"

"It keeps me sane."

I shuffled over to get more comfortable on the cold bench, stuffing layers of light wool from my cloak beneath me. "Listen. I need to ask you something."

At my somber tone, Rosanna kept her face neutral and came to sit beside me. "What's on your mind?"

My fingers managed to lock themselves together somehow. I studied them to see just how they had accomplished that feat.

"Alex."

"Did you know" — one finger wiggled free as I continued— "that Khrista hasn't been feeling well?"

"Yes, and she won't admit the truth, as though I'm not intelligent or observant enough to notice, forgetting I bore two of my own children, not to mention watching Lauryn carry the twins." Rosanna looked on the point of adding something else, and I wondered if she and

Anders had ever discussed my fear of bearing a child whose parents merged such turbulent bloodlines. But she said nothing, and I didn't want to ask a question for which I didn't want to hear the answer. "Khrista's paler than she should be, and this grandchild of mine is too active."

Another finger wriggled free. "Ah." And another. "Did Khrista ever, ah, show any mage talent at all? Even a trace?"

"No."

"Never?"

"No, Alex." Rosanna put a gentle but firm hand under my chin and forced my eyes to meet hers. "What are you trying so desperately not to tell me?"

I swallowed and tried to look away but Rosanna held me fast. "Khrista was raped," I whispered, hating to be the bearer of such news, "when she was held captive."

Rosanna's eyes turned cold. "By whom?"

"It must have been another renegade mage," I explained, finding the courage to meet her gaze. "One we never saw. Khrista said she was feverish and ill much of the time, and thought it was a dream."

"Why didn't anyone tell me?" Rosanna demanded, discarding the gentle, unassuming air she often carried. "As her mother, I had a right to know."

"No one knew," I said, trying not to flinch from the hardness in her eyes. "Only now, just some minutes ago, I forced the truth from her. She—" I broke free of Rosanna's grasp and turned my face away, unnerved and on the verge of tears.

Rosanna took my tense shoulders in her hands and gently turned me back to face her. "There's more."

I nodded, keeping rigid control over my emotions. "I wouldn't have suspected had she not complained of a sensation of fire and ice. I—Rosanna, I don't know what to do."

All color drained from Rosanna's face as realization settled in. "Come." She stood without warning, straightening her wool cloak. "We need to send word to your father." When I hesitated, she rested a hand on my head in understanding. "It won't be easy for any of us, Alex. But in the end, it will be important for all of us."

* * * *

"Sernyn, thank you for coming so swiftly."

Elder Keltie waved away Rosanna's gracious thanks as she studied the woman standing beside him. "My wife, Anessa." His deep brown eyes darted in my direction as I mumbled a polite greeting. I appraised the small, delicate woman whose light brown hair fell well below her shoulders. Warm, deep brown eyes returned my scrutiny in silent curiosity. Taking refuge in the overstuffed pillows scattered before the fireplace in Rosanna's parlor, I sat down, pulling Anders with me for comfort after he'd murmured his own courteous words.

Rosanna offered wine to her guests, along with cheese and a loaf of raisin bread, breaking the ice with small chatter about their journey. I tried to listen, but my fears kept intruding, until Rosanna tapped me on the shoulder. "Your mind is wandering. I'm afraid to ask where."

"Escape," I murmured, glancing beyond her chair to where Sernyn and his wife were seated. I took a deep breath. "You know why Rosanna asked you to come?" When they both nodded, I leaned against Anders, taking comfort in his warmth and solidity. "There's something I have to ask you. I don't—" Meeting Sernyn's steady gaze, I clutched the copper mage pendant hanging alongside Gwynn's wooden one against my chest. "I don't ask this lightly. Or," —I laughed, mocking my own feelings— "believe it or not, to hurt you."

Anders' arm came around my shoulder and squeezed.

My father stayed calm, though wary. "Then ask."

Easier to say than do. "When did my mother start feeling ill when she was carrying me?" Ancient pain and heartache flashed in Sernyn's deep, brown eyes. "I'm sorry," I whispered, startled to realize that I was, in fact, genuinely sorry, "but it's important."

"I understand." His sigh was heartfelt, and he thought for a moment, as Anessa took his hand and squeezed it with as much reassurance as Anders's gesture had meant to me. "Emila was in her fifth month."

And Khrista in her sixth.

"Did she describe the fire and ice from the beginning?" When Sernyn nodded, not flinching from my gaze, I wondered if he truly believed that I meant him no harm. I closed my eyes and sagged back against Anders.

"I've been thinking." Eyes fixed on Sernyn, Anders cut into the awkward discussion. "We don't know if Khrista must be a mage to feel the effects of a mage child. Emila was the only woman I knew in that situation."

"Remember my mother's notes?" I sat up, thinking hard, recalling what she'd written. "She wrote about the women brought to Glynnswood by the Crownmage. His experiments to merge bloodlines didn't work."

"Still." Anders was thoughtful. "If Khrista's not a mage, perhaps the pain won't be so disruptive."

"If she's not a mage, she can't control the baby's raw talent," I said, trying not to sound so negative with Rosanna listening. "We need to find out whether she has any mage ability, anything at all."

"Is it possible she wouldn't have felt anything? Showed any signs as a child?" Rosanna asked Anders and me. "Whether or not you believed it, Alex, you had the ability and knew it, though you denied it. All it took was coaxing to get it back into the open. Can a person have mage talent and not know it?"

Realizing she wasn't giving me grief, but simply needed to know, I reassured her. "Look at Gwynn. He never showed any sign of a mage gift until Elena's life was threatened." I caught Anessa's quiet gaze, a small smile tugging at her lips. "Maybe for some people, it stays hidden until something brings it to the surface. I don't know, but I do know Gwynn swore he'd never had any stirrings until that night, despite the fact both his parents are mages." I glanced at Sernyn's face, flushed at the reminder of magic he rarely used, and the result of his secrecy ending in my mother's death. But it wasn't the time or place for such talk. "And if Khrista is a mage, then maybe—" I faltered, deciding it was better to tug on a loose thread that was unraveling on one of the embroidered pillows.

My father spoke into the heavy silence. "Then we can teach her to control her talent enough to lessen the baby's destructive surges." At my involuntary shiver at his words, he added softly, "I am sorry, Alex. Maybe," —he turned to Rosanna— "there will be no trouble for your daughter. Khrista will at least have a chance." Eyes downcast, he sat still as stone.

For the very first time I listened to him talk about my mother, and I pitied him. I just didn't have the courage to admit it aloud. "Would it be an imposition for you both to stay for a short while to see if Khrista possesses any talent?"

Sernyn nodded without hesitation. "Anessa is a healer. We can stay as long as you need us. I realized my error too late for your mother, Alex. But maybe for Khrista, it will not be too late. If I can help her—"

"It won't bring my mother back," I said, unable to stop the rush of bitterness. Lords of the sea, how I despised the old tiresome grief and the way it ripped me apart, making me hateful when I never meant to be.

"No."

"I'm sorry," I whispered at the grave acceptance in his eyes.

"I know you are." His eyes locked with mine as though we were the only two people in the parlor. "Alex, you had twenty-five years to wonder about me, and two years to despise me. If you can find it in your heart to even consider forgiving me, even for a moment, I will not give up hope."

"I'll make it easier on all of us," I said. "I may not be here for the next few weeks."

"May I ask why not?" Anders pulled at my sleeve.

"I'm going north."

"To Edgecliff," Anders answered his own question. "And you're taking me along, aren't you? Sernyn, can you arrange for your scouts to meet us along the way? Even though your son did his best to teach your daughter to move with stealth, she still sounds like a huge beast crawling through the undergrowth."

"Of course." Sernyn didn't dare smile at Anders.

Rosanna looked from one of us to the other, trying, or so I thought, to ascertain my mood. "Are you going to find the renegade who assaulted my daughter?"

"Possibly." I settled back against the cushions. "There may be others. We need to find out what's going on. I need to know. The woman we destroyed six months ago spoke a language I wasn't familiar with. Maybe it's a Spreebridge dialect. Anyway, accepting Elena's title of Mage Champion drags me into all this annoying responsibility. We'll be back before the baby's due."

Sernyn cleared his throat. "Alex—"

I caught the warning look in his eyes. "No."

"I wish you would not be unreasonable."

"Absolutely not."

"What are you arguing about?" Anders scratched his head in bemusement.

"She will not take Gwynn."

"Ah."

"There's no need."

"There is every need," my father cut in. "More so, possibly, than during your last journey to Edgecliff. Besides," —Sernyn had the audacity to allow a small smile to escape— "you told Gwynn he is sneaky and underhanded. Admirable traits for a scout, don't you think?"

* * * *

"Alex!" Loud pounding on the cottage door jolted me awake. "Alex!"

"It's Gwynn," I mumbled into Anders's warm back. "It's my nuisance half-brother, banging on the door in the middle of the night, when he should be in bed."

"He sounds frightened."

I jumped out of bed and grabbed my discarded clothes, my instinct agreeing with Anders without any conscious thought on my part. Almost tripping twice, I flung open the door and found him on horseback, an extra mount at his side.

"Lady Khrista's ill," he explained as I stuffed my feet into cold boots. "She—" Gwynn shook his head, setting unruly brown hair in motion.

"She what?" Anders peered at my brother's face as I stretched for my cloak. "What's happened?"

With a fearful glance at Anders, he shook his head again in bewilderment. "She tried to kill herself."

Without a word, I fastened my cloak snug around my neck and bolted onto Gwynn's horse, locking my arms around his skinny waist.

"Alex, wait—" Anders snatched the other reins from my brother and followed after us, galloping along the darkened winding road to the manor on the hill.

Gwynn urged the horse on, Anders's grumbling growing fainter as he fell behind. I jumped down hitting the ground hard, the moment Gwynn neared the gate, and ran through the main hall to the stairway leading to the top floor.

Jules, disheveled and wrinkled, leaped up to greet me from his vigil at the top of the stairs. Worry evident in his eyes, he led me toward a smaller room where the family huddled together, waiting. "Mother and Kerrie are with her. And your stepmother," he added, the word sounding strange to my ears.

"What did she do?"

"Poison." He ran a shaky hand through rumpled brown hair. "It's lucky Anessa and mother saw the lamp lit in Khrista's parlor. She's been keeping odd hours, and they were worried. They managed to avert the worst of the effects, so she's all right, Alex. But—" Jules sighed. "Khrista's weak and disheartened and terribly unhappy."

"Where was Kerrie?"

"Sleeping in the adjacent guestroom. Since she's been so restless, Khrista asked him to sleep elsewhere, for fear of keeping him awake all night." Jules raked a hand through his hair, messing it further. "Kerrie's beside himself. He doesn't know how to comfort her. Nothing he says— It's as though she doesn't believe him."

Through all his rambling, I'd been keeping tight rein over my emotions. Nodding mutely was the best I could manage.

The door to Khrista's room opened as Anessa stepped out. With a nod in my direction, she told Jules, "She is finally sleeping. When she wakes, Alex," —she turned clear dark eyes on me— "if you would speak with Khrista, it may help." Anessa's words died as my father, in silence, dragged me to the far corner of the room, away from the others.

"I know that look in your eyes. If you think to take the blame for this," he kept his voice low, "you are wrong."

I started to walk away but he grabbed my shoulders and held me fast. "Get your hands off me."

"Not until you think with your head instead of your heart. You cannot take the blame for Khrista's actions. It was her choice."

"The knowledge I gave her led to that choice." I struggled to break free, furious at having this confrontation with others present.

"She had to know the truth eventually to face the baby's birth. Without it—"

"Without it, maybe it wouldn't matter, anyway. We don't know, do we? Now, let me go." I struggled to break free of his possessive grasp, but Sernyn held me tight. "You presume far too much on one conversation," I snarled at him.

"And you presume far too much on the influence you have over people's lives," he judged, finally releasing his grip on my arms.

I shoved him aside, past the others, to find comfort in the dark, but only found bitter cold. I felt lost and alone. Huddled in Rosanna's garden, balanced on the edge of a stone bench, I shivered, not so much from the cold night air but the pain of my father's stinging words.

I never meant to be presumptuous or arrogant, but things were different these last two years. Everything I touched always seemed to touch others. I'd fought so long and so hard against caring about the people I held dear. And now that I did, and willingly, was I so wrong to think I had a bearing on what happened to them? I couldn't win, so why try? Lords of the sea, Sernyn had me feeling sorry for myself, when it should have been Khrista I pitied.

Tired of shivering, and frightened of feeling so lost, I dragged my boot heels back to the main hall and found Gwynn sitting companionably side-by-side at the bottom of the huge carved stairway with an unexpected visitor.

Elena Dunneal, monarch of Tuldamoran, glanced up at me, dark blue eyes appraising my mood. "I've wanted to meet the young man who saved my life. And," —she paused, eying me with hesitation— "apologize to his sister." Without waiting for a response, she turned back to Gwynn. "We thought you'd come back inside, sooner or later."

"I didn't want to."

My brother had the same look in his eyes as that day in Edgecliff when I slapped Anders beside the bridge.

"Why is it," I demanded, "that whenever I get angry in front of you, I feel guilty?" When the boy looked down and studied his fingers, I knelt in front of him to force his attention. "You're like my conscience."

"I hate it when you are angry," he admitted, clasping his hands together. "I am afraid—" He dropped his eyes again.

Relieved Elena had returned to her senses and our friendship, I exchanged a look with her, baffled. "Of what?" I asked, running a hand through his thick, disheveled hair.

"That you will go away."

Elena's bland expression spoke volumes as to why she had waited with my brother, listening to his fears. She'd had Brendan around far longer than I'd had Gwynn.

"I'm not angry with you."

Gwynn shrugged. "It does not matter. If you are angry, you are not, well, it is hard to explain, Alex, but you are not you. You are someone else who frightens me." He tugged at his rebellious lock. "I do not know what father said to you to make you so furious."

"And I won't tell you," I said with an affectionate smile to soften my words, "or you'll drag yourself into the middle of an argument that's not yours. And believe me, Gwynn, you'll only get hurt."

"Can I come with you to Edgecliff?"

At his abrupt change of subject, Elena met my gaze evenly. "Anders told us what happened and what you plan to do. I'll send troops if you need them."

I leaned on Gwynn's head as I stood up, ignoring his feeble protest. "Maybe not at first, but I'd feel better knowing we could count on them if necessary."

"Shall I have an extra troop stationed at Bitterhill?"

"Yes, thanks." I nodded toward Gwynn, who was still muttering beneath my restraining hand. "And thanks."

"Just returning the favor." She smiled, watching Gwynn with open affection, reminding me of all the times in the past I'd kept an eye on her younger brother and heir when he was squiring here in Port Alain.

The two of them followed me up the stairs. Rosanna, sitting alongside Anders, jumped to her feet the moment she noticed us. With a wary expression, she crossed the room to meet me at the doorway. Elena and Gwynn squeezed past me to give us privacy.

"How is she?" I asked, firing the first arrow.

"Restless. She wakes now and again, then drops off. Kerrie won't leave her side."

"Will she speak to me?"

Rosanna hugged herself as though she caught a chill. "I don't see why not." She kept her eyes fixed on mine. "But I won't let you talk to my daughter, Alex, unless—"

"Don't you dare say it," I kept my voice pitched low. When Rosanna put her hand on my arm, I shrugged free and walked past her, ignoring the others, especially Sernyn Keltie.

Khrista was sleeping, Kerrie at her side. "Alex." Kerrie started to stand but I motioned him back down. "She won't listen to a word I say. She's all I care about, you know that. Nothing else matters. Can't you convince her of that?"

Before I could comfort the poor man, Khrista muttered something, eyelids closed tight. She tossed beneath the wool coverlets, finally opening her eyes. I turned to Kerrie. "Would you leave us for a bit? Please."

With a silent nod, and quiet confidence in my ability to make his wife see reason, he left us alone.

I took his place at Khrista's side. "That's a flamboyant way to get attention." As she shut her eyes in defiance, I tugged at her fingers. "Did you think Kerrie would abandon you? He doesn't care about anything but you and the baby. And the baby. Do you understand that?"

She spun around to face me, her cheeks spotted with scarlet. "Kerrie will always know that he's not the father."

"You don't give him very much credit," I said, trying to shame her. "Let your husband decide that for himself. Don't throw his feelings aside." When she blinked away tears and pulled the wool coverlet closer around her shoulders, I helped tuck her in. "Should your mother and the old duke have thrown me out because I wasn't their child? They never treated me any different than you or Jules." When she didn't answer, I persisted, "Would you rather they had thrown me out?"

"Fool." She huddled under the blankets. "Mother said you blamed yourself for what I tried to do. That's ridiculous."

"That's ridiculous? What you did was ridiculous."

"Well, then, we're both fools."

"Listen." I gripped her arm beneath the coverlet. "I won't blame myself if you won't try this again. Deal?"

"If I agree, will you stop squeezing my arm?"

I laughed in relief, simply because I trusted the look in her eyes. "Yes." Standing, I stretched the kinks from my back. "Now get some sleep so the rest of us can do the same. The last person I want to see on my doorstep in the middle of the night is my nuisance of a brother."

"Will you tell Kerrie to come back in?"

"Sure." I turned to leave.

"Alex—" Her expression turned solemn, eyes bright. "I'm really frightened. I don't want to die."

"And you won't," I pronounced with all the confidence I could muster. "We know more about mage births than my mother did. Besides, you won't be alone. Sernyn and Anessa promised to stay with you until Anders and I return from Edgecliff."

"You be careful."

"And you behave." I closed the door behind me once Kerrie went inside.

Anders left Rosanna's side to meet me. "Are you all right?"

"Yes." I didn't fight his arms around me as he held me close.

"Your brother's been fidgeting for the last two hours," he whispered.

"He wants to come," I muttered into Anders's chest.

"Should we let him?"

I looked up into cool seagray eyes that held no hint of judgment or disapproval, only concern and deep love. "Yes. But don't tell him yet."

* * * *

"Am I disturbing you?"

I glanced up from the notes I was writing to Lauryn about my students and their upcoming lessons to find dark blue eyes appraising me. "Even if you were disturbing me, most esteemed and majestic majesty, you have a right to command my attention."

Elena grinned. "I hate to pull rank on you."

"But you do it so well." I pushed the papers aside. "Anyway, you're not my first visitor. No matter how hard I tried to hide, they all found me. Jules, Rosanna, Lauryn, Kerrie."

"Your father?"

I slanted Elena a dark look. "Not yet."

"Ah." She looked over her shoulder at the door. "You know Gwynn's been sitting outside on the steps all day, don't you?"

"No. Why?" I scratched my head, moving the stool further back from the low school table so I could stretch my legs.

"I don't think he means to lose sight of you until you leave." Blue eyes twinkled. "Are you taking him?"

"Yes." I laughed quietly. "But I don't want him to know just yet."

"Lords of the sea, you're cruel."

"Believe me, he deserves it. How long are you staying?"

Elena toyed with a loose thread in her tunic sleeve and pulled it out. "Until tomorrow morning. I think I've imposed on Lauryn's good graces long enough. She refuses to blame me for what happened with Jules all those months ago. Unlike me, who unfairly blamed you for Erich's treachery and my execution of the traitor—" Elena's expression was so vulnerable it nearly broke my heart when she waved aside my attempt at dismissing her words. "Lauryn's got a generous heart."

"If Jules didn't love her, she might feel differently. But he does. And besides," I stressed, poking her in the chest, "what happened, or didn't happen, wasn't your fault. Jules was the fool in that little drama."

"Nevertheless. And you? How is it possible that you don't despise me? I treated you intolerably."

"You were grieving." I squeezed her hand, forgiving the months of distance between us. "You're still grieving."

"He betrayed me."

"Doesn't matter. You loved him."

"When did you become so wise?"

"I just fumble through the shadows and hope to find my way."

"You do, eventually. Listen, Alex, my troops have orders to stay at Bitterhill until they receive word from either you or me. It's the least I could do to keep my Mage Protector in one piece."

"Mercenary," I complained, brushing back a stray curl. "I knew you had an ulterior motive." I squinted at Elena, only then hearing the peculiar words. "Mage Protector?"

"You asked for another title."

"Yes, but, Mage Protector? Couldn't you come up with something a little less– A little more— A little something else?"

With a grin that made her look no older than Gwynn, Elena stood to leave. "Be careful, Mage Protector."

"You be careful. You're the one always getting into scrapes."

And who was going to save me? Particularly from the civilized knocking at the schoolroom door an hour later.

"May I come in?"

I didn't bother to look up at the polite tone. "I'd rather you didn't."

"Then I will leave."

"Lords of the sea, come in!"

Sernyn Keltie entered the schoolroom with open hesitation. "I want to apologize for what I said."

"Why?" I kept writing. "You meant every word."

He sighed and perched on a low stool opposite me. "Not the way in which you chose to interpret it."

"I didn't think there was more than one way to interpret it." I shoved the papers to the side and reached for a stack of well-worn books, looking for the lesson on local government.

"There is your way, Alex. And there is my way."

I started sorting through the pile, searching for what Lauryn would need for reference while I was in Edgecliff.

"When you did not come to apologize—" Though his words faded, he didn't flinch at my sudden glare. "Well, then, I knew I had hurt you deeply."

"That's the first intelligent comment you've made so far," I said dryly, uncertain how this would end, uncertain, even, how I wanted it to end.

"I am sorry, Alex. But I cannot help reacting to your reactions. We have far too much history between us when it comes to guilt and blame." His eyes were sad again, as they were when I first met him in Glynnswood two years earlier.

Thoughtful, I rested my chin on my hand. "And you make it so easy to pounce on anything you say."

"How can I make matters less troublesome for you?"

"That's as impossible as getting rid of my bodyguard." I waved in the direction of the door, where Gwynn was keeping guard.

"He wants desperately to come with you."

"And you desperately want to send him."

"Yes. Of course. Glynnswood must play a role in capturing the renegade mages." His expression shifted with a quiet transformation, until Elder Keltie, with all the burdens that entailed, was seated in place of my father. "Besides, Alex, as the queen's Mage Champion—"

"Mage Protector," I said, tongue-in-cheek. "Haven't you heard? The royal witch has changed my title again."

With Sernyn's restrained sense of humor taking over, he seemed to consider my words, as well as his answer, but chose not to comment, simply nodded. "The point I am trying to make," he went on, back to being Elder Keltie, "is that although the queen feels there has not been any involvement by Glynnswood mages in this matter, there is still the link with Spreebridge that makes it our responsibility to aid you. So, I wish to send Gwynn with you, as well as another excellent scout—" He allowed a small smile to escape for a moment, though he didn't explain why. "I would simply feel better if you had help from people you can trust."

"You're suggesting I can trust Gwynn? And what about Anessa?" I added, before he could respond to my sarcasm. "Isn't she worried about her son?"

My father smiled openly, a frank genuine smile that made me think about my mother and how easily she could have fallen in love with him. So much so that she respected his wishes to not use magic in front of him. "The thought of her beloved son sitting in Port Alain, moping inconsolably while you were gone, changed her opinion the moment I mentioned it. Alex—" He placed a hand under my chin in gentle defiance. "I am sorry, truly, for so many things. And if I can help Lady Barlow's daughter, I—" Though I hadn't yet scolded him for daring to touch me, Sernyn dropped his hand to the table and studied it intently. "I know it will not bring Emila back or make the heartache go away, for either of us."

"No matter the reason, we're all grateful."

"Grateful enough to take Gwynn with you?"

"Do I have a choice?"

* * * *

Exhausted, my brain scrambled and eyes bloodshot, I'd just completed my notes to Lauryn, along with stacking the books and supplies she'd need on the low table I used for my desk. My thoughts were a jumble, and I had an almost uncontrollable impulse to hide in the cottage for some peace and quiet. But there was one last person who hadn't yet sought me out, one last key player in the unfolding drama whom my conscience urged me to see. Apparently, she had the same thought to visit me, for reasons of her own, and arrived at the end of the day.

A soft insistent knock at the schoolroom door brought me to my feet with guilt when I identified my visitor, Sernyn's wife, the woman whom Jules had called my stepmother. She stood waiting permission to enter my hostile territory. Across the width of the empty room, Anessa and I studied each other in silence, measuring, considering, looking for the right words. To her surprise, I was the first one to speak, and my words were not what she expected.

"I was trying to get the courage to come find you."

"Me?" Her quiet manner betrayed her startlement. "Because of my son? Has he troubled you again, Alex? That boy. If he—"

"He always troubles me. So yes, because of your son. And more, because of your husband. And even more, because of you." I watched the expressions shift in her eyes, saw humor, kindness, alarm, curiosity, each take their turn, to be replaced by simple patience. If Gwynn were the example from which I had to judge, I'd have to admit Anessa had been, and continued to be, a damn good mother. "Come in and sit down, if you don't mind a child's stool." I sat on the edge of the table as she entered the spacious room, curiosity getting the better of Anessa's good manners as she scanned the walls. She took in the bright colored paintings, maps, charts, flowers or weeds, I couldn't tell the difference, but was betting she could. "I was putting my notes together for Lauryn. She's a wonderful good sport, always taking my place without complaint, when I'm not here."

"I was just thinking" —taking a seat on a low stool not very far from me, Anessa waved a slender hand at the bright illustrations of sailing ships the children had drawn some weeks ago—"that our own schoolmistress back home could learn a thing or two from you. The room is so bright and vibrant, and their teacher so caring." Guileless eyes met my own, smiling as I flushed at the unexpected compliment. "It is true, Alex, though you cover it up so well. That is part of the reason I came to find you. My son, well—" She laughed, brushing a strand of dark brown hair behind one ear. Anessa wore it long, well past her shoulders, and it suited her attractive face. "You care very much for Gwynn, and I cannot tell you what that means to all of us. And so, though I worry when he is traveling far from me, I am reassured you will do everything in your power to keep him alive and safe, as you did on the bridge in Edgecliff."

"That little incident," I said, envisioning my brother dangling over the bridge, "nearly stopped my heart."

"And mine, when he told me the tale as only a boy could, full of bravado." She smiled again, her adoration of the nuisance quite evident. "But Alex, I am also reassured he will do everything in his power to keep you safe, too, and that," —she paused for a deep breath, as though she were afraid of my reaction— "is just as important to me. And before you question my words or doubt them—"

"I don't." And somehow, I didn't.

Her smile was warm, its affection this time, intended for me. "I had hoped you would not doubt them. Alex, though it may be hard for you to understand, I, too, read with interest every letter Lady Barlow sent to Glynnswood, speaking about you, detailing your life. I knew from her words you had grown into a beautiful and honorable woman, knew from Gwynn's devotion that you would be a good and loving sister to him, and I knew—"

"From your husband that I was an unforgiving, cold-hearted—"

"Hush." Her maternal scolding was as effective as Rosanna's as she stood in front of me, holding my gaze. "I do not need my husband to tell me you have been desperately hurt by his abandonment and the circumstances of your mother's death. You have every right to be unforgiving."

"Do I really?" I whispered. "What happened in the past can't be changed. Anessa—" I shut my eyes against the compassion I read in hers. "I'm trying hard to make my peace with him. I owe it to my mother. I owe it to myself. I'm not sure, however, if I owe it to him. Maybe I do. But it's awfully difficult. Sometimes, I feel—" Opening my eyes, I gathered courage to admit, "Sometimes I feel as though in my own heart and mind I can talk to him not as Elder Keltie or Sernyn, but as my father. And then, before I can stop it, the ugly specter of my mother's death comes between us, and I revert back to childish behavior that shames me," I said quietly, not really surprised that this gentle, kind woman plucked such a confession from the depths of my soul.

"Do you understand how miraculous that is?" She squeezed my fingers and smiled with pride. "To hear you admit that brings joy to my heart, Alex. And your father, because he, too, knows you have been trying. But he will not push you. Sernyn told you long ago he does not want you to need him, only to forgive him," she reminded me of the painful encounter months ago. "And I would add to that, Alex, one thing. If you can find it in your heart, then it would be a joy to love him, too."

"No wonder Gwynn's the way he is." I scratched my head in bewilderment at this amazing woman. "He's got your heart and his father's sneakiness." Smiling when Anessa laughed, her face and manner relaxed, I added, "I did want to talk to you about Gwynn, about taking him along. But more than that, I wanted to—" When she stopped laughing, sensing a more serious thought was lodged in my throat, I sighed and gave in. "I wanted to know you, too, not only as Gwynn's mother, but—" though I couldn't use the word stepmother, I said instead, "I thought you and I should become friends, if you were willing."

The immediate answer I got was a warm embrace. "Alex, I have wished the same, but feared to push my presence on you."

"That's your husband's doing," I grumbled, trying to cover up my embarrassed relief she hadn't outright rejected me. "And Rosanna, telling you what a monster I am."

"Do not forget Anders. He, too, has been telling tales." Anessa's smile was one of conspiracy as she touched my cheek. "The only one who swears you are perfect is Gwynn, and I am afraid," —she laughed— "that the longer he cozies up with all those traitors, that he, too, will start telling tales."

Chapter Twenty-Four

We were some miles north of Jendlan Falls, three days into our journey. Anders, Gwynn, and myself; a ragtag band, first in search of a Glynnswood scout, and then renegade mages. I really preferred to be back at the cottage, snuggled in bed, with or without Anders, preferably with him.

"Be a good apprentice," I told my brother, "and change that pile of wood to a campfire to keep me warm."

Before Gwynn could move an inch, Anders cut in. "That would be a waste of his talent."

"You never said that to me when I was apprenticed to you," I complained, "and you forced me to do the same thing, as I recall."

"As I recall, you were difficult, slow-witted, and reluctant." Anders dodged the bedroll I tossed at him. "Your brother gives me hope."

"For those nasty words, I could challenge you to a mage duel. But since we don't have time, and Gwynn needs discipline—" I tried to distract Anders by pointing at my brother as I aimed a coil of rope at his backside and succeeded.

The old beast grumbled, disentangling himself from the rope. "You need discipline."

With a foolish grin, I snapped my fingers. "The campfire?"

"Talent should not be used for frivolous purposes," Gwynn intoned, in a perfect imitation of Anders's voice, reminding me of his mother's recent warning.

"Elena's troops are waiting at Bitterhill, and your father's scouts are even closer. Whose company do you prefer?" I challenged the boy.

Gwynn ran a hand through rumpled brown hair and met my stern gaze with preposterous innocence, so very much like Anders. "How large should I make the blaze, Mage Protector?" Before I could respond to his cocky question, Gwynn started to concentrate, a burst of flame appearing at the center of the woodpile.

"That is an impressive campfire, Master Keltie."

Gwynn jumped, losing his focus, at the unexpected voice. The flame sputtered and died.

I laughed aloud at Gwynn's scarlet face. "It's good to know someone can sneak up on you," I said, one eye on my brother, the other fixed on the edge of the wood where our visitor was likely to appear.

"My apology for intruding unannounced, Mage Protector, Crownmage." A scout stepped lightly from the cover of the trees and gave us both a polite bow before shooting an impish grin at my brother. He, no, lords of the sea, she, looked no older than Gwynn. No wonder Sernyn had a devious smile on his face when he mentioned another scout.

"My apology for being rude." I studied the young woman. "But do they train you as scouts the day after birth?"

"Alex." Anders tapped me on the shoulder. "You're being very rude."

"Oh, no, Crownmage," the young woman assured Anders with a ghost of a smile, "in Glynnswood, Alexandra Daine Keltie is well known, as are her brave exploits and courage in the face of danger."

"What, ah, precisely, do her virtues have to do with her rudeness?" Anders looked befuddled as he scratched his head at the young woman.

The scout grinned openly. "Along with her virtues, she is known to be direct and not very shy when seeking knowledge."

"That's the politest way I've ever been called rude," I admitted, not sure whether to be insulted or not.

"Your pardon again." The young woman turned sober. "I meant no disrespect but your humor is also known. If I have taken liberties, I apologize and will make amends."

"No, please. Don't worry. Everyone else takes liberties. Come join us." I took a seat by the nonexistent campfire opposite my brother as the scout sat on the hard ground, legs tucked beneath her. "What's your name?"

"Maylen Stockrie." Gwynn sliced through her answer with a look of undisguised and uncharacteristic disgust.

"You know each other?"

Maylen's foot sneaked out and nudged my brother's boot. "I was born one year before Gwynn Keltie, and he still will not admit that I am wiser, more skilled, and a better hunter."

"Because you are not," muttered my brother, dodging her foot as it snaked out again to nudge him.

Hiding a smile, I exchanged an amused glance with Anders over my brother's head. "Now who's being rude?" I kicked Gwynn's other boot playfully. "I thought all you Glynnswood people pride yourself on being polite and civilized."

"Sometimes difficult circumstances make it impossible to be polite and civilized." Gwynn's tone was so serious as he tugged at the rebellious lock of hair that I immediately covered my grin with a cough.

"I see. Well, then. Gwynn, why don't you—" I shook my head, visions of a burning forest clear in my imagination. "No, never mind. I'll make the campfire. You get our guest some food. And Anders—"

"Why don't I get some Marain wine?" he suggested amiably.

"Why don't you?" I closed my eyes and called on the fire and ice, merging their sharp sting to cool warmth, envisioning the dry wood as a merrily blazing campfire. I soon felt the heat nip at my fingers. "Much better." I sighed in satisfaction and released the talent with regret.

"Now then," I continued as Anders and Gwynn provided food and drink, "what news do you bring?"

Maylen tossed a long, blonde braid over one shoulder and sipped the wine with thanks. "There is no further word of dangerous mage sightings in Edgecliff or anywhere else nearby. But there is another matter." She paused to bite into an apple, wiping the juice from her chin with one slender finger. "There have been stories of women disappearing, and sometimes children."

"All in the same area?"

"Yes. All within twenty miles of Edgecliff. The people missing live at the edge of Glynnswood, on the border." Maylen looked disturbed, but said nothing further as she took another bite.

"Maybe there's a mage who wants to merge bloodlines again," Anders suggested, digging in the dirt with a stick, eyes thoughtful. "Isn't that similar to what we overheard six months ago in Elena's court when Erich suggested he send Barrow's Pass troops to investigate?"

"Nothing was ever brought to light."

"Yes, well, my guess is that Erich likely never sent troops." Anders caught the apple I tossed his way. "Or never bothered to report on what they found."

"Good possibility either way, according to Elder Keltie," I agreed, recalling our recent conversation. "But why kidnap Khrista and Kerrie and the boys? None of them are from the area Maylen mentioned."

"Maybe they were a mistake." Anders bit into the apple with a crunch. "Maybe there's no connection. Maybe they're not particular about whom they kidnap."

"It doesn't make sense."

"It does not, Mage Protector. I agree. We need to find out more," Maylen said, adding with a bland expression, "Elder Keltie asked that one of us meet with you again in two days. That should give you enough time to reach Bitterhill." Anders nodded, lost in thought, staring past Gwynn at nothing in particular, oblivious to Maylen's diplomacy regarding Sernyn Keltie. With a graceful motion, Maylen stood. "Then I will leave you now."

"But you haven't even rested," I said, looking up at the young woman in confusion, trying hard not to feel centuries old and a doddering fool as I envied her energy and grace.

With a sidelong glance at my brother, she hid a smile behind a raised hand. "I do not need as much rest as some others do."

"Let her go, Alex." Gwynn's uncharacteristic annoyance prompted a hundred thousand questions, but I held them back. "We will be better off without her. There are other scouts."

"Do not miss me too much, Master Keltie," Maylen's voice dripped sweetness as bright blue eyes danced with mischief. "Elder Keltie has asked me to meet with your party again and relay the news."

At Gwynn's indignation, I caught back my teasing words. "Well, then," —I kept rigid control over my laughter— "if Elder Keltie has asked you to take on such important work, then he must value your skills."

With a completely disarming smile for me that Gwynn couldn't see, she nodded. "Indeed, Mage Protector, he does."

* * * *

"What was all that about?" Anders whispered in my ear later that evening as he crept closer for warmth, on the opposite side of the campfire from Gwynn.

"Typical."

"Typical what?" Anders snaked a hand into my bedroll and pinched my backside.

"Ow! Flameblast you, Anders."

"Hush. Your brother's trying to sleep. Now what were you saying?" he asked me. "Typical what?"

I rolled over and glared. "Typical man."

"I'm missing a critical piece." Puzzled, Anders leaned up on one arm, intrigued.

I shoved his arm and toppled him over. "You men always miss a critical piece." Dodging vengeful fingers, I grabbed his arms and held them to his side. "Gwynn is a typical boy."

"Young man, Alex. Or haven't you noticed?"

"Yes. But not mature enough to enjoy a female's interest," I whispered, slanting a glance in my brother's direction to be sure he was asleep beneath the elm and not just pretending.

"Interest?" Anders whispered back, looking even more befuddled. "She was goading him on purpose, the little imp. Just like—" He stopped suddenly, recognition apparent in his eyes. "Aha. Just like you goad me."

"I knew that old head held some intelligence."

"Oh, my."

"Amusing, don't you think? Particularly if Sernyn really sent Maylen, knowing full well she's skilled and has an undisguised interest in my little brother." I laughed, keeping my voice low. "I didn't think he was that devious, but Elder Keltie had distinct mischief in his eye when he spoke to me of the other scout he would send our way. Rosanna must be corrupting him."

"Oh, my," Anders repeated, squirming free of my grasp. "You won't torture the poor boy, will you? That would be cruel."

"You know me better than that."

217

* * * *

"So—" I munched on a wedge of cinnamon loaf, the very next day, and sipped cool water fresh from the stream out of the neck of my leather waterbag. "Is Maylen really wiser, more skilled, and a better hunter than you?"

Gwynn sent me a disgusted look, something he would never have dared only weeks ago. "I cannot believe you would ask me that."

"Is she?"

With a melodramatic sigh, he took a long swallow from his own waterbag. "Of course not. She is good," he admitted, after long consideration. "She would have to be or she would not be allowed to scout for the village, but she is not better than me, Alex."

Still hungry, I reached for an apple. "What does your father think?"

The boy frowned, tugging at the lock of brown hair standing on end. "She is skilled."

"Better than you?"

"Alex!" Anders scowled across the cold campfire, trying to comb his hair into a semblance of neatness.

Gwynn threw Anders a grateful look. With another sigh, he turned a somber face in my direction. "She is very skilled. We were taught together."

"So you're friends?"

"No." At my raised eyebrow, he grimaced. "No, Alex. She is a terrible pest. We are not friends."

"I didn't think so." Packing up my belongings, I let the matter drop, ignored the issue even as we traveled northwest for the remainder of the day. But on the following day, as we approached the far borders of Edgecliff, I took a closer look at the situation as our new scout reappeared.

"Definitely not friends," I muttered to Anders behind my hand. Maylen materialized from the dense thicket closest to the bridge at Edgecliff, over the Jendlan River; that same bridge where I had slapped Anders in a rage.

That bridge.

"It all depends on whose eyes you're peeking through," Anders whispered with a crooked grin as he nodded to the Glynnswood scout.

Gwynn ignored Maylen, who caught my eye and beamed. I started to laugh in feminine support until Anders jabbed my side with an elbow. Restraining myself, I slanted a sidelong glance at Gwynn, who was busy unpacking his gear, my gear, and Anders's gear, but decidedly not Maylen's gear.

The young woman shrugged with an easy smile and perched on a log in one fluid movement. "I have received word from Elder Keltie." She tossed a braid over her shoulder, pretending not to notice my brother's sudden stillness. Keeping her pretty young face exquisitely neutral, she added, "He has given me explicit instructions depending on the information our scouts have gathered."

I didn't know what was coming, but I held my breath. "And?"

"Elder Keltie has commanded" —a swift glance at Gwynn to be sure he was listening— "that if we found any sign of other renegade mages in the area, I should accompany you."

"Did you?" Gwynn blurted, almost losing his balance and tumbling over the dusty packs.

"No."

Anders caught back my arm as I stretched behind Gwynn to shove him over, cool seagray eyes scolding me in eloquent silence. I ignored Anders and grinned at my brother's blatant relief, which would somehow be short-lived. The mischief in Maylen's bright blue eyes warned me. So, of course, I baited the hook.

"Ah. I see." I coughed and settled my chin in cupped hands, which rested lightly on my knees. "What were, ah, Elder Keltie's orders if you didn't find any trace of renegades?"

With a bland look in my direction that assured me she knew what I was doing, Maylen took the baited hook and dangled it in front of the fish. She looked straight at my brother. "To accompany you on your journey."

With a loud, impolite curse, my ever-polite brother toppled on his side as I shoved him over.

"Alex." Anders's expression was stern as he crossed his arms in disapproval. "At least have the decency to look contrite."

With a somber expression, I reached over to help Gwynn sit up. I changed my mind, laughing at his surprised expression when I pushed him over again.

Chapter Twenty-Five

"Alex, I don't mean to tell you how to deal with your family." Anders hesitated. I kept pace alongside him as we forged a path through the woods near Edgecliff. "But really—"

"You were never shy before."

With a glance over his shoulder at Maylen and a glance forward at Gwynn, he whispered, "Gwynn's just a boy." When I hummed under my breath, quite content, he said, "It's not fair. And you know it."

"Gwynn needs to develop a sense of humor about women sooner or later. He'll survive."

"He feels betrayed by your teasing."

I shot Anders a quick sidelong glance. "How do you know?"

"He told me."

"Foolish nuisance. I'm not serious."

"He thinks you are. Alex, he's hurt by it only because he's so young and embarrassed and new to all this maneuvering. Please stop torturing him." Anders drew his brows together in a scowl. "And what's worse, Maylen is as bad as you."

"You're serious."

"Quite."

"I'll consider the situation." And I did, finally agreeing the poor boy was in need of consolation. Feeling guilty, and cranky because of it, I manipulated Gwynn into sharing a private walk while Anders and Maylen set up camp for the night. My brother kept his head down, shoulders slumped, kicking at twigs along the way, until I grabbed his shoulders and forced him to sit on a tree stump. "You're mad at me, aren't you?"

Avoiding my eyes, Gwynn shook his head.

"Liar."

Gwynn shook his head again. "I am not lying."

Sighing with heavy drama, I thought back on the chat we'd had with Elena a lifetime ago. "It's all right to be angry with me. I won't run away."

A quick blink indicated he was listening, considering my words, until he finally raised his head to look at me. "I do not understand why you are saying these things to me."

"Have I hurt you?"

Gwynn's handsome face flushed scarlet as he turned away, breaking my heart.

"Have I?"

"Yes."

Anders was right, which infuriated me all the more. "I'm sorry."

"It does not matter."

I put both hands on my brother's face, felt the soft stubble of a beard, and forced him not to look away. "It matters to me," I said quietly. "It matters very much to me. I was only teasing you, Gwynn, because Maylen likes you."

Hurt and uncertainty vanished, replaced by disbelief. "Likes me? She is a pest, Alex, and a nuisance. And that is what she thinks of me, too." He was so adamant, I stepped back and crossed my arms. "She provokes me. It is not possible that she considers me a friend."

"Don't I provoke Anders all the time?"

"Yes, of course, but—" His face flushed even brighter as he reconsidered.

When I laughed, it was not at him, but with him. "That's why I've been teasing you."

Speechless, Gwynn gestured lamely. "Is it really possible?"

"From how I torment Anders, and you, too," I added with open affection, ruffling his unruly hair, "I think it very possible. How does she act with other scouts?"

"She laughs and teases them, but not—" Gwynn's expression was so incredulous he appeared no older than Jules's twins. "Not as she does with me. She is always provoking me, making fun of me. Lords of the sea, Alex, she is very much like you in that way."

"Does it trouble you, if she's, ah, interested in you as more than just another scout?" Gwynn's blush deepened as he tugged furiously at his rebellious lock of hair. "What?" I prompted, as he became intrigued by his dusty boots, which I nudged with my foot. "Tell me."

"I would like that."

"Then why not be nicer to her?"

Gwynn looked at me as though I'd suddenly sprouted horns and claws. "Do you think it would work?"

"It did for Anders." I laughed at his sudden transformation. "Besides, she'll still provoke you, but you'll certainly catch her off guard. It's worth a chance. Men can fight back, you know."

His smile was infectious. "I will try. Can I speak with Anders about this?"

"I'm not sure that's a good idea, since Anders is a terrible influence. Your mother even admitted that to me," I said, realizing from his grin she'd repeated at least some of that conversation. "But now, I want the truth." I gave him a stern look. "Were you angry with me?"

His smile faded. "Yes. A little."

"All right. But you have to be obvious like me when I'm mad so I'll know when to apologize. I'm sure Maylen already knows that trick."

That trick and many more. But Gwynn did manage to catch her off guard the next day to his immense delight.

* * * *

We made our cautious way across the Jendlan Bridge, with Anders keeping his comments to himself as I flew across the span in sheer panic. We were a day's travel closer to the Bitteredge Mountains, and I was uneasy, without knowing why. I stayed clear of the children, who'd declared an odd sort of bickering truce, no different really than Anders and me.

But all the while, as we traveled, I couldn't dismiss the feeling of danger.

"What is it?" Anders asked for the hundredth time that day, seagray eyes scanning the woods in all directions.

"I don't know."

"When you're irritable and restless like this, it worries me," he complained, unable to keep the anxiety from his own expression.

"It should."

"Why?" he snapped, looking in every direction but at me. "What's wrong?" When I didn't answer, but braced, swiftly coaxing forth the fire and ice, he grabbed my arm. "Alex, for—"

"Can't you feel it?"

Eyes shut tight, I reached out, merging the fire and ice to cool warmth, shivering at the alien mage talent surrounding us, creeping closer, sending chills up my spine. Without warning, Anders shoved Maylen and Gwynn down and out of sight. I gasped with shock as I was caught unbalanced before the elements had smoothly merged, distracted by coarse ropes thrown over me. Fire and ice sliced through every inch of my body, sharp as knives, as I tumbled unconscious to the ground.

* * * *

"My apologies, Mage Protector, for the rough treatment."

Muttering a vicious oath about my captor's parentage, I opened my eyes and found indecently attractive green eyes set in a seductive handsome face topped by short black wavy hair, watching me. It wasn't lost on me that he was using Elena's latest title for me.

Cautious amusement danced in those eyes as he kept his distance. "It was necessary to get your attention."

"It would have been far more polite to send a courier to Port Alain," I said, trying to ignore the nagging ache in my head, "if you wanted favorable attention."

"True," he admitted, "but knowing your reputation and skill, I could not take the chance that you would not overwhelm me before I could explain."

"Hmmm." With utmost discretion, I began to coax the fire and ice back from their sleep, hoping the pain wouldn't disable me.

"Ah, no, please." The pirate's apology actually sounded sincere. "I cannot have you doing that. The children—"

Hiding my panic, I looked around for the first time since opening my eyes. Anders looked uncomfortable, tangled in rope, as he eyed me in warning. Surrounded by dark-clad guards, Gwynn and Maylen huddled together, defiance all too evident on their young faces.

"The children, I am sorry to say, will suffer if you use your quite respectable and impressive talent." As the brigand edged closer to them to emphasize his point, Gwynn moved to trip him. I cried out in warning as our jailer caught his balance and slapped Gwynn hard, rocking my brother's head back against the tree trunk.

"Lay a hand on him again, and I promise you, I'll rip out your heart and stuff it down your throat."

"Your brother, I would guess." Folding his arms across his broad chest, the stranger peered back and forth between us, verifying the similarity. With a sigh, he walked back across the clearing and crouched beside me. "I desperately want to avoid anyone getting hurt. I have information you need and a deal to offer." Bright green eyes studied me. "My name is Jackson Tunney. I am a mage." He edged so close I could feel his warm breath on my cheek. "From Spreebridge."

Spreebridge.

"If I have your word that you will listen and not try to escape, I will have you and the Crownmage untied."

"And the children."

"I cannot take that risk. I need some assurance of your good faith," he said, keeping those indecent eyes locked on mine.

"You'll have to trust me."

"Not if you want the information."

"Flameblast you, Tunney!" I snapped, losing all patience. "I have no time for this nonsense. We wouldn't be here if you didn't need something from us in return. Now either set us all free or rot in a watery grave."

Tunney glanced at Anders in mock sympathy. "Is she always this contentious?"

"Only when she doesn't get her way. Now be a good mage and listen to her, or we'll all regret it. She does have a valid point, you know," Anders added, his tone so amiable, I was tempted to knee his groin the moment I was set free.

Tunney scratched his curly head. "I am not very skilled at negotiating, but I do need you to listen."

"I can hear much better if I'm comfortable," I muttered darkly.

"I am sure of that, Mage Protector." Jackson Tunney suddenly grinned and got to his feet. With an order for the guards to keep close watch, he released all of us, including my sullen brother.

"Are you all right?" I asked Gwynn, as he rubbed the back of his head, nodding at me, while shooting daggers in Tunney's direction.

"I understand" —the mage ignored my brother's glare and gave me an innocent look— "that you also hear better with a glass of Marain Valley wine in your hand." At a wave, one of the guards brought two bottles of wine, as the foreign mage helped me to my feet.

"Does everyone in Tuldamoran know my affairs?" I complained, trying to stretch the kinks from my aching legs without aggravating the pain in my head.

"There are certain, ah, aspects to your affairs that are widely known." Tunney handed me a glass. "And others of which only a few are aware. Such as your new title, Mage Protector."

"What else?" I prompted out of perverse curiosity.

"Why you are here and who you are tracking."

"We're traveling for pleasure." I met his insolent gaze without blinking, examining the glass as though I hadn't a care in the world.

"You are traveling with a definite purpose. And I can help you. We know about Duke Barlow's sister. And before you say a word against us, which would be your right," he added, surprising me, in a tone of apparent sincerity once again, "we were too late to help her. We knew the renegade mages were kidnapping people."

"There are more then, aren't there?" Anders cut in, taking a wedge of bread from Maylen's outstretched hand before she passed it along to my brother.

"Yes. We have been following them. You know about the history of Glynnswood mages and Spreebridge, from which they originated." At my silent nod, he went on. "The elders in Spreebridge do not usually pay attention to affairs here in Tuldamoran, but word came back to them that some renegade mages were starting trouble again. And to be honest," —he glanced at Anders and then me, cheeks flushing with some emotion or embarrassment, I couldn't tell— "they might have done nothing if the two of you had not made such a flamboyant appearance."

"Meaning?"

"No offense," Tunney apologized to Anders, "but a Crownmage after five hundred years was enough to start an uproar. But then a Mage Champion shows up with unexpected talent eerily reminiscent of the old Spreebridge tales. They were curious, as well as concerned." The mage looked thoughtful as he washed down his bread and cheese with some wine. "So they sent me to investigate."

Convinced now the wine in my glass was not poisoned or drugged, I took a sip. "Why you?" I asked, resting my chin on my hand, instinctively picking up on some hidden message.

His handsome face turned twice as crimson as he said what I'd already guessed, "My talent is, ah, very like yours."

"I see."

"Do you?" He snatched up another chunk of bread.

"Well, for one thing, I see that I'm no longer unique. And that'll take some getting used to." I gave him a crooked grin.

"You'll always be unique to me, heart of my heart." Anders leaned over and patted my knee, sniffing with indignation when I shot him a dubious look, which, of course, prompted him to grace Maylen with a sidelong grin.

I turned back to Tunney with a shake of my head, forgetting the pain, and wishing I hadn't moved so fast. "Are there a lot of you?"

Green eyes shone with a hint of deep mischief. "No. You and I are still somewhat unique. The elders kept me a secret for quite some time."

"For good reason."

"Probably. But anyway, here I am, and what I have discovered is that there are several renegades scattered across the Edgecliff-Glynnswood border, kidnapping women and children to use in merging bloodlines." Taking a deep breath, he shook his head. "As I said before, Mage Protector," —his eyes were downcast— "we were too late for the duke's sister. I am very sorry."

"I wish you hadn't been, but the damage is already done."

"Has she—" Fumbling in his haste, Tunney stopped his words after a swift glance at Gwynn and Maylen.

"She has. And they know."

"You are here for justice, then?"

Weary, I leaned back against Anders and closed my eyes. "I'm here to stop what's happening before anyone else is hurt."

"We will help you." His simple statement caught me unawares. As I blinked my eyes open, he added, "They are renegade mages from Spreebridge," he admitted, "and they are going to cause trouble between my kingdom and Tuldamoran. We want them stopped and punished as much as you do."

"Why haven't you done so already?" There was a hard note to Gwynn's voice I had never heard before. I regretted, deep in my heart, that I ever had to hear such a tone from the boy. Anders gave me an inscrutable look as I craned my head to glance at him.

"Before I answer your question," Tunney said with respect, "I wish to say that I am sorry for striking you earlier. I thought you were trying to escape."

When my brother didn't acknowledge his apology, Maylen's hand crept along his arm and gently squeezed. "Why haven't you stopped them?" she demanded.

"We have been tracking them with great caution." Tunney's voice lost its apology. "We did not know then how many there were. We do now. There were six before, five now, since the woman you fought at Edgecliff fell to her death." He shrugged at Gwynn in explanation. "Their organization is loose, volatile, as some of the mages are more or less rational than others. But now we know."

"And if I hadn't conveniently walked into your backyard—"

Tunney cut me off with a disarming smile as he poured wine all around. "I would have sent a courier to Port Alain."

"I see."

"Well, I don't." Anders took a long sip of wine and stretched his legs around my body, effectively hemming me in. "You said you'd help us and explained why. But I still feel I'm missing a point somewhere. What's really in it for Spreebridge?"

"Spreebridge wants only to be left alone. To be frank, we fear Tuldamoran will blame us, invade our peace, and demand retribution."

"Elena can be vicious."

Anders tapped my head with a light finger. "Our host is being serious."

"So am I."

Jackson turned a stunning smile my way. "I would like to offer our help for the queen's promise not to exact vengeance on Spreebridge. And that is where we thought you might help us."

"I'm not a good negotiator, Master Tunney."

"Neither am I, as you can see from our introduction." Another smile blazed across his face. "But you, at least, have the queen's ear."

"Actually, she pays far more attention to Crownmage Perrin."

"That's because I'm more civilized."

"And if I were civilized," —Tunney stood, without waiting for an answer as to whether or not we'd help him— "I would let my guests get some sleep. We can talk again in the morning."

"Are you civilized enough to trust us?" Gwynn challenged, solemn eyes fixed on Tunney.

"Yes, of course, Master Keltie," Jackson Tunney bowed formally. "I misjudged you as a child. It would seem I was very wrong."

Chapter Twenty-Six

"I thought it best, Mage Protector, to use you for bait." Jackson's expression never wavered as he informed us of his plan with which to address the renegade mages.

"Why not me?" Cool seagray eyes studied him closely.

"Jealous?" I nudged Anders in the ribs. As he gave me that if-that's-what-you-think-it-is look, I grinned and turned back to the foreign mage. "Well, why not Anders?"

"Pardon, Crownmage." Tunney's face turned bright scarlet. "No insult intended toward your talent, of course, but the Mage Protector's magic is more intriguing." He blinked, looking decidedly embarrassed. "That is, to the renegades, of course," he added, as I started to chuckle.

"Then why not you?" Gwynn's quiet voice sliced through my amusement, and I regretted once more that my brother had lost something innocent on this trip when he should have been left at home, boyish and cocky. "In fact, why have you been able to evade capture?"

"For the simple reason that I have kept my distance, as well as my power, from them. My companions have come closest to spy on their camp. Besides, even were the renegades to know that I am a mage, they would still not know what kind of power I wield. And I am unknown to them, Master Keltie. Unfortunately, your sister is well-known throughout Tuldamoran—and more of an attraction."

"But she is not unique," Gwynn persisted in a calm manner that made even Anders sit up and take notice. "So you can make yourself known to them as my sister did," he emphasized the word, tugging at the lock of unruly hair, "when she trapped the female renegade some months ago."

I stretched over to grab a fistful of Gwynn's wool cloak. "Yes, he can. But they know about me, which makes it easier. Besides, we don't have the time or luxury for a well-developed plan. We need to be back in Port Alain before Khrista's baby is born."

Gwynn stared at me for a long time in silence until Maylen grabbed a fistful of the other side of his cloak and tugged. "She is right."

When my brother started to say something, I stopped his words with a hand to his lips. I knew that dangerous expression in his eyes. "I'll make sure you're there to keep an eye on me. Between you and Anders, I'll be perfectly safe."

Tunney blinked long lashes over his green eyes, sidestepping the family drama. "Once we have caught the mages, we will give them a draught to keep them sleeping until we decide what to do with them."

"And then?"

Anders planted a kiss on the tip of my nose. "Must you always ask difficult questions?"

"Someone has to."

"I would leave that to the queen's justice," Tunney answered, glancing at each of us in turn, including Maylen and Gwynn in the silent appraisal. "If you would intercede for me, Mage Protector, I would ask the queen's restraint from holding Spreebridge to blame."

"I should think Elena would be fair-minded. But still," I mused, considering the logistics, "five renegade mages will need careful watching."

"And justice." The foreign mage's expression transformed to a harshness I hadn't yet seen. "Some of them are truly mad and not at all rational. Others are simply cold-hearted and vicious. It would seem only fair that Spreebridge take responsibility for dealing with them."

"I'd like to see them stripped of their talent, but I don't see how that can be done without killing them," I murmured, hugging my knees close to my chest.

"There is a way." When I stared at Tunney, dumbfounded at his confident words, he explained, "Spreebridge elders have found a peculiar draught to block mage talent." He raked shaking fingers through short black curls, obviously as uneasy with the concept as I was. "Feyweed. If taken in too strong a mixture, it may be fatal."

My thoughts flew back to Port Alain. "Could we use it for Khrista's baby? And can it be reversed?"

"It is risky. The child might die. And" —he stuffed his hands deep inside his cloak— "when I left Spreebridge, the elders were no nearer to finding a way to reverse the damage. There were rumors but nothing I could believe with confidence."

"But feyweed—could it save the duke's sister?"

Jackson shrugged in sincere apology. "I am sorry, but I do not know."

"Alex." Anders gripped my shoulders tight. "That's a decision for Khrista to make."

"I know. But it's a choice." Finding little comfort in the arms he held around me, I murmured, "Then we'd best take care of these renegades and go home."

"The sooner the better."

"We know where they have made camp. It is where" —Tunney blinked again, considering his words after glancing at the young people— "they have taken women and children hostage. If we distract the renegades and capture them, my people can free the villagers."

"Yes." Anders nodded in agreement. "And I have a plan."

* * * *

Anders ripped the collar of my tunic, and Jackson bound my wrists tighter than I expected. "Lords of the sea, Anders—" I stopped, appalled at the fear in my voice.

His fists caught in my cloak as he started to rip the edge of the material. Cool seagray eyes met my troubled gaze. "I won't let them touch you, or Maylen."

"There are five of them."

"And four of us." With a quick apologetic smile at Maylen, he added contritely, "Mages, I mean."

"I always prefer the advantage."

Anders took my face in his gloved hands and lifted my chin. "We have the advantage." He kissed me with tenderness, all pretense at being witty vanished. "We have you."

"Flatterer."

He grinned and winked at my brother. "I want to enjoy some private time with you when this adventure is all over. Ready?"

I rested my head against his chest for a moment, anxious to feel his warmth, and then nodded. Anders led the way. He sent Jackson scurrying behind to coordinate the plan with his guards. Once outside the safety of the hidden clearing, no one talked. If we were near their camp, there'd be sentries about. I eyed Maylen, whose own clothes had been ripped and muddied, and fretted about her safety. My brother caught my eye and gave me a reassuring smile.

We stopped to rest after a short while as the woods grew denser, trees menacing in their closeness and unseen heights, roots reaching out to catch our awkward feet and slow our movements to a crawl. Even I, who knew nothing about trees, sensed the vast age of this part of the forest. My body shivered involuntarily, instincts alert.

Gwynn inched ahead to see whether their camp was still where Tunney's escort had last found it. As stealthy as ever, he crept back, catching me off guard. Maylen and I huddled together against the late afternoon chill.

"There is a sentry beyond the next cluster of oak." With a grin for me, he added, "I will tell Lady Barlow on our return that you could not ever make a good scout since you do not know the difference between an oak and a rose bush." The imp scampered out of reach as my bound hands darted in the direction of his head. Serious again, he glanced at Anders. "If we announce ourselves as we get nearer, it will alert Jackson Tunney, and his people can take their positions. I saw him hidden at the far end of the camp," he said quietly. "Alex? Can we . . ."

Something in Gwynn's voice and the hesitation in his question prickled my instinct into further wakefulness. "What?"

Gwynn studied his hands, wrapped in smooth leather gloves.

"What is it?" Anders prompted my brother after exchanging a worried look with Maylen and me.

Gwynn sighed, tugging at his fingers, his gesture painfully reminiscent of me when I was reluctant to express what I was thinking. "Can we trust Mage Tunney?" He glanced up to meet my gaze, brown eyes wide, looking no more than a frightened boy of six.

"We'll have to, won't we?" When he nodded, I whispered, shoving him playfully, "Lords of the sea, I trusted you. And you lied to me about your father and a hundred thousand other things."

"It isn't the time for family squabbles." Anders stood and pulled me up. "Ready?"

"I suppose so."

"Maylen?" Anders appraised the young woman and shot her an approving grin as she stood up on her own before Gwynn could yank her upright. "Good luck to both of you."

"And you," I said dryly. "You're protecting us, remember?"

* * * *

Anders and Gwynn were talking in loud voices, practically shouting, as we approached what I presumed to be the cluster of oak trees. They pulled Maylen and me along behind them, an act for which they both would dearly pay when this nightmare ended. Gwynn muttered something rude to Anders and yanked at Maylen's cord. Two scruffy men stepped in their path, arrows held cocked and ready before them, pointing at Anders and Gwynn.

"Stop. Go no further."

"Put those damn bows away." Anders growled. "We're just passing through. No business of yours."

The scruffier of the two pointed his weapon at Maylen and me. "No one just passes through this part of the old forest. And not with two prisoners." The brigand narrowed his eyes, spat noisily, and wiped his mouth with the filthy sleeve of his tunic. "Especially female prisoners." He took a closer look at me, and then my twin mage pendants, one copper, the other wood, which Anders wanted in plain sight outside my tunic.

"Well, we do." Anders held his ground and yanked my rope, causing me to stumble at his feet, scraping my knees against the branch-strewn earth. Lords of the sea, he really would pay. "Bounty hunters on our way to Edgecliff." He raised his arm to shove past the men and started to walk ahead, dragging me after him in the dirt. "Let us by."

Judging from the arrows aimed at his heart, they were inclined to disagree. "There's someone who might be interested in your bounty."

"For a good price, maybe." Snarling in disgust at the men, Anders pushed aside one bow with his gloved hand. "And I doubt you're the type to offer any price I might consider."

"Insult us, will you?" The other sentry answered, stepping back but keeping his bow targeted on Anders while his partner raised his weapon again. With a harsh shout, he stepped back and waited, eying Maylen and me with open interest, until more ruffians appeared from the dense growth and surrounded us.

Tugging at my rope, Anders darted a quick glance my way and pulled me to my feet with unexpected roughness. I lunged at his chest to punch him in the heart, but he grabbed my arms and held me fast. He may have thought I was acting, but I was ready to strangle him.

"Well, then." He slanted a questioning, fierce look at me. "I hope there's at least the chance for some hot food. I'm starving."

"There will be." The sentry near Anders grinned, a nasty expression that revealed stained and crooked teeth. "Come along."

I pleaded fervently the fool truly knew what he was doing, prayed that Jackson Tunney was trustworthy, and held to the belief we'd all come out of this horrid affair alive. But I would have been lying if I said I had no doubts at all.

Gwynn's trained eyes swept the edges of the clearing, beyond the perimeter of guards scattered around, as we were led further into camp. Armed sentries clustered in the far corner, where I guessed the prisoners were held. The area to which we were led was nearly empty but for five solitary tents set in a circle, facing each other, as though none of the renegades trusted any of the others. If Gwynn caught sight of Tunney or his men, well hidden in the depths of the undergrowth, he gave no visible sign. Watching him with such intensity, I fumbled and tripped, landing on my face, bound hands caught under me, in a muddy ditch.

"One hopes she has more grace as a brood mare."

I looked up, spitting mud from my mouth, at the sound of that hideous cold voice, and caught my breath at the sight of the scar on his chin. Khrista's tearful face sprang into my thoughts. With forced calm, I coaxed mage talent awake and merged the fire and ice in readiness.

Rational, cold, and arrogant, the mage kicked me sharply in the ribs though not before bending down to inspect the mage pendants at my neck. "This one is for my personal experiments." As he gestured for a sentry to take me away, four others stepped closer, two men with the same cold, rational lusting look, and two women, tattered and unkempt, and undoubtedly mad, which made me wonder why the women were the ones who went mad. "You can share the child between you." The scar stood out against his weathered skin as he kicked me once more for no apparent reason. "I like my women to have experience. And this woman" —he eyed me from head to toe, cold eyes clearly recognizing my face— "is a prize I will take off your hands."

"No way in hell," I spat at the mage, startled when Anders kicked me into the mud.

My face smacked the ground, the earth shook beneath me as Anders reached deep into the earth with his magic. Concentrating on the rope binding my wrists, I changed the coarse fibers to air, freeing my achy hands, and doing the same for Maylen.

Flames erupted all around, as Anders guided the campfires toward the renegades and their tents. Screams sounded from the far edges of the camp where Jackson Tunney's band, or so I assumed, struggled with the armed guards. The three male renegades fought the distracting flames and Anders's attacks. I turned my attention to the two screaming women unleashing raw power in the same uncontrolled, random destruction as the woman Gwynn forced off the bridge. With a focused effort, I brought forth a gale wind from the water in the muddy ditch to smash the two women against the trunks of nearby trees. As they were knocked unconscious, I caught sight of Maylen being dragged away by one of the male renegades. Before I could shout a warning to Anders, the mage with the scar lunged at me in fury with a sword.

Just as Gwynn stepped between us.

Trapped beneath my brother's falling, bleeding body, I smacked my head against a rock, and darkness reached up to snatch me away.

* * * *

I awoke, groggy, sometime later to an eerie silent scene of devastation. Uprooted trees, smouldering fires, and, lords of the sea, blood spattering every surface. Gagging with nausea, I sat up, immediately dizzy, and fell back against strong arms.

"Easy." Anders set me against a tree, propping me up with soft blankets. "I knew you'd be seeing double for awhile. Sit still until your vision clears." Obedient, which had to have surprised him, though he made no comment, I took his hand and waited. "The female renegades are sleeping at the base of the trees you flung them against. I managed to pry a strong sleeping draught into their mouths as a precaution."

"The others?" My voice croaked from the raw, smoke-parched tightness of my throat.

"One mage is dead, another missing. The gentleman who insisted on your experienced company is bound with the two women. I was lucky. I caught him unawares."

And he'd caught my brother with his sword. I gripped Anders's hand in panic as the scene replayed itself in my head. "Gwynn—Anders, where is he?"

Cool seagray eyes watched with a guarded expression. "Gwynn was hurt."

Hurt. Not dead. "He saved my life. Anders, where is he?"

A barely perceptible nod in the direction of a flickering campfire. "He's resting. He—" Anders looked away, his face ravaged by grief. "Your brother lost an awful lot of blood by the time I found the two of you. Alex, I've done all I could for him." When I tried to stand, shaky as a newborn colt, he held me upright, until my blurry vision cleared, gripping my shoulders. "His fever is dangerously high. Alex." He caressed my cheek, a warning in that touch, saying words I'd never expected to hear. "The sword tip was poisoned."

I spun to face Anders, grabbing his cloak as I lost my balance, and started to cry at the compassion in his eyes. "He won't die." I brushed away tears. "He wouldn't dare. He's a nuisance, Anders, and drives me mad, but he won't die."

Not bothering to answer, Anders simply held me close against his chest as I wept my frustration and fears. Pulling away, I wobbled toward the campfire, stumbling twice, Anders catching me, guiding me along. I knelt at Gwynn's side, appalled at the fevered delirium he suffered as the poison wormed its way through his slender body. Helpless, I wiped the sweat from his forehead with the cloth Anders had left alongside my brother's head. Helpless and a little mad, I laughed at the rebellious lock that refused to lie neatly, still misbehaved, though sweat drenched his hair. I tugged at it gently, and started to cry again.

"Maylen knows something of healing," I said, breaking the silence. "Where is she? Anders, she—" I glanced about, but the scout was nowhere in sight. "One of the renegades was dragging her away right before Gwynn was hurt."

"Jackson's men are searching the woods for both of them." Anders studied his dirt-streaked hands very closely. "And Jackson, too."

"I didn't see him when the fighting started."

"And I didn't see him when it ended." He shrugged, fatigue clear in his tired eyes. "He's not my concern right now. Maylen is, and so is Gwynn." Anders knelt beside me and took my face in his hands. I shivered as he traced the path of tears along my cheek. "There's not enough time to get Gwynn back to your father's village. Our only chance is to find Maylen. Stay here with Gwynn, while I search for her."

In case he dies, so he's not alone.

I shut my eyes at Anders's unspoken thought and leaned against his chest. "I'm older than him," I whispered. "I should have been the one protecting him."

"You love him. That's all he's ever asked. Besides, Gwynn always felt he should protect you." Anders kissed me softly on the forehead. "Now it's your turn to keep watch. I'll be back as soon as I can." With another kiss, he vanished from sight.

I pulled my cloak tighter round me, chilled despite the wholesome fire, oblivious to the muted sounds at the far end of camp, survivors settling down for the night, weary and wounded, and finally, for the villagers, free. Leaning back against a log, I took Gwynn's burning hand in my own and settled down to wait.

* * * *

Warmth on my face prodded me awake, though I was uncertain where I was; uncertain what was nightmare, what was real. Gwynn was real, his young handsome face ravaged by pain and fever. Jackson Tunney, bending over my brother, long-silvered knife in hand, was real. I snarled and threw myself at the foreign mage to drag him away from my brother before he killed him outright.

Strong, gentle hands pulled me back with a struggle. "It's all right." Anders held me close, safe within the protection of his arms, as I stared at him in bewilderment, only then noticing Maylen at Jackson's far side, holding a length of cloth for the mage to cut into strips. Tunney darted a confused look my way before turning back in response to Maylen's terse instructions. Her young face was grim, filthy, as she applied a foul-looking poultice to Gwynn's chest. While the mage held my brother's skinny body motionless, Anders brushed tangled curls from my face.

"Jackson killed the other mage and freed Maylen." At the question in my eyes, he said softly, "We can trust him, Alex. Maylen saw him fight before she was dragged away." Anders squeezed my hand. "He went after Maylen to bring her back."

Jackson slid his knife out of sight and helped Maylen tuck Gwynn's tunic back together, wrapping blankets around my brother's shivering body. Crouching at my side, the mage eyed me with caution.

"I'm sorry." My throat was still raw from smoke and weeping.

Green eyes flashed in confusion. "Why?"

"I doubted you."

Jackson regarded me gravely as he kept his balance. "I see."

"I had no reason to doubt you." I gripped the edges of my cloak, bundling myself deeper inside its warmth as Anders pulled me close. "I saw the knife and I thought—" Shrugging, I didn't try to defend my actions further.

"You thought you had reason to doubt me."

"Yes."

Mischief danced in those indecent eyes as he answered in a bland tone, "The queen's Mage Protector could not possibly be wrong. I believe you were distracted and solicitous for your brother's welfare. As you should be," he added, with a wink at Anders, who laughed, keeping me snug within the warmth of his arms.

Maylen sat back on her legs, studying my brother, her braid loosened, face marred with dirt and scratches.

I pulled free of Anders' protective embrace and knelt beside the girl. "Will he be all right?" The clear blue eyes that met mine were full of grief and anxiety, no longer child's eyes, not ever again. She nodded, and I hugged her close. "You all right, too?"

"Yes."

Jackson cleared his throat with delicacy as I pulled back from the young woman and wiped my eyes. "We need to deal with the surviving renegades."

I looked beyond him, to where the prisoners were bound. There was a harshness to their features, an aged, weathered look, even in the ease of sleep in the two women. I felt their madness as a power in itself. I shivered involuntarily and turned back to Jackson. "Can you prepare the draught?"

"Of course." He rummaged through his pack until he found the small leather pouch that held his herbs and assorted odd-looking ingredients. "Some wine, please?" he asked Maylen. "Or water. That will do as well."

"I hope you have the recipe," Anders muttered, watching Jackson's nimble fingers grab a pinch of this and a pinch of that, "and share it with us."

"Of course." Jackson mixed the powder into the cup Maylen offered. "Sorry to waste your good wine, but it is for a worthy cause." Smiling in apology at me, the mage brought the glass close to his nose and sniffed. "It has its own peculiar sweet odor which somewhat reminds me of a dead whale that has been beached for days."

"Pleasant."

Jackson flashed me a grin. "Here."

"No." I shook my head. "I'd rather not."

Jackson's bright green eyes met mine with an appreciative look that acknowledged my reluctance as a reaction to the potion itself, not the odor. "Then I will."

In silence, he pried open a waterskin and poured it over the head of the mage with the scar on the left side of his chin. Sputtering for breath, and groggy from the sleeping draught, he accepted the cup Jackson brought to his lips with a look of utter confusion, drinking its contents. As his eyes cleared, his face took on a strange expression. I clutched Anders arm so hard he nearly lost his balance. There was confusion and anger and betrayal, and most evident, a naked urge for vengeance in the mage's eyes as he searched inwardly for a talent that had vanished. With a vicious oath, he lunged for Jackson but his hands and legs were still bound tight. Jackson's fist left the renegade mage unconscious again, but not before I saw the final emotion that blazed clear and bright in his eyes.

Utter and complete loss.

"Can you handle the rest?" I asked Jackson, fighting back nausea.

"Yes." He exchanged an anxious look with Anders. "It is my responsibility."

"Maylen?"

"Yes?"

"Can you stay with Jackson for a moment in case they give him any trouble?"

"Yes, of course."

"Good." I turned to leave and fainted dead away.

* * * *

"Mage Protector—"

"Alex," I interjected, stifling a yawn. "We've been through too much together for formality."

"We have, yes." Jackson sighed, his handsome face strained with fatigue. "If you have no objections, I will send the renegades back to Spreebridge under heavy guard. I know we spoke of having the queen dispense justice, but in truth, I have been thinking that they are Spreebridge criminals and deserve Spreebridge punishment." Running a hand through his black curls, he waited for my answer. When I nodded my agreement, too tired to argue, as long as the renegades were taken away and dealt with, Jackson turned to give the order to his small band of woodsmen.

When he was finished, I grabbed hold of his cloak. "Are you all right?"

The mage graced me with a crooked smile. "If it were not my responsibility, I would have fainted right beside you."

"I'm glad you didn't," Anders said, putting on a brave face. "I couldn't catch both of you at the same time."

Green eyes flashed in appreciative humor. "Well, then." Jackson turned back to me. "We can leave for Port Alain whenever you wish."

"I can't leave until I'm certain Gwynn is safely out of danger."

Maylen appeared at my side, braids neat and tidy, her fresh young face scarlet from scrubbing. "The fever is already leaving him. He is all right."

"Still—" I shrugged, uneasy at the thought of abandoning the boy. "I'd feel better if he were awake himself to tell me that. It's not that I don't believe you," I reassured Maylen, "but, well, he's my responsibility as much as I'm his." I growled at Anders's smug smile at that particular admission. "And besides," I argued with the young scout, whose face was bland, "Khrista's baby isn't due for six more weeks."

"Without horses, we have barely enough time if the baby's the slightest bit early." Anders stood behind me and massaged the tension from my neck. "But if you'd rather wait and babysit your little brother, I'll stay with you."

Maylen tugged at my cloak when I tried to swat Anders. "I promise you Gwynn will be all right. He would not dare prove me wrong."

"I hope you're right."

"I am. Now go. I will tell him you wept endlessly at his bedside."

Chapter Twenty-Seven

"Thank the lords of the sea, you're back." Jules raked tense fingers through disheveled light brown hair when we appeared on the road. He'd been waiting for us since morning at the fork that led south to the manor, having gotten word from one of Jackson's band who detoured through Port Alain. "Khrista started labor hours ago. At least, that's what your stepmother said."

"It's too early for the child," Anders protested in vain, as Jules spun his nervous horse around, nearly running over Jackson in his haste. "Alex, wait! Damn it, wait for me."

But I couldn't, and mounted behind Jules as he urged his horse up the long winding road to the manor house. A young stablehand grabbed the reins as I bolted from the mount's glistening back and flew up the stairs to Khrista's chambers.

"Alex." Sernyn Keltie jumped from his seat next to Lauryn by the blazing fireplace in Khrista's sitting room. He grabbed my hands and held me still as I caught my breath. "Her labor started this morning, some ten hours ago, but it has been a slow, painful process. The child would not wait, but now that labor has started, she is quite stubborn and determined to escape."

"She?"

Sernyn smiled as Lauryn squeezed between us and embraced me. "Definitely a girl child. Anessa discovered that weeks ago, but Khrista is in wrenching pain." His eyes darkened as I squeezed his fingers tight, knowing both of us were overwhelmed by memories of my mother.

"Still no sign of magic?"

He shook his head. "I wish there would be. At least then she might exert some control over the child."

"Can I see her?"

"Yes, of course. She has been asking for you." He released my hands, but held me back as I turned toward Khrista's bedchamber. "Are you all right? This childbirth will be difficult for you."

"I'll have to be all right, won't I? Besides, it's worse for Khrista." At the sound of boots pounding up the stairs, I added, "There's a mage from Spreebridge journeying with us. Talk to him. And—" I hesitated, unable to meet his damnable perceptive eyes.

"There is something wrong." Not a trace of judgment in his voice, but yet he knew all the same, and braced himself for the bad news. "Is it Gwynn?"

"He was hurt protecting me." I glanced up with hesitation, found myself saying with pride and heartache, "He saved my life. I didn't want to leave him behind, but Maylen promised he'd be all right. She said he wouldn't dare not be."

"Ah." His eyes filled with loving concern for Gwynn and loving concern mixed with bemusement for me. "Then he will be."

"Sernyn—"

"If you are going to say you are sorry for what I know in truth you would have done for Gwynn had your positions been changed, I will surely lose my patience." At my guilty expression, he sighed with exaggerated drama. "Go see Khrista. She has been asking for you all day."

Speechless at his reprimand, I didn't bother to reply and crept into the master bedroom. Damp hair plastered to her forehead, Khrista seemed to be asleep, or at least resting. Clutching Kerrie's hand in a crushing grip, she lay very still. Anessa and Rosanna, speaking in the far corner, rose together as I shut the door behind me. Rosanna's hug was fierce, and frightened. Anessa hesitated, a question in her eyes.

"Gwynn was hurt protecting me," I blurted, all thoughtful consideration swept away as I blinked back tears. "Maylen is nursing him."

Anessa met my worried gaze evenly. "He went along to protect you, Alex. I am not surprised that it happened." She shrugged as though his battle wound was of no consequence, though I knew better than that.

"I should have been protecting him."

"My son does not seem to see it quite that way." Anessa's smile was warm. "And as long as he is under Maylen's care, he will be all right." When I started to protest, she repeated, "He will be all right. Gwynn would not dare disappoint his elder sister or Maylen Stockrie." She squeezed my arm in gentle reassurance.

I smiled back, knowing I wouldn't win this argument, not with Anessa, or Sernyn either. "How is Khrista?" I kept my voice low.

"Suffering," the healer apologized, as though it were her fault. "We cannot seem to ease her pain."

"There's a mage from Spreebridge with us." As Anessa's dark eyebrows inched up with interest, I explained, "He has a draught that blocks mage talent. It's very dangerous, but—" I looked at Khrista's sleeping form. Turning back to meet Rosanna's gaze, I said quietly, "It's dangerous. The amount of potion to still the baby's raw talent might kill the child. Or hurt Khrista. I thought you should know if things become desperate, and we need to make a decision."

Rosanna caught the edge of my cloak as I approached the bed. "Should you be here?"

"You mean, can I handle this?"

The old witch didn't blink. "Well, yes."

I tossed my cloak on the armchair behind me. "As I just told Sernyn," —I kept my expression neutral beneath Anessa's quiet scrutiny— "I'll have to, won't I?" Rosanna didn't say anything further as I went to the bedside and knelt by Kerrie, touching his arm to let him know I was there.

Khrista's eyes fluttered open, and widened as she recognized me. "Alex. I've been waiting for you." Her voice was hoarse, her smile weak, but still there.

"I didn't plan to wake you."

"I wasn't sleeping." She squeezed Kerrie's hand as a spasm gripped her abdomen. As though it never happened, she went on. "I thought you'd never get here."

"And I thought you'd wait for me."

"My daughter was impatient." As she flinched in pain yet again, Kerrie threw me a despairing look.

"Then she has your beastly temperament. Let's get something straight," I said with firmness. "You'd better show her who's in charge before you send the little imp into my schoolroom. Particularly if she behaves like Carey."

Khrista laughed softly, eyes closed, as the door opened and Lauryn slid into the room. Anessa sent me a guarded look and went out, presumably to speak to Jackson and Anders.

Lauryn stood by Kerrie's shoulder, one hand resting on his bowed head. "Why don't you get something to eat?"

"I'm not hungry."

Lauryn tugged at a lock of his hair. "Once your daughter decides she's ready to come out, you won't have a chance to eat. Now go. Jules is waiting for you. Hurry before he and Anders devour everything in sight." She winked at me. "From what I hear, when Anders travels, he has the appetite of three ravenous whales."

"Go." Khrista released her grip and waved him from the room. She smiled when he had finally gone, and heaved a deep sigh. "Men."

I laughed and took Kerrie's seat. "I know what you mean. Between Anders and Gwynn and Jackson—"

"Who?"

"A mage we picked up along the way."

"A mage with incredible green eyes," Lauryn cut in with a lusty grin, handing me a glass of Marain Valley wine from the bottle sitting on the nearby table. "Indecent, really."

"You're not kidding." I sipped the wine, my parched throat grateful for the liquid.

As time dragged on, I tried to distract Khrista and let them speculate and gossip about Jackson, tossing in a controversial comment when necessary. I unobtrusively nudged my magic awake, merging the fire and ice into familiar cool warmth. Tentatively, I tried to sense the child, but she was devious, a true Barlow, and not one to welcome intrusion. It took long silence and patience, but finally, finally, I found the little beast.

There.

Lords of the sea, she flung out her raw talent, as I had done to my own mother. Reacting with my heart, I blinked back a tear as Rosanna, caught by the subtle change in my expression, studied my face. Ignoring the question in her eyes, I tried to soothe the child as I had tried to soothe the renegade woman at Edgecliff. Not that I had helped her, me efforts instead only inflamed her. But maybe for Khrista, it'd be different. I held my breath, reaching out with the cool warmth that tingled through me. I gasped uncontrollably and shut my eyes tight as the child lashed out in furious denial, prompting a moan from Khrista.

"Alex." Lauryn knelt beside me, peering into my face with undisguised concern as I opened my eyes.

"Your niece doesn't like to be pushed around." I forced a smile as I turned to Khrista. "Sorry, I thought I'd try to be polite and make her acquaintance." Feigning the need to stretch, I stood up and placed my wine glass, forgotten in my hand, on the low table near the bed. "I'll be right back. Since none of you thought to ask if I were hungry," I said dryly, "I'll have to take care of myself. Not that there'll be anything left." At Khrista's brave smile, I went to find some help and snuggled gratefully into Anders's welcoming embrace. "The baby doesn't like to be pushed around."

"What did you do?"

"I tried to soothe her to see if I could control the way she lashed out with that mage talent of hers." I murmured in contentment as Anders massaged the tension from my shoulders.

"Didn't work?"

"She wasn't impressed." I shook my head. "Stubborn child fought right back." I peeked out at Jules. "That's definitely Barlow blood."

Jackson cleared his throat. "What if three of us tried to control her together?"

"I was hoping you'd say that."

"Well, then." Anders kissed my neck. "Let's try."

I led them back inside, introduced Khrista to the Spreebridge mage.

"Oh." Khrista smoothed back her damp hair at the first sight of Jackson's handsome face. "Oh my."

"Indeed." I grinned at Lauryn, when Khrista smoothed the damp sheet over her swollen abdomen. "We're going to try to restrain that willful, stubborn child of yours," I explained, adding in apology, "but she may protest."

Khrista took hold of Anders's outstretched hand as Jackson and I settled together on either side of the bed, coaxing the magic awake one by one. I was conscious of Sernyn and Anessa sitting quietly at Rosanna's side. When I felt that Anders and Jackson were ready, I nodded, focusing magic gently on the child, flinching against her fiery lashes, thrusts of magic that grew stronger and bolder and wilder. Anders sent me a guarded look, but I ignored him until Khrista cried out sharply in pain. As one, we abandoned the effort.

"Stubborn little wretch," I muttered to Khrista as Lauryn wiped perspiration from her sister-in-law's face. "That trait comes from your mother." I winked at Khrista, grateful she could still smile though the pains were coming faster and stronger.

"I'll ignore that, Alex," Rosanna said so loudly I knew she was putting on a brave front for her daughter.

"I've never spoken anything but the truth," I said, taking noting of Sernyn's distressed expression. "Be right back." I patted Khrista's hand and dragged him away from the two women. "Should you be here?"

"Do you mean," he said gravely, "can I handle this?"

As I swore with a vicious oath, his eyebrows rose in amazement. "Does that old witch tell you everything?"

His smile was mischievous, rather uncharacteristic, considering our fragile relationship. "Only what she thinks I should know. Still, Alex," —he caught my hand in his and admitted the truth— "I would rather be anywhere else but here, but I will stay in case I am needed."

"You've done enough."

He shrugged, looking as weary as I felt. "It is not over yet. She may have need of me somehow."

"All right." At the piercing cry behind me, I broke free and ran back to the bedside. Khrista's face was distorted in agony as the baby fought her way free and flexed her magic.

"Help me, Alex." Khrista was crying softly now, clutching Anders's hand so tight his knuckles were white. "Alex!"

I turned to Jackson. "Get the feyweed ready." When he glanced at Anders and then back at me, I snapped, "Do it! If we need it, we'll at least have it ready."

"It's not your decision to make," Anders said, for my hearing alone, cool seagray eyes stern with warning.

"I won't see her die like my mother," I whispered, blinking hard to keep back my own tears. I held Khrista's other hand, aware Anessa had gone out with Jackson, aware of Rosanna inching closer to the bed, and fully aware of Anders's magic trying with quiet desperation to calm the child. "Khrista—" Finding courage, I pushed a damp strand of hair from her forehead. "Listen to me." Eyes closed tight, she squeezed my hand. "We may be able to block the child's talent with a draught." I met Kerrie's eyes as he entered behind Jackson and Anessa.

"Will it harm her?" Khrista's voice was shaky and hoarse with exhaustion, but clear. "Will it? Tell me the truth, Alex."

I looked at Sernyn across the width of the chamber. At the sight of his tears, I buried my own. No time.

"Alex . . ."

"We don't know. It may harm her. It may—" I couldn't go on.

"Coward." Khrista clutched my hand so hard I whimpered. "Don't lie to me now, Alex. You've never lied before. Don't start now."

Traitorous tears had a will of their own. I couldn't stop them. "It might kill her," I whispered in misery.

Khrista fixed me with a grave look, an expression in her eyes that needed no words. "Then promise me you won't give it to me."

Kerrie rushed over, frantic. "Listen to me, then." He took his wife's sweating hand from mine. "I want you safe. We'll have other children."

Khrista seemed oblivious to her husband's pleading as she kept her eyes locked on mine. "Promise me."

"I can't," I whispered, unable to take that oath. "Damn it, Khrista, my mother never had a fighting chance, but you do."

"I do, too." She screamed so suddenly I thought the child had pushed herself free without our help, but Khrista's face was, well, odd. She was straining to catch her breath, confusion clear in her eyes. "Alex." Her voice held a peculiar mixture of wonder and fear and hope.

I leaned forward as she beckoned me closer, catching a hint of another mage talent. "Lords of the sea, I don't believe it."

Anders's eyes widened as he recognized what I had felt. Grinning from ear to ear, he gripped Khrista's hand in encouragement. "Easy. Remember what Sernyn taught you."

At the sound of his name, Sernyn watched in confusion, until he too, recognized what had happened. He flew to the bed and took Khrista's hand from Anders, placing his free hand on mine. "Remember what I taught you. Focus on the sharp sting and force it gently, easily, to a comfortable level inside you." As Khrista cried out again, he spoke gentle and reassuring words to her over and over as she fixed her eyes on his, trusting him implicitly.

I watched in amazement as the full pitcher of water at her bedside evaporated to steam. "A flameblasted seamage," I muttered. "That's all we need in this house."

Sernyn grinned with pride at Khrista, distracting her from the baby's protests. "Calm your daughter," he urged.

She turned frightened eyes to me, and then back to him. "I'm afraid."

"Nothing to fear," he said with confidence. "Just show her who you are. You can do it, and we shall all help."

Struggling, sweating, crying, and gasping for breath, Khrista eased the ferocity with which her daughter unleashed her talent. As she did so, Anders, Jackson, and I blanketed the baby with soothing calm over and above her mother's touch. It was not so very long before Kerrie cried out he could see the child's head. And not so very long after that we heard a loud shrieking wail from the defiant little girl plucked from a warm womb by Anessa's skilled hands.

I ran exhausted fingers through disheveled curls and shook a finger at Khrista in warning. "I'm telling you now, woman, if you don't discipline that little beast before she enters my schoolroom, you'll be teaching her yourself."

"Don't you threaten my granddaughter." Rosanna's damp eyes shone with relief, gratitude, and deep affection as she hugged me close.

Delirious with relief, I wiped my eyes and dragged Anders from the noisy room, only to find Gwynn, pale and thin, propped up between Maylen and the Queen of Tuldamoran.

"I was told you did not care to wait for me, to see if I would live." Gwynn's large brown eyes were overflowing with sorrow and accusation as he struggled to stay upright on shaky legs.

Though my impulse had been to run to his side, I stopped in mid-stride, my heart beating unbearably loud, at a loss for words.

At the stricken look on my face, Maylen jabbed Gwynn sharply with her elbow until he cried out in pain. "That is a cruel joke. Apologize to Alex. Now!"

Apologize? "You little—" I lunged for my brother as he hid behind Elena, who crossed her arms and barred my way. "Don't you have a kingdom to rule?"

"My very efficient counselors and heir do that for me." She grinned, pulling Anders and me into a warm embrace. As she caught sight of Jackson, walking out of the master bedroom with Sernyn, Elena went very still.

Anders looked at me, vastly amused. "Oh, my."

"Indeed. Could be interesting, don't you think?" I punched his arm playfully as Sernyn joined us. "Thank you." I hugged him close, surprising us both. "Mother would've been proud of you."

He touched my cheek, slightly dazed. "She would have been filled with pride for her daughter, too."

"After how I treated you?" I asked quietly. "How can you say that?"

"Because I know well what Emila would have thought. Alex, believe me." Sernyn's smile was warm and unrestrained. "She would have been proud to see how you've grown."

"Are you?"

He read the uncertainty in my eyes and kissed my cheek. "Never more than today."

"Even though I lied?" When he stepped away and blinked in confusion, I explained, "I told Rosanna, and I told you in no uncertain terms, that I didn't need or want a father. That was a lie."

"You were confused."

Relieved at his smile, I pushed my father toward Gwynn. "Your son is feeling neglected." I grinned at my brother before turning back to Anders, an odd, wondering expression on my face as a peculiar thought entered my mind.

"Now what?" He crossed his arms, eyes alert with suspicion.

"I have an idea."

"I was afraid of that."

Taking the plunge, I beckoned him closer with my finger until we stood eye to eye. "I was just trying to figure out, what with our crazy bloodlines, precisely what kind of little mage you and I could create."

Cool seagray eyes widened in undisguised surprise as he caught the wistfulness in my whisper. "You're serious, aren't you?"

"Quite."

With an impossibly bright grin, Anders swept me up in his arms. Flashing a bemused look at Elena, as she turned to us in surprise, he shrugged. "I know it's the middle of the night, and you do so love to come knocking at our door, but would you mind not visiting until morning?"

Elena's smile matched his in delight as she waved us away. "And Alex always said you were so old. I never believed her for a moment."

About the Author

Virginia G. McMorrow has worked as an editor/writer for more than 30 years, after a career in human resources. In her professional capacity, Ginny has worked for business publishers as an editor of books, journals, reports, and newsletters targeted for clients, and now works as a freelance editor/writer. She has also had numerous articles on both professional and writing topics published, along with several short stories. As a playwright, Ginny has had 28 short one acts and one full-length play produced off-off Broadway by Love Creek Productions in a black box theater, as well as two short plays performed on a west coast radio show. She now lives and works in Venice, Florida.

Coming Soon!

VIRGINIA G. MCMORROW

MAGE EVOLUTION
THE MAGE TRILOGY
BOOK 3

Mage Evolution, Book Three of The Mage Trilogy, continues the tale of Mage Alex Keltie—her husband Anders the Crownmage, the Barlows, and her dear friend Queen Elena. Five years have passed since the confrontation of the Spreebridge renegade mages, and a new character has entered the saga, four-year-old Emmy, Alex's precious daughter, who possesses mage talents from both her parents. Yet Alex is desperate to protect her daughter, even as a conspiracy sweeping the land takes away all mage powers-even her own.

**For more information
visit:** www.SpeakingVolumes.us

Now Available!

VIRGINIA McMORROW'S

MAGE CONFUSION
THE MAGE TRILOGY
BOOK 1

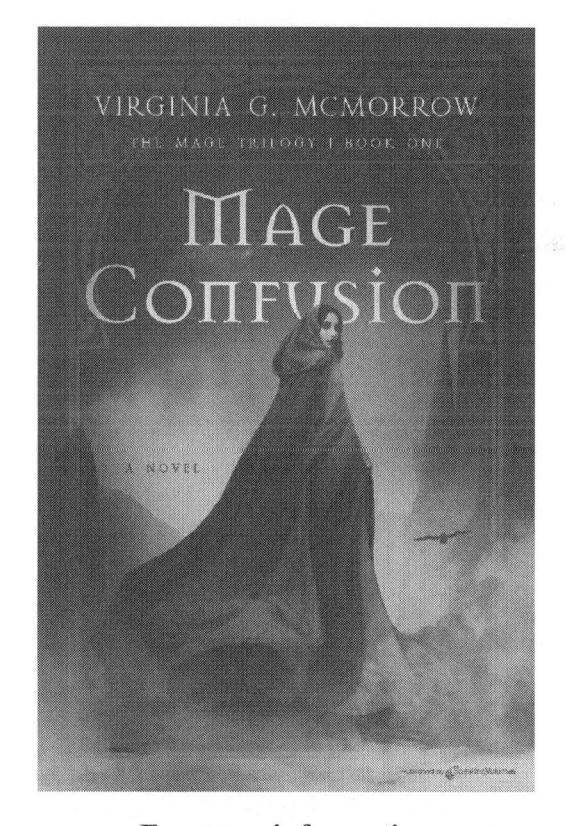

**For more information
visit:** www.SpeakingVolumes.us

Now Available!

JORDAN S. KELLER'S

ASHES OVER AVALON TRILOGY
BOOK ONE

**For more information
visit:** www.SpeakingVolumes.us

Now Available!

P.M. GRIFFIN'S

STAR COMMANDOS SERIES
BOOKS 1 - 8

**For more information
visit: www.SpeakingVolumes.us**

Now Available!

JACK HILLMAN'S

GIANTS WAR TRILOGY

**For more information
visit:** www.SpeakingVolumes.us

Made in the USA
Columbia, SC
10 April 2023